Jane Slavin is an actress. She lives
Writing on the Water is her first novel.

WRITING ON THE WATER

Jane Slavin

BLACK SWAN

WRITING ON THE WATER
A BLACK SWAN BOOK: 0 552 99781 1

First publication in Great Britain

PRINTING HISTORY
Black Swan edition published 1998

Copyright © Jane Slavin 1998

Set in 10/13 Monotype Melior by
Deltatype Ltd, Birkenhead, Merseyside

Black Swan Books are published by Transworld Publishers Ltd,
61–63 Uxbridge Road, London W5 5SA,
in Australia by Transworld Publishers (Australia) Pty Ltd,
15–25 Helles Avenue, Moorebank, NSW 2170
and in New Zealand by Transworld Publishers (NZ) Ltd,
3 William Pickering Drive, Albany, Auckland.

Reproduced, printed and bound in Great Britain by
Cox & Wyman Ltd, Reading, Berks.

For my mother,
Sheila,
who gave me the whole world.

I fancied you'd return the way you said,
   but I grow old and I forget your name:
I think I made you up inside my head.

I should have loved a thunder-bird instead,
   at least when spring comes they roar back again.
I shut my eyes and all the world drops dead.
   I think I made you up inside my head.

Sylvia Plath: 'Mad Girl's Love Song'

He was drinking coffee and I had cappuccino and outside the moon shone upside down. He held my hand over the table. A woman came in carrying a basket of old fruits, dead from age. The fruits had once been exotic; I could see that much even through the shroud of mould. The woman looked slightly mouldy herself; her hair was lank and black and straight where mine was red and curled and clean.

'You have ruined my life,' she said, and threw the fruits onto the table. She had grey tracks of mascara running down her cheeks and bloodshot eyes. She wore a shirt not unlike a strait-jacket.

'A cup of boiled water please,' she shouted to the waiter, and looking down at me she said, 'The boiled water's for you. For when your life is over like mine.'

When she moved away I saw she was barefoot and her feet were filthy and bloody.

He finished his coffee and I finished my cappuccino and we walked out into the night and in a street off Leicester Square we had silent hasty sex in the doorway to the surgery of a twenty-four-hour emergency doctor. Before we had finished a woman in a white coat came through the door. She had a stethoscope round her neck. She didn't speak. She didn't seem even to see us, though we were in her way. She ignored us so utterly we later doubted she was ever really there.

At my flat there was a note stuck on the door which said 'These fruits are for you. Such fruits you will feed from for ever,' and inside, all over my home were thirty or forty baskets of fresh, sweet, exotic fruits and together we sat down and ate. Such sweet peaches I had never dreamed of. Some of the fruit we couldn't even name.

'Such sweet fruits could never die,' he said to me, and I believed him, and in a haze of nectar we slept, woken only once by the cry of a woman, a woman we hadn't heard approach because her feet were bare. Once she had padded away we slept on and he held on to me as though he were drowning and I was his lifebuoy.

When I awoke there were no baskets to be found and no fruit at all, apart from a thin-skinned orange which I could tell would be sour. But I could taste the sweetness of the mangoes and cherries I'd eaten in the night even after I smoked my first cigarette, and I was warmed by the memory of the man in my bed even though I had woken alone. For most of the day I smiled, even when I realized the night had been an illusion and the sweet fruits nothing but a dream.

Chapter One

London steamed. Its buildings breathed sweat. I could see it happening. There would've been a mass of people peeling away their clothes and seeking out patches of green all over the city, but it seemed anyone capable of travel had fled to the beach, the country, anywhere other than here. For a fleeting moment that morning I had wished for a car, a family, a lover, but the moment passed and was forgotten and I carried on with my day.

The phone rang all day long; a hot bank holiday in August when everyone I knew was apparently gripped by chronic boredom or loneliness. I had a lot to do and it would've been wise to just switch the answering machine on, but I picked the phone up every time it howled. My flat was in total chaos; I was in the middle of decorating it. I should also have been looking at a script for the next day's work. September the first. It felt like it would be the beginning of a new year. I saw the London air turning crisp and cool over night; summer's end. I watched the sunshine drifting off toward some other city. It would leave without me, as it always did. Around that time of year I've been known to go quite loopy with desire for eternal summertime, with fear of winter. But it was not like this then.

The job – yes, the job. Well, it wasn't about to propel me into any dizzying heights of fame and stardom. It was only for a few days and no-one would ever see the finished result, well, nearly no-one, but I was looking forward to it; four days filming in an ancient studio in Holland Park with a bunch of actors and a director I'd never met. It would be amusing if nothing else. It might even pay off one of my debts. I looked around the bedroom to see if I could see the script under all the debris. I spotted it lying neglected on the bare, paint-splattered floorboards, in between the kettle and a tin of cream gloss.

I'd moved into the flat about ten weeks before, and then gone away on tour with a play called *The Sugar Man* and hadn't even bothered to unpack. The play had then come into the West End for a limited run and had closed two days ago. I'd pretended I had no time to spare for practicalities. In actuality all I'd had to do was turn up at the theatre every night. The play was only ninety minutes long; there had been more than enough free hours to sort out my belongings and paint a few walls, particularly as the flat is spitting distance from the West End. But I am lazy. At least, I was then. In the five weeks I'd been back in town I'd done nothing but unpack the kettle and the odd teaspoon and open my rucksack and I'd wandered into town every night and done my bit for British Theatre. I had waited for this bank holiday thinking *then* I will paint, *then* I will get back in touch with everyone, *then* I will sort the flat out. Now the day had arrived I was trying to do a million things at once, which is just typical of me; sometimes I will brush my teeth and read my mail and go to the toilet all at the same time, like this is going to save me some time, like I can't afford to waste even a minute, and after this I'll sit thinking and staring into space for forty minutes or more and then look at my watch and wonder where all the time has gone.

I look back on that day all the time, as though it holds some profound significance. In reality it was simply a typical lazy summer's day; lying around smoking, listening to music, talking on the phone.

Outside it seemed like London was melting; like the heat had closed up all the openings of the shop doors and seized all the engines on the roads. At least tomorrow there would be traffic again and people on the streets. The shops would open up and the trains would run their regular hours. I hate bank holidays. They are those bastard days when families get together when they mightn't otherwise; when people get out of the city; when lovers lie in bed together, drinking coffee and making love all day; when people celebrate having the day off work. Celebration. As if. Never ask an actress to celebrate having a day off work for she will spit in your eye. We love to work, we can't get enough of the stuff. Too many months of our lives are spent deprived of it. Bank holidays are like an extension of unemployment. We want to work all the time partly because when we do, when we're working, we think *This job might be the last*, we worry that no-one will ever want us again. I'd done all right for more than twelve months, I'd worked almost constantly and earned some money and worked with some good people, but I still had the usual actor neuroses about starving in the street somewhere and niggling doubts about self-worth, only this time around there wasn't much in my behaviour to reflect this insecurity. For instance, I'd spent all my money and more. I'd ordered stripped pine furniture from an antique dealer in Camden; I'd bought a washing machine and a video and a cooker and a fridge. I'd had bookcases made by a master carpenter in Islington. After the shopping binge I found (and it was no real surprise) I'd left myself with about three pounds in loose change in the pocket of my jeans and about sixty quid in the bank. My fridge was empty. Even the coffee jar was nearly empty and I'm a regular addict. But I was happy in my new home; years of flat sharing with nutters who drank aftershave and idiots who didn't know what it was to pay a bill before disconnection day had sent me quite mad. My new flat was a haven of long overdue solitude and quiet. My bills were all my own. My living room was my own. I was in love with the place from the day they gave me the rent book. I had little address stickers printed out and sent them to the world and his brother with little covering notes saying, 'Free. At last.'

I contemplated the money crisis. Tomorrow I would whip the rest of the money out of the bank before it was eaten up by a standing order or a bank charge and I'd buy some more paint and some more coffee. The furniture I'd ordered would start to arrive in the course of the next couple of weeks. I figured if I was going to be out of a job for any length of time at least I would be surrounded by lovely things; I might be hungry but at least I'd be comfortable. I was as happy as ever before. Happier. I carried around inside me an optimism that almost burned a hole in my gut.

I ran out of paint and the short bursts of decorating ground to a lazy halt. I went out and spent a couple of hours burning through the streets looking for some shopkeeper somewhere who had chosen to ignore the holiday. I turned down so many dead ends in the unfamiliar streets that eventually I gave up and strolled home sweating and paintless, spending some of the three quid on a stupidly expensive ice-lolly, resigned to the fact I'd have to wait till tomorrow for a new tin of County Cream gloss. The lolly, however, was a revelation; it tasted like some dream I'd had, the details of which I couldn't quite remember. Walking by the South Bank sucking the thing I felt utterly euphoric. It was so magnificent, so amazingly fruity and juicy and cold, so extraordinary it made me gasp out loud and I found myself thinking I must write to the manufacturers of this lolly and congratulate them because it really is a winner. I would phone my friends when I got back and advise them all to go out and buy one. I'd tell them all what I'd discovered, what a miracle I'd found. Later on when I told my friend Lottie about that lolly she asked if I was all right, was I a bit depressed, over tired? Was I eating properly?

But I was not depressed. I sang in the street. Frequently. Since I'd moved into the new flat I'd started talking to strangers in shops, chatting to anyone who would chat back. I woke in the night not from fear or loneliness but from a fierce, unshakeable optimism; from some excitement, some vague notion of impending change. I would get out of bed at 4 a.m. and make coffee and sitting smoking in the kitchen, I would wait patiently for the new beginning; listening to the early-morning traffic, wondering where all these people were going at such an odd time of day.

In spite of the fact I hadn't got my paint I got back home feeling refreshed, the taste of iced fruit lingering on my lips. I stood in the living room for a moment or so and imagined what it would be like if ever I finished it; when my books were on the bookcases and the walls were painted and the carpets down. Impulsively, I started to rummage around, vaguely thinking of making a start on it there and then. In one of the boxes I found some tins of food given to me by Alice on the day I moved in. I wondered how she was getting on with her new kid. She didn't seem to be enjoying motherhood much. Anyway, she'd given me a box of goodies and I'd gone away the same night and it had been forgotten. As well as the tins there was some pasta, a bottle of vitamin pills and a wet looking brown paper bag of something. In the bag I found pounds and pounds of cherries, covered in green fur. I only recognized them as cherries from their stems. I put my hand into the depths of damp mould; it reminded me of some woman I'd met somewhere but I couldn't remember her name or even her face. I couldn't remember where I'd met her or when, but I remembered the mould. The phone screamed at me and I dropped the fruit in shock feeling guilty like a burglar, listening to the startling rings for several seconds before I remembered who I was and ran to answer it.

'Why are you out of breath? Who've you got there?'

'Alice. I was just thinking about you. Just now in the . . . I've just discovered your food parcel in my living room.'

'What?'

'The cherries.'

'What are you talking about?'

'Never mind, it doesn't matter. How's it all going? Have you had him adopted yet?'

'I wish. Oh, it's OK. Work's fine. Ish. David's sort of OK, but shit, don't have kids, Elle. Not until you can afford a nanny. I have to book an appointment just to have sex. I feel like he's staying awake just to annoy me. I'm sure he knows he's sending me mad.'

'I thought you were going to have someone in.'

'David says he doesn't want him being looked after by a stranger. I say what does it matter? He won't know it's a stranger, I mean he's a baby, he knows nothing, does he? David says he knows us, his mummy and daddy.'

'He'll come round to the idea, you know David.'

'Yeah, maybe. Maybe I'll go away for a day or two, see if he changes his mind when he hasn't slept for forty-eight hours. How's the filming? Has it started yet?'

'Tomorrow.'

'Have you got a good part?'

'I've no idea. God, I haven't really read the script yet. Not properly. It's not an award winner though, I can tell that.'

'What've you been doing then?'

'Oh, y'know. Catching up. Answering the phone. Had a fabulous ice-lolly walking by the river. A moon beam or a sunbeam or something.'

'Are you stoned?'

'No! I'm serious. I've never tasted anything like it, it was a really, really good lolly, really fruity and juicy and, shit, Alice, it was beautiful.'

'Ellie—'

'I wonder if you can buy them in bulk . . .'

16

'I worry about you.'

'Don't. I've never felt better.'

'Oh, God, listen to that.' Jack the baby screamed in the background. 'I suppose I'd better go. I just wanted to see how you are. Enjoy tomorrow. I'll call you again in the week.'

I dragged my thoughts away from Alice and her life and read the script. Written by a lesser-known writer from Donegal it was called *The Bard's Tale*: A fictional account of the life of William Shakespeare. The main bulk of it was Shakespeare himself chatting to the camera, documentary style. A few other characters pop in and out, but none of them says a great deal. I was playing Ophelia, desperately in love with the bard but hopelessly mad, kills herself in the last scene; and Rosalind, a woman obsessed with dressing up in boys' clothing. Reading it in the bath I knocked a whole packet of cigarettes into the water. Later on I tried to dry them under the grill but quickly abandoned the idea and got dressed again and wheeled my little yellow push-bike round to the 7-Eleven. I bought a packet of ten and came home and in my bed that night with stale, damp cigarettes in my grill pan and mouldy cherries in my living room I fell asleep thinking it a blessing that I lived alone. What man or woman would want to live with a beast such as I?

I was standing outside a church at the edge of a lake. It was my wedding day and all around me my family and friends were saying, 'What did you say his name was?'

But I found I couldn't pronounce his name and when I looked around for the man who was to marry me he wasn't there and when I tried to picture him he had no face.

'What's his name again?' they said, and a woman I didn't quite recognize came out of the crowd wearing a long black dress. As she drew closer I saw that the long black dress was just rags, and when one of the guests touched her arm a cloud of dust billowed into the air and people started to cough. The woman in rags came even closer to me, so close I could smell the mildew on her breath.

She said, 'Whatever his name is he's dead now,' and turning around in a cloud of her own dust she said, 'Just like me,' and with a look of unconstrained grief she threw seven dead roses at me. 'For remembrance. You will remember me.'

When she disappeared into the crowd of guests my father came over. 'There's blood on your dress.' A dead thorn from a dead rose had cut into me. I looked down and saw I had no shoes on and my feet were bloody and filthy.

'He's in the water.'

'Who?' said my father.

'I can't pronounce his name,' and I waded in up to my neck. Someone whispered 'Ellen!' and I followed the sound of my name to the bottom of the lake where a dead man lay. At his side was my mother, dead for three years now.

'It's too soon,' she said.

'But I want to spend my life with him.'

'Who?'

But I couldn't pronounce his name.

Chapter Two

At the studio reception desk in Holland Park I was given a
cast list. A mad drunken actor who had once been the toast
of The Theatre was playing The Bard, an actress called Rose
Mullholland was playing the roles of Juliet and Portia and
someone called Harrison Mellor was playing The Boy. I
went straight to the canteen and bought coffee and a bar of
chocolate and across the room I saw the drunken actor
having a cigarette and a bottle of Guinness. Standing at the
side of him was a man; an ordinary man, a man you might
see in the street and look at only once. They both looked
over as I made my way to their table. The ordinary man
looked right at me and the coffee spilled down my hand and
if I remember correctly I may have collided with a chair.

'Aedan O'Brien.' An Irishman. The director of the film. He
put his hand out.

Aiden. It is pronounced Aiden. I said the name over and
over again in my head. Aedan.

'Ellen.' I held his hand. Blue eyes, though some would say
grey and some would say green; some would say unremarkable and until the moment we shook hands I might have
agreed with them. His teeth were crooked. He had lines
under his eyes, weary lines, weary eyes, but in them I saw
myself. I wondered if he saw recognition in my face. I let go
of his hand and sat down at the table feeling slightly drunk,
as though I were on some precipice and had an irrepressible

urge to leap. I stared at my coffee and read the label on the bar of chocolate. A whole conversation took place before I could even bring myself to look up but I was not surprised to find that when I did he was looking right back.

'Aedan O'Brien,' I said, and he said, 'I know you.' And nobody heard except us and no-one imagined that anything strange had taken place.

Ask me about the job and I can tell you nothing except that during it I met a man named Aedan. Some would say they wish I'd never been given the job, that I had never met Aedan and he had never met me. Some would say he ended my life and some would say I ended his right there and then in the canteen of a studio in Holland Park.

Chapter Three

I painted the flat like there was a deadline to be met. Exhilarated rather than exhausted from the filming, I was filled with a new sense of urgency. Instead of going home and crashing out for an hour which is what I might normally have done, I lugged all the new tins of paint through the flat, opened one of them and painted the kitchen without even taking my jacket off. At about 8 p.m. I took a break for a coffee and a cigarette and then I laid the carpet, moving the fridge and the cooker around the room with apparent ease, like this was something I did every day of my life. By ten the room was wet but finished. By the time the delivery man got to me with my new washing machine the following morning, I'd given the bathroom its first coat of Chelsea Yellow and made a start on the hallway.

For the next two days I can remember working and decorating and not much else. I occasionally answered the telephone but kept conversation to an absolute minimum. 'The job's fine. The flat's coming together. I met a man.' I met a man. An Irishman. According to my filofax I spent one evening that week at the theatre but I have no memory of what I saw or where. Whatever else I did, at night I sat sleepless on the new blue carpet in the kitchen, thinking, drinking wine or coffee till daylight shook me into action and I would paint some more before going to the studio.

We ate lunch together, me and the Irishman. Every day.

While the crew and the cast looked on we talked of Ireland and London and ourselves and eyebrows were raised. I became unable to hold any sort of intelligible conversation with anyone when he was anywhere near me, which suddenly became all the time. I went home with the smell of him in my hair.

But this is not a romance.

He lived alone, he told me, in Dublin and he had a place in Belfast he was trying to sell, though for the last six months he'd spent more time in a flat in Oakley Street in Chelsea. He said he felt that London was his home again; he'd lived here before, years ago when he was an actor. He told me that in about two weeks his contract here would be up and he was due back in Ireland where he had a house and some work to do and baggage. Emotional baggage; he remarked on my lack of it. He said I was 'untroubled'. Maybe he was right. Maybe at that time I was.

Two months, he said, he would go back for a maximum of two months and then he'd come back to London. 'I like the people,' he told me. 'I have to come back. Especially now.'

I said, 'Come back soon!' in the same way a child might, and he said, 'How could I not?' and just like a child I believed him.

One time in the canteen he said, 'Will I bring us something nice back?' and I asked, 'What?' And he said, 'A surprise!' and came back with fruit for me which was no surprise at all.

I spent the last filming day in a state of perpetual nausea; sick with the fear that at seven o'clock, when all the work was done, the whole story would end and he would get on one train and I would get on another and that would be that. Years away he might not even remember the colour of my hair. Of course the day didn't finish at seven, it merely transferred to the local pub, where cast and crew drank Guinness in the beer garden. Sitting out there in the cold our legs collided more than once, which made us laugh because really there was plenty of room. I think he even came out with the age old line of 'You remind me of someone,' or something similar and I laughed very loudly and said, 'Your mother?' It got colder and he gave me his jumper to wear and I asked him not to let me get drunk for fear of saying a hundred stupid things. I asked him when he'd like me to bring the jumper back to him, maybe we'd have lunch or something. When would he like?

'Is tomorrow too soon?' he said, and we both laughed at foregone conclusions.

We had a meal. Six of us, in a Greek place off Regent Street. When it was all over and everyone was saying goodbye and going home, we got in a cab to Chelsea, the two of us, where we drank Jameson's whiskey and talked all night and where at eight o'clock on Saturday morning we dozed together and eventually woke, locked together, fully clothed. I let him doze some more and crept downstairs to the living room in the basement where I lit a cigarette and tried with little success to look back at things in my life that had happened before I met this man. I tried to picture the people I'd known but the only name I could remember was his.

He wandered in, sleepy, in shorts and a white T-shirt. His legs were as unremarkable as the rest of him and he was out of shape and white. Such pale skin he had, with tiny, pale freckles on his arms. He sat down next to me and I put my cigarette out wishing I didn't smoke and he pulled open my lips and kissed the inside of my mouth.

'Will we get married?' he said, and I laughed and said yes and we went back to bed and slept.

'I have a son,' he told me.

'Are you married?'

'I'm not.'

'Your son's mother?'

23

'Cara. She lives in Dublin with Louis.'

'Oh.' I felt that perhaps in some bizarre way I already knew this.

'Louis is eight.'

'When did you split up?'

'About eight years ago.'

'Oh.'

He said, 'And you? Are you married? Do you have a lover?'

'I don't. You?'

'I did. Frances. She's on my shoulder now.'

'Will you tell her about me?'

'She'll want to be at the wedding.'

'She'll hate me.'

'She wants me to be happy.'

'Are you in love with her?'

'I'm not.'

As we undressed each other I said Poor Frances, and the face of a woman I'd never met screamed out in pain No! and then was silent.

We talked a lot.

Later on we had our first fuck.

We made love.

We screwed each other.

Whatever. It was not something I could describe. I lost myself utterly with this stranger. Aedan. The Irishman. We were reckless. We came over and into each other a thousand times. Later I found condoms in my bag and realized we'd been careless and said next time we really should use these. What about AIDS? But this isn't about that and as luck would have it we'd both been tested and were OK. What about kids? He said he'd like to plant his seed in me, which made me laugh. I said it was a nice idea but impractical and we really should grow up. We didn't. We behaved like adolescents only worse. At one point I even held him inside me as he was coming and said fuck me and give me a kid, and the idea of making me pregnant made him come and so I did it again and again because when he came he looked like he was in agony almost and I enjoyed that look and couldn't have enough of him and he said For ever For ever For ever and I said yes.

Over dinner we talked about where we would live. A house in Highgate, maybe. Maybe we'd stay in the flat till we found the right house. All the things I'd never had any desire to do suddenly became a talking point, a need. We needed a house because at some point we figured we would have kids, and anyway we wanted a lot of space. We needed a garden at the house for the kids to play in, for us, where we could have breakfast and bonfires. Where once we'd wanted to live alone, now we couldn't.

'You have the key to life,' he said, and I said, 'I do. I have the key.'

At such a moment he ripped open my mouth and kissed the very inside of me. People in the restaurant stared disapprovingly in our direction.

'They're jealous,' he said, 'because they know we're dining on perfection. And they aren't.'

Chapter Four

We planned the wedding. We made a million phonecalls, breaking the news to the world as it were. It seemed that in spite of the circumstances no-one was really surprised, at least, no-one seemed shocked. No-one asked me did I know what I was doing. No-one asked, 'Why the rush?' No-one mentioned the lengthy five-day courtship. Perhaps they thought I'd finally lost my mind. My father telephoned from Sydney to say he'd buy me the dress, did I want him to fly over? He would if I did. I didn't.

We devoured each other in the streets, in restaurants, in the Chelsea flat, on tubes. When we weren't snogging like teenagers we were talking, incessantly, about everything. We never slept. Once we went to the theatre to see *The Theban Plays*, the Oedipus trilogy. It was one of the best things I've ever seen. It seemed like even that had been blessed. We sat entwined through the six hours of Greek tragedy. During one of the intervals I remember him saying, 'Why do I feel like I've known you for ten years?' and he held on to me so tightly he broke a piece off my hair and nearly broke my back. At the end of all the drama we drank champagne and wandered through the city slightly drunk. Elated. Familiar.

I am not a stupid woman. I did question what was going on. I am not particularly romantic. In some ways I am quite horribly cynical, but with every question I asked of myself and of this man I felt completely certain. I never doubted for a second. He said that at thirty-six he had thought he would never do something like this, that he imagined he would never meet someone like me. He said I was the only woman he'd ever wanted to marry. He said we were destined to be together.

What happened to us? What was it between the two of us that inspired such ludicrous certainty? Lunacy? Did we make it up inside our heads?

My grandma telephoned.

'Beware the Irish flannel.'

But it was too late to beware anything. I remember lying beside him in a sort of half sleep one morning and he woke me suddenly and clutching my face like a madman, an animal, he said, 'Tell me you love me!'

'Yes. I do. I love you.'

'For how long? Tell me!'

'Till we die,' I said, which was the only answer he would accept and the only one I could give and then he lay down again and we clung together as though death was just outside the room. We broke new records of insomnia. Sleep seemed such a waste of precious time. When we did sleep we squashed so tightly together we might have stopped each other's breath. We pressed against each other as though by letting go we might wake up alone. Clinging together like that we got so hot it always seemed a miracle we didn't turn to ashes in the night.

His last night in London arrived; a bit of a shock but more of an inconvenience. He might be gone for several days, there was a lot to sort out in Ireland, but we had the phone. We had no doubt. Not really knowing what we should do on such an evening and not wanting to put any significance into our first separation we took ourselves off to a restaurant on Kensington High Street and ordered fish and good wine and drooled at each other over the table.

'You've set me free,' he told me.

'From what?'

'From whatever. Despicable, isn't it? We've become that awful couple, that couple we've despised all our lives. We've turned into one of those couples we've always laughed at.'

'The ones who walk around pawing each other in public. Snogging on tubes.'

'We *are* that couple.'

'I'm very cynical,' I said.

'Yes. Well, you were.'

'I don't believe in love at first sight. It's crap.'

'No. Neither did I.'

'I'm not even romantic . . . not really, not in reality.'

'But you promised you'd love me till we die.'

'I meant it.'

'So did I.'

'Romantic.'

'Worrying.'

'Terrifying.'

'Has it been like this before? I mean, was it like this with Michael?' Michael was my last boyfriend.

'Not even similar. I mean I suppose he loved me . . . quite a lot, but . . . well, it was nothing like this. And Frances?'

'Yes. Well, Frances loves me.'

'Will you see her when you go back to Dublin?'

'Yes.'

'Does she wish I was dead?'

'She wants me to be happy. She says she's only worried about the age gap. She says, "Sleep with her, Aedan, if you really have to, but for God's sake don't marry her."'

'Oh, for fuck's sake, it's only twelve years. How old is she?'

'Forty-two.'

'Huh. Menopausal.'

'Now now.'

'When did you last fuck her?'

'About three months ago.'

'What sort of relationship is that?'

'She's married.'

'Oh.'

'To a chiropodist.'

I felt a bit giddy, slightly sick.

'Are you all right?' he asked.

'Feel a bit strange.'

'So do I. Let's get some air. It's too hot in here.'

On the street it was too cold. We went into a cinema but the film was terrible and we staggered out after only fifteen minutes, dropping popcorn and sweets everywhere and laughing at all the disapproving tuts. On the journey home we started to sweat and got giddier and wondered if maybe the wine had been off. Unlikely.

Back at the flat we fell straight into bed. He looked ill, his face a sort of greenish colour.

'You look poorly,' he said to me.

'Not as poorly as you.' We started to make love but after about ten minutes I had to climb off him to go to be sick. I imagine with anyone else I might have been slightly embarrassed; I was quite loudly ill in the bathroom. No deterrent. Still sick we clawed relentlessly at each other's bodies. There was a moment when I thought he was just about to come but he slid out of bed to the bathroom where he was violently ill as well. All night we alternated between bed and bathroom. At six, with the September sun creeping through the curtains he said, 'I'm dying,' and I lay over his chest, exhausted, and said; 'So am I. It must have been the brill.'

'You had salmon.'

'I had a mouthful of your brill.'

'We've been poisoned!' he wailed. 'We're going to die!'

'Well, if we go, we go together.'

Chapter Five

He went back to Ireland that night. Sunday. I remember I felt elated. I was not sad at his going. It felt as though he'd left a piece of himself beneath my skin; like he hadn't really gone; like now I would not be alone again.

He phoned. All the time. In the following two days we spent a total of nineteen hours on the telephone. I sent him two letters and received three and a card and a tape of Sting's latest CD. Undeterred by distance we had sex from every available phone at every available moment. From detailed descriptions I got to know his place in Dublin as intimately as if I'd lived there; we did it in every room. He stood on the coffee table in his lounge and watched himself in the mirror over the fireplace while I listened from London. We even did it from an office at the Irish TV buildings until we were disturbed by a security guard.

And then on the third day he came home for two hours; said he couldn't wait a minute longer. He turned up on the doorstep, steeped in insecurity.

'I missed you too much. Did you miss me?'

'I don't feel like you've been away.'

'But didn't you miss me? Is it still the same?'

'It is the same. It's worse. I pine for you.'

'Marry me.'

'Yes,' I said, and meant it, though I wondered when we'd have the time to organize anything. My agent called to say

Liam Johnston was directing *Thérèse Raquin* on film and he wanted to see me for Thérèse. How old was I? How much filming had I done? How much theatre, etc., etc., etc? I met him at a casting office in Soho the next day. He asked me a hundred questions, I answered them, we made each other laugh. I went to meet the producers and then some more producers. I got the job. Thérèse. The Big Break. The part of a lifetime. Wow.

Back in Dublin Aedan whooped congratulations down the phone. Flowers arrived within the hour. 'But you might not love me now you're famous, now you're a superstar.' More flowers arrived; a bunch so vast the vase tipped over from the weight. And then a week later he was home. I wandered over to the family planning clinic before he arrived, vaguely thinking of getting a coil or something as it appeared we were never going to be disciplined with rubber. I asked the doctor how reliable a coil would be.

'One hundred per cent,' she told me. It sounded a bit permanent, put like that, irrevocable, and so I left the clinic with thirty-six condoms. My period started on the way home, mocking me, a signal from my womb perhaps, letting me know we'd been let off for the month's utter stupidity. I was reminded of fertility and chance.

He came home and sprayed us all over with Bollinger. Now I was a movie star, he said, we could afford such behaviour. Undeterred by the period we had sex on the kitchen floor and again in the hall. The little bag from the clinic sat forgotten in the corner of the room, laughing at us. I caught sight of it and thought next time we must use those. But this time we're all right. We'll be all right. We're safe. Protected.

We woke in the morning looking like the victims of some terrible massacre; our whole bodies caked in dried blood, the sheets thick with it. He said maybe someone had come in in the night and shot us dead. We looked for bullet wounds and made love on the bloody sheets.

I wring out each of my senses in search of the way his skin felt under my fingers; I relive the memory of that time of my life more frequently than any other; I wring out each of my senses in search of the way his skin felt under my fingers. There is a slight scar on the back of one of my legs from a crushed champagne glass which sometimes I attribute to that time even though I think that was much, much later on. I look at that scar to make certain I had lived those days and not made them up inside my head.

He was meant to stay for three days but the three days turned into five and then ten. We left the radio and the TV switched off. We didn't buy a newspaper or open any mail. The only thing we bought from the local shop was a bottle of Famous Grouse. We didn't even cook, except once I made a sort of pasta-bake thing to show I wasn't as mad as I looked and could actually prepare a meal, but we went to bed while it was in the oven and when we finished it was a bowl of carbon. We didn't visit anyone and no-one visited us. We didn't even pick up the phone. I would've introduced him to all my friends but there didn't seem any need and as he would have to go back to Ireland at some point we were selfish with our time and barely even left the flat. There was one day when the sun was shining and we went and had a browse at the shops on the King's Road and he bought me a fruity-looking fruit bowl and we looked at furniture and wedding suits, but that was our only contact with the rest of the world.

He missed several return flights and stayed a bit longer and a bit longer. He missed a meeting with some lunatic writer he knew and couldn't get hold of anyone to arrange an alternative date but he didn't seem to care. We missed Black Wednesday; the pound died a death and we didn't even notice. I forgot about the rest of England. I believed he was the perfect man, if such a being existed. He said I was the perfect woman. I spent the happiest week of my whole life. Were it not for the fruit bowl and the now empty bottle of whisky I would think it had never actually happened, we had not spent those days like adolescents, like kids who hadn't yet learned the necessity of self-preserving cynicism.

When eventually he really had to get back to Ireland and I was alone again in the flat, he stayed with me on my shoulder, in my mirrors, in my bed. He was in every room, shadowing every thought in my head. A note left under my pillow said, '*Think of me every minute as I will think of you.*' In the kitchen there was an arrow pointing to the fridge and in the fridge I found a box of mangoes and where the eggs normally go he'd put cherries. In the salad compartment I found strawberries and kiwi and a note saying, '*Sweet fruits. For you. Until we die. A.*'

We were having dinner in a candlelit room with two friends of Aedan, Simon and Jenny Peterson. I thought Jenny was just about the saddest woman I had ever seen. She looked utterly bereft as she served up the fifteenth course, a fish dish. When the meal was over I found myself in a very small room – so small it might have been a cupboard. Aedan was with me. He was looking for a swimsuit for me.

'But I can't swim!'

'I won't let you drown,' he said.

We left the cupboard through a door that opened up into the depths of a dense forest. Narnia was mentioned and we both laughed, and then Aedan said, 'Jenny's dead. Had you realized that? She's been dead for a month.'

'But she served up fifteen courses.'

'Exactly. Have you ever seen anything quite so absurd?'

'But we talked to her . . . we had a conversation with her.'

'Dead for a month now. Longer.'

'Can we talk to the dead then? I mean, what about my mother? Can we talk to her? I miss her. Can we talk with her? Can we?'

But as we came out of the woods and into a field I turned

around for the answer to my question and Aedan was gone. I climbed over a stile and into another field. I walked through a kissing gate but there was no-one there to kiss. In the distance I saw a group of people. They looked like they were walking towards me. Moments later I went with them into a vast, palatial sort of house, only inside it was derelict, squat-like. In the crumbling mansion the people who'd taken me there started doing acrobatics; not your average cartwheel and forward roll, they were bouncing fifty feet into the air and running on their hands and tying their legs behind their necks.

'Try it! It's easy!' said a man, jumping to the ceiling.

'I couldn't.'

'Try it!'

'How do you do it? How do you do all these things?' I asked.

Someone said it was because they were all dead. They could do anything. An old friend of mine came over. I noticed he was wearing ballet shoes. When I asked him what he was doing with all those crazy people, he said, 'Some petrol leaked into my garage. It set me on fire.'

The penny dropped. Not before time.

'I shouldn't be here! I'm in the wrong place,' I said. 'I'm alive. I'm not dead.'

A hundred pitying faces closed in on me.

'Ellen. You were murdered on August the seventeenth.'

'No!' I cried. 'It didn't happen!'

'Terribly sad. A tragedy.'

'But I want to spend my life with Aedan!'

'Who?'

'Aedan.'

'No. You'll be happy here.'

'No! I'm going back!'

I woke up and turned all the lights on and looked in every room and boiled water for coffee. I felt sick and scared. It wasn't the dream that frightened me but something quite separate; some worry, some fear; the first of its kind. A doubt. It was four o'clock. I'd read somewhere that that was when people died in their sleep; when the body is closest to death.

Just a dream. It doesn't mean anything.

'Nothing!' I said aloud, cutting the silence with the word. I got back into bed with coffee and Aedan's letters and stayed awake for the rest of the night.

In the morning he phoned, a call which went on till about six that evening and so the night was all but forgotten. We lunched together courtesy of British Telecom. By the end of it all my face ached from laughing. We were safe again.

It seemed my whole life plan had changed. When I was a kid I had one single ambition and that was to be an actress. My mother said to me, 'Well you won't be able to have a husband and a family as well; the two just don't mix.' I really didn't care, and while my friends were playing Housey games I was improvising bizarre plays into tape recorders, playing all the characters. I put on ballets and plays for the family at Christmas. I dreamed of being on the stage at Stratford or in the West End, or staring down from a cinema screen. It was the only thing in the world I really wanted. I never dreamed of white dresses and wedding bells; nothing could've been further from my mind. Even the very first time I thought I was in love I never imagined marrying the guy; it wasn't important. It wasn't part of the plan. I did think that maybe I'd be someone's mother at some point, but perhaps when I was thirty-five or forty and perhaps alone. When my friends started to meet people and settle with them I watched from a healthy distance. From the age of seventeen to twenty-four I moved house nine times. In that time I met men and loved them and they loved me but they were never for ever. I couldn't imagine choosing one and forsaking all others; I liked change and excitement and more than anything I liked my independence.

And so when I met Aedan I was happily single. His arrival in my life and how it made me feel was unexpected, and suddenly I wanted this one man and no other and it was intense and all-consuming. I was besotted, in love, possessed by him. It had happened in a single moment. Alice said she'd expected it to happen all my life, because my life had always been like a film. She said it was not like real life where things fade into question and doubt; it was like a dream. It felt like one. I believed I would never wake up.

Chapter Six

At seven that evening a deeply frustrated make-up artist from the *Thérèse* production company telephoned to ask about my hair; what colour was it, what length, what texture? Copper mesh seemed to be the most accurate description I could give; it is fair to say my hair is damaged. It looks OK, so I'm told, sort of long and red, but it feels like straw.

She said she'd been trying to get hold of me all day – had my phone been off the hook or was there a fault on the line? Was I ready for tomorrow's read-through? And would I mind if she cut off some of my hair? I told her she could give me a skinhead if she liked, it was all the same to me.

I sat with the script and the novel and the mountain of notes I'd made. It occurred to me that most of the notes were irrelevant and half of them were nothing at all to do with the script. Quite a lot of them were about a woman sitting opposite me on the tube one day; I'd noticed she was doing the *Sun* crossword with a dictionary and it had obviously taken up the whole of my thoughts. Fortunately I'd read the novel five or six times before the job had even been thought of so I knew it inside out. I (Thérèse) am married to the sickly, doltish Camille. I meet Laurent, a healthy, virile artist. We embark on a wild affair, fall in love and drown Camille. A year or so later we get married but the union is confounded; we are consumed with guilt, haunted by the sickly white face of our victim. Everyone dies. Not a happy tale. I made some more notes about the script and read some more of the novel. Undoubtedly a masterpiece, by anyone's standards, the book certainly had the edge on the screen adaptation, which had more sex in it than torment. I took a break from it at midnight and called Aedan. I wouldn't have time even to breathe the next day; I had to get the first train to Manchester where I would meet the rest of the cast and where we would read through the script and drink wine and discuss our characters and any problems we might have. Filming was scheduled to start on the Monday.

'Hello, you've got through to the phone maid, Aedan speaking, sorry I can't—' Bloody machine. Where was he? I waited for the appropriate beep and asked him to call when he got home, regardless of the time.

I sat on the edge of the bed looking at the phone. At twelve-fifteen I picked it up to see if it was working. At twelve-thirty I called again, got the machine again and hung up. I'd never had much respect for people who wait for the phone to ring, sad and desperate, I liked to think I was above that sort of thing. Obviously I was wrong. By one o'clock I was really quite worried. I felt sick. One-fifteen and I was sure something was wrong, though the licensing laws are different over there so it was quite feasible he'd gone drinking with friends. Well, there was nothing wrong with that. I poured a glass of wine and tried to pack my imagination away.

I put the script into a little overnight bag and tried to find some clothes for the week away but I couldn't remember what the weather was like outside, whether I'd need a coat. Was it winter yet? I lit a cigarette and looked at the possibility of death. If he was dead would I know this instinctively? I had known when my mother died – or had I? Had I rewritten that memory in the three years since she'd died? If he *wasn't* dead then where was he?

I looked at the film schedule to see if we were going anywhere exotic on location. Manchester and London and possibly Budapest over a period of seven weeks. Budapest apparently looks more like Paris than Paris does and it's cheaper to film there. I imagined Aedan coming out to visit me, fucking me on the banks of the Danube and the thought made me feel slightly better. Well enough to pack seven pairs of knickers, two shirts – including one Aedan had left behind which still had the smell of him all over it, a very warm cardigan, a pair of trousers and my jeans which I would wear to travel in. It didn't look like I was going to get any sleep so I put them on. One-thirty now. Even if he'd gone drinking he would surely be home by now. I called again. Nothing. I took the jeans off and got into bed and chastised myself for overreacting. I got out of bed again and sat on the kitchen floor, listened to the traffic for five minutes, made coffee, threw it away, smoked, waited. At two-fifteen the phone rang.

'Hello, babe. It's only me.' It was Alice. I couldn't keep the disappointment out of my voice.

'Oh. Hi.'

'What's happened?'

'Aedan. I don't know. He hasn't called. I think he's going to leave me.' As I said it I realized that was precisely what I'd been thinking about since that bloody dream.

'Don't be ridiculous. He'll be asleep at this hour. Have you been fighting? Has something happened?'

'No.'

'Well, when was the last time you spoke to him?'

'Today.'

'When today?'

'All day.'

'You were on the phone *all day*? Shit, Ellen, whose bill was it on?'

'I don't know, his, I think.'

'What on earth did you talk about for so long?'

39

'Nothing. I mean, we laughed a lot. We talked about a million things. We wanked.'

'So what makes you think he's about to leave you?'

'I've no idea. It's just this feeling I have.'

'He could be at a party, or asleep or out somewhere or dead even.'

'I'd know if he was dead.'

'Ah, bollocks. How?'

'I just would. It's not normal, I mean, we aren't normal. We were never normal from the start. I'm sure I'd know.'

'You're imagining it. I'm sure there's nothing wrong.'

'It's two o'clock in the morning. Why did you call me?'

'I just did. I often do.'

'But why tonight?'

'Jesus, I don't know. I was feeding Jack and . . . well, you were on my mind so I called you.'

'Precisely.'

'Precisely *what*?'

'You *knew* I was in trouble.'

'But you're not in trouble.'

'You knew I was awake and you sensed I was in trouble and I sense that he's going to leave me.'

'Ellie, this isn't like you at all. Look, you're always awake. You're a fucking insomniac for Christ's sake. I simply called for a chat. That's it. As simple as that.'

'Something's gone horribly wrong.'

'Ellen. The man loves you. You're getting married. Do you suddenly doubt all that?'

'No. Not at all. Listen, babe, can I call you back? Only he might be trying to get through.'   ·

'Look, phone me. Any time. And don't worry so much. It's not like you, it's really not.'

'I'll let you know what happens.'

'Any time. Love you.'

I lay down on the floor and dragged the duvet over me and stared into space and shouted *Why why why*? into the stillness of the room. I am too crazy for him. A mad woman. A woman mad. Is that it? Is it London? Does he hate London? Is he afraid? Six weeks. Not a long time to know someone and be sure. Thirty-six and never been in love; he must be terrified. Suddenly meets a mad woman. Thinks it can't be real. I can't be real. A woman mad. A dream. Maybe I'd got it all completely wrong – maybe he *was* dead after all. Would I rather he was dead than alive without me? Such poisonous characteristics we see when we look too closely into the mirror.

Three fifteen. His voice at last. He sounded like a different man; cheerless. I knew.

'What's happened?' I whispered. Such a bloody long silence. A minute or more.

'Hello?' he said.

'I'm still here.'

'I don't think I can come over.'

I sat up and took a very deep breath, dizzy. When I tried to speak, nothing happened. I put the phone to my other ear like it would make a difference.

'Ever?'

Big pause.

'I don't think so.'

I whispered no no no no again and again so that whatever had just been said might be blotted out, so we could sleep and wake up and such words would never have been spoken. This was a mistake.

'I'm sorry.'

'Aedan . . .'

'I'm sorry.'

'Aedan, think about what you're saying.'

'I have thought.'

'I don't believe you.'

'I can't do it.'

'I don't believe you. You're scared, that's all. Moving, selling your house, me, it's a big step, marriage . . . We don't

41

need to get married. You don't even need to move. I never wanted to marry anyone – we can carry on as we are. I don't care, I love you.'

'It's not any of those things.'

'Is it Louis? He could live here – we could live with him here.'

'No.'

'He'd love it. Great schools. Parks. Opportunities. He'd be—'

'It's not Louis.'

'Is it Cara? Does she hate me? Does she want you back? Do you want *her* back?'

'No. No, we don't even like each other any more. It's not her.'

'Well what is it then? It can't all suddenly just *stop*, can it? Has someone said something? Frances! Is it her?' Oh God no, not her. 'Can't she just concentrate on her fucking husband? It's her, isn't it? What about her kids? She's got three fucking kids, what about them?'

'It's not Frances.'

'Have you seen her today? Has she been poisoning you?'

'Of course she hasn't.'

'Did you fuck her?'

'No.'

'Did you kiss her?'

'Not in the way you mean.'

'It's her, isn't it? Oh, shit, no Aedan.'

'It's nothing to do with her. It's me. I can't do it. I can't come over.'

'Has it all been lies?'

'No.'

But I no longer believed him.

'What about for ever then? And all this love and marriage crap? Has it all been lies? Are you making fun of me?'

'I love you.'

'Then what's the problem? Have we gone too fast? We

42

could slow down. We could live apart. We could just be normal.'

'We couldn't.'

'We could. We could take our time. Take it really slowly.'

'No.'

'For fuck's sake! We can't just *stop*!'

'But I can't come over right now. I just can't.'

'Then I'll wait until you can.'

'I won't let you.'

'You can't stop me.'

'Elle . . .'

'We could phone and write and meet up and I could visit you there and you could come here and we could always make love, I mean we can't simply stop. Don't you ever want to make love with me again?'

'Of course I do.'

'Then I'll wait.'

'I don't want you to waste your life on me. You're twenty-four.'

'It wouldn't be wasted. It's my life. It'll be wasted without you.'

'No it won't. You don't understand . . .'

'No, you're fucking right, I don't fucking understand at all.'

'Look, you're going places, you'll be a star.'

'Oh, fuck off. Don't patronize me, Aedan.'

'I don't mean to.'

'I'm going to be sick.'

'What?'

I was sick all over the film schedule.

'Are you all right?'

'Do I sound all right?'

I wandered into the bathroom with the phone under my chin, mopped myself up and sat on the edge of the bath.

'This is madness Aedan. Do you know that?'

'Yes. I think you're right.'

43

'You'll regret it.'

'I know. I already do.'

'Well, doesn't that tell you something?'

'Yes.'

'I'll change your mind.'

'You probably will, yes.'

'Look, tell me you'll think again.'

'I have thought.'

'I don't want to be without you.'

'You'll forget.'

'Never.'

'You deserve better. You don't want some long-distance relationship.'

'I want you.'

'It might be years before I move to London.'

'Then I'll wait years. It's worth it. Perfection, that's what you said it was. Remember? It was all perfect. Wasn't it? Wasn't it all perfect?'

'Yes.'

'So why throw it away?'

'I don't deserve you.'

'Bollocks. You're talking shite and you know it. You must have a better reason than that. What is it? Is it me? Am I too mad? Is that it?'

'I love you. You're more beautiful than anyone I've ever known. I'm astounded by you. I'm compelled. But I can't do it. I don't want you to change my mind. I don't want you to try.'

'How long were we on the phone yesterday?'

'All day, I know.'

'Were you leading up to this? When we were wanking were you thinking about this?'

'No.'

'I tried to call you all night tonight.'

'I know. I'm sorry.'

'I knew something was wrong. I knew it.'

44

'I don't know what to say.'

'It's my read-through tomorrow – today – for *Thérèse*.'

'My timing isn't very good.'

'Your timing's shite.'

'I'm sorry.'

'Oh, stop fucking apologizing.'

'Where've you to get to?'

'Manchester.'

'What time's your train?'

'Seven or eight. Eight, I think.'

'Are you ready for it?'

'I was. I don't know. I think so.' I actually didn't know anything. If someone had asked me my name right then I would probably have said Susan. The room looked exactly the same as before. I felt it should have altered in some way. Dried peach roses, stripped pine, everything the same. I looked the same. I still breathed the same air. I could change his mind.

'Maybe you could come to Manchester. We could talk. Properly.'

'Perhaps at the end of the week.'

'Yes. Yes, meet me in Manchester.'

We went on to talk about filming and Louis and food and money (I had none). He was always a bit worried I wasn't eating enough. He used to send me cash through the post and order me to buy food with it. It was beautiful Irish money and I was always loath to part with it. He asked me what clothes I was taking with me, did I have enough money, was I confident, scared, excited? We talked our throats dry until at six-thirty I left the flat and headed, exhausted, for Euston station. I got there way too early and called him up and asked him if he'd changed his mind. He didn't know. Perhaps. He would call me at the hotel. Was I all right? I'd been sick again. What had made me sick, he asked. He had.

'I've given you baggage, Ellie, when before you had none.'

'No. You haven't given me baggage, Aedan. I've got a bug. I'm as undamaged and baggageless as when we met.' I didn't believe it. 'Aedan,' I said, 'we won't be put asunder.' Ever the queen of drama.

I threw up at the ticket office, all over the floor. I'd looked for a waste-bin but they'd all been removed or sealed up. Bomb threats.

I bought sweets to take away the taste of sick. On the train I sat tearless, reading the script. I didn't feel like crying or thinking. I didn't feel much at all, except perhaps inside me somewhere there was a fight waiting to begin, and determination, alive and hot and strong which just about dried every other feeling up. I could not believe it was finished. This is only the beginning. And then away from all the love and the pain I felt something verging on hatred for him for doing this to me on the morning of my read-through. Damn him. Didn't he know how important this day was? Didn't he remember? Damn him. And then I couldn't damn him anymore because I suddenly smelled him on the shirt I wore and I remembered I had promised him the moon and meant it.

Chapter Seven

Cast and crew of *Thérèse* gathered together in a conference
room in the centre of Manchester. Food and wine was laid
on, the producer and the director talked animatedly in a
corner and the rest of us sat or stood around a long table,
scripts under arms or on chairs. We drank coffee and
smoked and discussed our journeys and the hotels we were
staying in, though as I'd come straight from the station I
hadn't actually seen mine yet. Some people already knew
each other and were busy catching up on personal news. It
was a very convivial atmosphere, which was not surprising;
a group of actors all working, all being paid and fed and
plied with alcohol will never be an unhappy assembly.

As Thérèse I was required to brood a lot and stare moodily
into nothingness. It was not difficult. By the time we got
round to actually reading anything I had no feeling left in
my brain. I sat next to Ian Turner, an actor with a sickly
blueish pallor who looked severely undernourished; ideal
casting for my husband, Camille. When Turner read, he was
so tense the veins in his neck stood out like he was about to
have some sort of coronary and his hands shook so badly
someone had to light his cigarettes for him. On the other
side of me was Matthew Howard, a bright young thing who
was quite clearly about to become a star. He was playing
Laurent. Not quite such ideal casting; unlike Zola's description of the artist as tall and dark, he was a redhead like

myself and his skin was fair. He was very beautiful though and I could see why they'd given him the job. Either way I didn't care. Liam Johnston seemed like a man who knew what he was doing.

We all read our lines with absolute indifference, which is something actors do at read-throughs though I've never learned why. When we'd finished Liam Johnston came over and hugged me and called me a pussy-cat and we all started on the alcohol and Ian and Matthew and I discussed the schedule and our characters and skirted around the issue of our lives. I did not speak of Aedan though it felt like every word that came out of my mouth was dripping in him. He seemed to have taken over my brain and my good sense. His voice was loud in my head. I thought more than once that I wasn't the only one who could hear it, that maybe everyone in the room was listening, but no-one mentioned it, no-one said, 'Where *is* that Irish voice coming from?'

Ian Turner, for some reason, was not staying in the same hotel as the rest of us. He had chosen to stay in a cheap little flat about five miles in the opposite direction. Perhaps he was as mean as he was nervous. Perhaps he was just frugal. Our expenses covered the hotel bill twice over so perhaps he was just making some money. Who cared? He said a very nervy goodbye and Matthew, Liam and I walked back to the hotel together. The two guys wanted to drink and talk and made a bit of a fuss when I said I was going to my room so I compromised by having a quick glass of beer with them, which tasted like poison, and then bolted upstairs where I could think in peace. I got into the bath trying to drown away the doubt and lay in the water till it was too cold to bear. It was impossible, I thought as I lay there freezing, to stop it all. It is not every day you chance on the missing half of your own self, and on meeting it, recognize it recognizing you. The two halves meet and melt into each other. To wrench them apart now would be to annihilate the whole soul. We couldn't have turned back then if we had tried.

I stood under the shower for a moment just to get warm again, at which point he phoned. He sounded tired and miserable. He said he was going to Cork to help clear his head. He would come back on Thursday to meet the writer of his next project which was to be about a very fat woman and a dwarf. Love prevented me from voicing any doubts about the artistic worth of such a venture and love prevented me from crying out loudly in selfish protest when he told me he wouldn't be coming to Manchester after all because he was going to meet Louis on Friday and would be spending the weekend with him. You cannot compete with a son. He would, however, endeavour to fly to London on Monday and we would talk then.

'Change your mind,' I begged, idiotically. There are few things in this world less attractive than a desperate mad woman on her knees.

'I'm going to disappoint you so badly, Elle.'

'You won't.'

I should have married him the day he'd first asked me. He'd said, 'Let's do it now, today, this minute.' What had prevented us? I remember a few days after that he'd phoned me from his office one afternoon and suggested I call the Register Office to find out what we needed to do. We could do it that day, he'd said. Would I mind? Was that what I wanted? Would I rather have a big white do in a cathedral? I got through to the Kensington and Chelsea Register Office and found out that all we needed was forty pounds and our passports. It was that easy. I'd slammed the phone down and thought *What am I doing? Are we serious here?* So I asked him. I called him back and said, 'Are you serious about this wedding bit?' and he'd said yes. Never more so. He'd said, 'This is how it should be. How it never is. Meet, fall in love, get married. Do it all in a week.' So when was he thinking of? 'Now. This minute. This week, this month. Not next year. Next year's not soon enough.' But what about our friends? 'OK, then,' he'd said, 'but if we have to wait let it be for only one month. We'll do it in November, in the Brompton Oratory, and all our friends will be there and we'll have a Mexican band. Can we have a Mexican band? Would you like that? Will we get married in November then, November the second?' And I'd said yes.

I took out my script to look over the next day's scenes but it might have been written in Swahili for all I could make of it. I was heavily distracted by the thought of Aedan and I dancing irreverently down the aisle to the strains of a Mexican band; a million friends leaping about around us.

I am not Bride of the Year material. I don't believe in God or the Church or religion. I would look ridiculous in a big white meringue of a dress. The last time I went into a church it was the middle of the night and I was very drunk and in search of my dead mother. Aedan, on the other hand, was a Catholic. Lapsed, he told me, but a Catholic nonetheless. Maybe *that* was why he wanted marriage so much. Maybe that was why he didn't. If I found that Catholicism was the problem dragging him away from me I would go and light a little Catholic candle and say a little Catholic prayer in a little Catholic church somewhere and then raze the whole fucking building to the ground.

When he phoned again at one in the morning to tell me he missed me and to wish me goodnight I asked him on a scale of one to ten how religious he was. About one and a half, he thought. Maybe less. Why did I want to know? Did I want him to light a candle for me? I said I didn't need a bloody candle, I was strong enough for the both of us. His voice was a tonic to me even though he had nothing positive to say. He told me he was afraid he'd said certain things that could never be undone, that he was a disappointment to me, that soon I would hate him for his weakness, his fear. I could not hate him ever and he would never be a disappointment. As for his words, I told him, nothing is irrevocable except death. Change your mind, I'd said again. He would regret it if he didn't. He agreed and I felt hopeful again and safe, safe enough to fall asleep at last.

The Pope married us. At least I thought he had; I couldn't be sure because he spoke in Polish. We turned around once our vows had been made and saw the Mexican band were having a break at the back of the church. One of them looked to be dead.

I said to Aedan, 'One of the band looks to be dead.' And he replied, 'Actually he is, but nothing could spoil this day.'

But it wasn't day it was night and as we opened the doors at the entrance to the church an icy wind battered its way past us. On the steps, just outside the door, a wolf howled up at the moon.

Aedan said, 'She sits on my doorstep all night and all day.'

The wolf howled again and looked at me with haunted eyes through the rain that was now falling.

'Better not get wet,' Aedan said, putting an umbrella up over me and the wolf.

'What about you?' I said. 'You'll drown in all this water.'

'Only room enough for two.'

'Yes. You and me.'

'But we can't just let her die.'

'Why not?'

Ignoring my last remark he took my hand and said, 'Will we all go home now?'

'I'm not sharing my bed with a wolf, Aedan.'

'She'll stay on the doorstep.'

'Always?'

'Looks that way.'

'Couldn't we find a home for her? With another wolf maybe?'

'How many wolves do you know?' He laughed. 'I've married such a crazy woman. Wolves indeed.'

And off we walked to our new home.

'Can't we just leave her at the church?' I whispered.

'But she wants to spend her life with me,' he said. 'And anyway, she's not a Catholic.'

'Neither am I,' I said, but I said it so quickly that through the rain he didn't hear. Even through the rain, however, we both heard the plaintive howl of the wolf as, when we got to our house, we closed the door on the beast and left it on the doorstep to get rained on. And we both heard the crash of breaking glass at the side of the house when, early the next morning, the wolf threw itself through the window.

Chapter Eight

When I woke I felt like I'd been badly beaten in the night, like my brain had been bruised. I went into the studios slightly early, hoping the feeling would wear away. I caught an horrific glimpse of myself in the mirror on the side of the extras' minibus. I hung around looking hideous until the coffee arrived and with the coffee all the questioning glances. Perhaps they thought I was an alcoholic. In the make-up caravan I had to endure a whole hour faced with my horrendous reflection. I thanked God or whoever that Kathy my make-up artist was exceptionally good at her job. She performed a veritable miracle on my hair which had seemingly died a gruesome death in the night and with several strokes of Clinique foundation she completely eradicated the blue lines under my eyes. Feeling too sick to eat anything I had more coffee on the coach and a cup of boiled water to settle my stomach. Matthew wandered over with a bacon muffin and orange juice and said I looked tired but a bit happier than I'd looked at the read-through – it's not my business etc., etc., but is everything OK? I said I wasn't unhappy at all but he looked unconvinced and for the rest of the day he had quite unnerving concern in his eyes. I think he tried to keep his distance but this was almost impossible as we had to shoot a particularly graphic sex scene later that afternoon. I was too weary to care and when it came time I stripped off without even thinking about it. I don't get embarrassed easily at the best of times. As soon as my knickers were off the cameraman left the room quite rapidly and Flo the dresser raced over with a bathrobe to cover me up but I couldn't have been less bothered. It was only a body after all. Matthew was not quite as uninhibited, but then I guess men are always a bit awkward about their willies. He looked deeply embarrassed as he peeled off the layers of clothing and he kept his knickers on till the last possible minute. We spent the rest of the day thrashing around together in this big old bed in a very cold room with Liam Johnston standing in the corner looking engrossed. He checked what paltry dialogue we had, made sure the lighting was right and the camera angles and whatever else it is that directors do, but essentially left Matthew and I to choreograph the thing ourselves. It was quite enjoyable. Any actor who says that filming sex scenes is a purely clinical thing is a liar.

By the end of the day however I felt wretched. I sat in the hotel bar feeling lost and Aedanless. I suddenly felt quite strange about the sex scene, as though in some way I'd been unfaithful. Someone other than Aedan had touched me, and even though it was just a pretence, some stranger acting out a role and getting paid for it, I felt it had somehow pushed me further away from Aedan, that I was losing him after all. I panicked at the idea that I might never make love with him again and that if I didn't, ever again, I would not have his fingerprints all over me but some stranger's, and a stranger who hadn't even wanted to do it.

I saw Matthew wander into the bar and got up to leave hoping he wouldn't see me.

'Ellie . . . Look, I know it's nothing to do with me but, well, whatever it is, if you want to talk about it, I mean . . . well, there's something wrong, isn't there?'

'I'm sorry. There is . . . I guess. I just feel that if I start talking about it then it'll be real and I'm trying to pretend it's not. Sorry I'm being such a bore. I'll sort myself for tomorrow.'

'It's not the job is it? I mean if there's something I can do?'

'No, no, it's not the job.'

'Well, I just thought . . .'

'No, it's . . . well, I think my boyf—' Was Aedan my *boyfriend*? It sounded ridiculous. Such a stupid label to stick on a fully grown man. So how should I describe him? My lover? My fiancé? Before I could think any further I'd said, 'I think my boyfriend's dying. Please don't tell anyone though. He might even be already dead. My fiancé.'

The colour, such as it was, drained from Matthew's face. Perhaps I'd gone a bit far. I've always found, though, that people are so terrified of death they don't interrogate you when you're touched by it.

'Shit. Elle, I'm really sorry. I don't know what to say. When did it? I mean, when did you . . . ?'

'All very sudden. Yesterday, before the read-through.'

'Bad timing.' Yes, I liked the man's style. He wasn't afraid at all. I was glad I'd told him. The relief of being able to talk, even such a pack of lies, was immense. '*Appalling* timing.'

'Mmm. Tell me about it. But hey, I haven't given up hope. I can't. Mustn't. It'll be all right. I promise I won't be a miserable cow all week. There's nothing worse, is there?'

'God, Elle, I'm really, really sorry. Have you been together a long time?'

Christ. 'I'd better be getting to my bed. Thanks for the chat. I'll see you at breakfast, then, shall I?'

What in Jesus' name was I supposed to say to people? Oh, yes, we've known each other for six whole weeks. We *were* getting married, until he jilted me. He proposed after five days and I accepted. I want to spend my life with him. If someone told me that I'd think *silly cow*. If I told people the truth about Aedan they'd think the same. *Mad fool*, they would say.

And they'd probably be right.

Chapter Nine

A letter arrived from Dublin. It was waiting on the bedside table one night when I got back to my room.

My darling,
I'm sorry. I cannot change my mind. I do not deserve you, never have.

It is not Louis or Frances that keeps me here but something in myself. With you in London I was completely happy. I felt freed. But I got back to Ireland and suddenly felt I must stay here. It seems the only thing we can do now is stop. I can't leave Ireland right now and in that I can only disappoint you. I can't bear any of this any more than you can. I did not deceive you, Elle. Everything I said I meant.

I'm so sorry to have to write such words but I don't know what else to do. I don't think I should come over as you suggested, perhaps that would only make things worse. I'm so sorry, love.
Your,
Aedan.

I read it over twice and mentally criticized the construction of it and thought that it did not sound like his voice at all, that he would never put words together in such a way. I dropped it onto the bed and said *Ha!* And moved quickly from bed to door to bag, clothes out on the bed, shampoo, script in hand, bath taps on – Ah, running water, such a sound as that – *Ha!* Again and again, clothes off, cigarettes out, lighter, coffee? Yes, room service – pick up the phone, the phone, coffee please, milky, sugarless, phone down, inhale, exhale, script down, pace, pace, smoke, the water runs, smoke, the coffee arrives and with the coffee a woman and behind the woman Alice stands. 'Surprise!' she says, her bags at her feet. And in a crumpled heap she found me and picked me up and steered me to the bed. I gave her the letter which she read rapidly and without expression. She poured coffee from the tray and passed me the cup and lit a cigarette from mine and we sat in silence and smoked.

'I'm learning to despise him.'

'Don't,' I said.

'I wouldn't worry though. He hasn't gone, he's just weak.'

'He's not weak.'

'Whatever.'

There were people in my life at that time who I know were of the opinion that this break-up was simply not worthy of analysis. A six-week affair hardly merited a breakdown.

I've spent years with people and not known them like I knew Aedan after only ten days. I've been in relationships that lasted months or years, that fizzled out or exploded. They were either good or bad, but either way they were temporary. Second best. I imagine there were people who thought the same of Aedan, that he was casual, temporary, second best. Alice was not one of the sceptics. She turned up that day and quite literally picked me up off the floor and we tore the letter into little pieces and laughed and then we didn't talk about Aedan at all. I had decided that he would have to come over the following week, whatever he'd said on paper. He would not be able to lie to my face.

And so I ignored the letter and started enjoying the job. I'd sort it all out when the week was finished. I had a few days off and we would see each other then and everything would be all right.

On Friday evening we finished shooting at around ten-thirty and I spent one last night in the hotel. I stared out of the window until the moon dissolved into sun whereupon I paid my bill and drank coffee in the foyer till it was time to go. He called just as I was handing my key back to the desk.

'Hello, my darling,' I said, chirpy. Worried, he said, 'Didn't you get my letter?'

'Oh, the blow out? Yes, I got it.'

'I'm sorry.'

'I think you should get over here. Whatever you've decided. Think we sort of owe each other a few words.'

'Are you very angry?'

'I'm not angry at all. So, when will you come?'

'Can't do it this coming week.'

'When then?'

'The next?'

'Fine.'

'Do you hate me?'

'Don't be absurd.'

'Have you had a good week's work?'

'What do you think?'

'Sorry.'

'No, actually it was fine. Everyone's very nice here. The crew's lovely.'

'I miss you, Elle.'

'Have you changed your mind?'

'I don't know.'

'Well your indecision is just killing me. Call me at home, would you? I've got a train to catch. Let me know when you'll be over.'

'Elle?'

'What?'

'I love you.'

'Good. Remember that.'

That was probably the shortest call in the history of our relationship. I almost went straight from the telephone to the airport to Dublin to knock some strength into him, some reason. To bring him home. If at any time he'd told me he didn't love me or want me, that it had all been a big mistake, then I would've given up without any fight, I would've stopped calling him, stopped all contact and got on with my life.

I would've let go.

But he said he thought of me every minute; that the idea of not having me in his life was a hideous one; that he loved me, missed me, that without me he was lost.

Well come home then. Come back to me.

Chapter Ten

In London I found that all the trees were dead. The grass was the colour of burnt sand and people were wearing coats and gloves and boots and walking with their heads down, fighting against the wind and the rain. The flat felt about as welcoming as a cold meat store. I spent half an hour trying to work out how to set the central heating, listening to the answering machine at the same time.

Lottie was back in town, which was a relief. Lottie and I had been friends since the first day of college. There was a message on the machine saying could we go out? She'd been away for more than two months, recording some songs she'd written with some oddball character who had a crush on her and lived in Cornwall in a renovated medieval church. I had missed her terribly.

Lottie was waiting for the Big break and/or a baby. She sounded like a cross between Shirley Bassey and Barbra Streisand to me; I was sure it was only a question of time before some record label snapped her up and offered her the world. As for the child she desperately craved, well, she'd be a great mother, I didn't doubt it, and perhaps that was only a matter of time too.

I called her and we arranged a time and a place to meet the next day and I ignored the other messages and lit the oven and tried to thaw out sitting on the floor in front of it. I felt angry and irritable. Winter is not my favourite time of year. Apart from the obvious discomfort and inconvenience of being so bloody cold all the time I always feel suffocated under the weight of winter clothes. I'm much happier in shorts and T-shirts. I prefer pure silk to pure wool. I'm happiest when I'm sweating and burning and collapsing from the heat. I like the grass to be green and wet and the nights to be long and warm and endlessly light. Londoners seem so unhappy and bloodless and constricted in winter; battling through the streets, buried alive by their woollies.

Aedan didn't call and I didn't sleep. In the morning I put on a heavy jumper and lots of restricting garments to keep me from freezing to death and went to meet Lottie at the National Theatre. We sat outside and drank coffee by the river. She looked tired.

'Is everything all right?' I asked. 'You're glad to be back, aren't you?'

'Yes.' She didn't sound it.

'Really?'

'Takes a bit of adjusting, that's all. Being back. I haven't seen Tom for three weeks.' She lived with Tom. As far as I knew they were very happy together.

'Is everything OK with you two?'

'I'm very tired, it's nothing more than that. I'm *weary*, y'know? I'm *disillusioned*. Jesus, it's been a whole year now. I'm terrified of becoming one of those women who sits by the bed with a thermometer and talks about fertility all the time. I mean, sometimes I think it'll just never happen, that I'll *never* get pregnant. And Tom . . . well, he just doesn't seem bothered at all. I mean he bothers that I'm upset but he's not upset himself. He says maybe it's a blessing that we have to wait.'

'Well, maybe he's right. Maybe it's not the right time for him. He's very young.'

'He's nearly thirty. Anyway I can't wait for ever. I'm twenty-four. I want to still be young when they're growing up.'

'You've got plenty of time.'

'You understand, though, don't you? You want to have kids with Aedan, don't you?'

'Sure, but not right now. We've not been together very long. I want some time on my own with him first.'

'Well, Tom and I have had five years.'

'I don't know what to say.'

'He spends most of his time with his bloody cartoons.'

'But that's his job. Put yourself in his shoes, I mean, if you suddenly got a big recording contract or something you'd want to spend all your time on that. Wouldn't you?'

'Yeah, but when's that going to happen?'

'Having a baby's not the answer to that problem though, is it?'

'No. But I've always wanted a family, even more than a career. I'm not like you.'

'I'm sure it'll work out.'

'I wish I was. Tom's just got work animating some fucking film in Germany. I'll never see him.'

'He won't be there for ever, though, and you'll be able to go and visit him. Think of the money.'

'Perhaps he's firing blanks. I can't wait around for ever only to discover we can't have them.'

'Lottie, that's terrible. Are you thinking about leaving him? I thought you were so happy.'

'I want to be pregnant. Now. This minute.'

'What if it were you, I mean, what if *you* were infertile?'

'It isn't. I've *been* pregnant. When I was sixteen I got pregnant by Mark Watt.'

'You never told me that.'

'I never told anyone. Not even Tom. I felt guilty ever since. Had an abortion.'

'I didn't know.'

'If I could turn the clock back . . .'

'Then what?'

'Well, I'd have my child.'

'Lott, you can't think that way. You mustn't regret something you can't change. You did what was right for you at the time. Just because it's not right for you now . . .'

'Maybe. Maybe not. Maybe I could've worked around it. I'd have an eight year old now.'

'Yes, and nothing else.'

'What else is there? Look, I don't know, you're probably right. Maybe Tom and I are just trying too hard. Maybe I should just be patient.'

'When is he off, then, to Germany?'

'Two weeks. He's coming back for Christmas.'

'What is it . . . is it a film he's animating?'

'Who cares?'

'Lottie!'

'How was *Thérèse*? Did you wow them all?'

'It was fine. Good. Ish. We've got a couple of weeks off. The director's gone off to Budapest . . . think we might be going on location there, all being well.'

'What are they all like?'

'Nice. I think. Didn't really get much of a chance to mix, it was mainly work. The guy playing my husband seems like a bit of an arsehole, but the other guy's all right . . . fabulous actor.'

'And what about Aedan? What's happening? Has he sorted himself out?'

'I don't know. I don't know what's going on. I think he's frightened. Can't really blame him, I mean, I'd be frightened of me. I think he's coming over on Thursday so perhaps we'll sort it out then.'

'What if he doesn't come?'

'He will.'

'What if this is it? What if it's all finished?'

A string quartet started to play over by the bookstalls. I turned round to watch them.

'Ellie, what if he isn't coming back?'

'Listen to that. Is it Elgar?' I watched the four musicians and then looked around in my bag for some money.

'Elle, think about it. What if he's not coming back? What if he's in love with someone in Dublin?'

'Do you want another coffee?'

'Yes. Ellie, listen.'

'No. I don't want to.'

'You can't wait around for him indefinitely.'

'Why not? Will I get you something to eat?'

'No. Just coffee.'

'Lottie, I know you're only thinking of my welfare. I appreciate it, I really do, but believe me I think about those things about as frequently as you think of having kids, or not having them. The thought of losing him . . . shit, the thought of losing Aedan makes me sick, physically sick.'

I got us both coffee and some more cigarettes and we sat in comfortable silence watching the river. I couldn't give Lottie a child and she couldn't give me Aedan, but we could at least let each other dream.

Chapter Eleven

I called Aedan three times when I got back to the flat. I left three messages. He didn't call back either that day or the next. I remember putting on a broken down old track suit that was neither black nor grey but a sort of sludge colour. I remember wearing it for days without changing it or washing it or even taking it off. I left the flat only to get cigarettes and milk. Once I bought a newspaper but left it in the shop and couldn't be bothered to go back for it. My agent called to sort out various things, Liam Johnston called, Alice and Lottie called. I performed for them, told them I was well and wonderful, rushed off my feet and excited about the next bout of filming and the money and my life. I told them I was having people over to stay in the hope they would all stop calling.

Eventually Aedan telephoned, full of inadequate apology for his long silence. I'd been losing hope of ever hearing from him again. He explained that a friend of his, Jim, had been rushed to hospital a few days ago and he'd been visiting him all hours of the day and night. He had chronic migraine this Jim who I'd never heard him mention before. 'Were there no telephones at this hospital?' I'd said, bitterly, instantly wishing I'd not said anything at all. Bitterness is never a winner. I apologized. He apologized. It had all gone wrong. He said that every time he spoke to me it seemed he hurt me a little bit more and this was not something he enjoyed. I said that not talking to him for several days was infinitely more painful and what was he playing at? I didn't believe the story about the friend and his fucking headaches for one minute. I didn't quite believe him when he said how much he loved me, missed me, wanted me, but madness in me said he would be back, he would be mine again, that we could repair the damage in an instant and forget.

I wandered around in my sludge shroud, going from room to room, staring at the walls. I put tapes into the stereo but they were never the right ones. I listened to Sting and 'Drowning by Numbers' because it was music we'd listened to together. I played the same two tapes over and over again. Ignoring the constant nausea I'd felt since he left me I set about getting him back but in a very listless way, like somewhere in me I'd lost hope. I wrote the odd letter to him, *odd* being quite an accurate description I see now when I re-read them. Some were light-hearted; a pretence. Most of them said, '*Come home come home I love you come home come home come home.*' I got his shirt out of my bag, the shirt he'd left behind, and buried my face in it and breathed and breathed but the smell of him had disappeared. I dragged out the four or five photographs I had of him but either his head had been cut off or he was too far away or out of focus. I pinned them all on the notice-board in the kitchen with the unpaid bills and postcards and receipts. I dredged my memory for details of our first meeting, the first time we ever slept together; I tried to remember the clothes he'd worn, the clothes I'd taken off, my clothes, the clothes he'd ripped away from me but the images were swathed in fog. I cried at my inability to conjure him up. I might have been someone else for the last two months, someone other than me. Memories pale so quickly.

Chapter Twelve

A stranger called on Thursday afternoon. He said he was
Aedan and he sounded like Aedan; they both had the same
soft Irish accent and they both seemed to know my name
and number but for the first half hour or so I talked to a
stranger. He asked about my life. I said I was coping with a
partially decorated flat and a mountain of debt and that the
weather was intolerable but apart from that . . . The stranger
kept saying, 'But what about *you*?'

'I'm fine. I haven't been out much. Looking forward to the
rest of the filming.'

'But what about *you*? Tell me about Ellen Millar.'

'What is there to tell?'

'Is she OK?'

'I need to see you.'

And the stranger hung up and Aedan said, 'Will we have
an argument if I say I'm not coming over next week?'

We might have done, had I not felt so debilitated.

There was an hilariously long pause.

'*Why?*' Sad and resigned. Perched on the edge of the bed I
was small and without defence, fight just dripping out of
me. My eyes fixed on the antique pine cupboard and the
dried peach roses. This home I'd tried to put together
mocked me as I muddied the peaches and lemons and
creams with my sludge. '*Why?*'

'I can't. I just can't.'

'Why not?' There must be something I could say to persuade him this was all wrong, this was not what we'd planned. If such a word existed it eluded me.

'I don't want to,' he said.

As simple as that. Not dramatic at all.

I slid down the edge of the bed onto the carpet, knocked over an ashtray and curled up on the floor, smaller than ever now, holding the phone like it was a dead animal I was trying to coax back to life, all the time knowing it would still be dead the next day and the next. Of course, he didn't see any of this and in the past he'd remarked on my spirit, my strength, and so I thought I must appear strong and in control and I must not weaken and I have the key to life and I know this because he told me, more than once he told me. He didn't see me disappearing in our bedroom, shrinking on the floor, and I didn't choose to enlighten him, though when I spoke I realized I'd started to cry. I was overwhelmed with defeat and such sadness I had never before imagined and all the words I wanted to say just did not want to be said. Instead I sort of choked great gulping sobs and I felt like I was drowning and somewhere I remember saying sorry, which he heard, and then I was fighting for breath and dignity, trying desperately to speak, for in speaking perhaps I could stop it all; make the clocks go backwards, make him see he was wrong. He was lying to me, he had to be because if he wasn't lying now then before might never have happened.

A voice came at last. 'Aedan . . . Aedan, if we've come to this, if you really mean – and you can't mean it – but if you do . . . Y'know, you say it stopped for you one day, as sudden as it started, and something massive changed in your life or maybe it was you, maybe you changed or were afraid or something, but *my life stayed the same*; nothing changed for *me*, and if for whatever reason you don't want to see me – and I can't believe that – but if you don't and you mean all this, then Aedan I have to see you, I have to see you one last time to tie up all the knots and touch you again and find out why you've done this to me and . . .' Sobbing and choking I'd made my speech and he had heard me, a different woman, all wailing and pleading, and this wasn't someone he'd fallen in love with. He fell in love with a woman who had the key to life.

'I'm sorry, love,' he whispered.

'What for?' I screamed, like a child. 'Why are you sorry?' He said nothing. It sounded like he was crying himself. Afraid now that he was just going to hang up and that would be the end of it all I said urgently, 'Aedan, please come. You have to. I won't try to persuade you to stay. I won't be angry. I won't get upset, I just need to talk. I love you. I'll let you go. I won't even touch you if you don't want me to.'

'I do want. I love you.'

'Then *be with me.*'

'I don't want it all to start again and if we see each other it will. I made up my mind. It's too complicated.'

'Why? It doesn't have to be.'

'Well, it is. I don't want to be in love with you any more. It's too difficult.'

'Tell me you love me.'

'I do.'

'Say it.'

'I love you.'

'But you won't see me.'

'I can't. I'm staying here. I've decided.'

Silence. Just me crying down the phone. I remember hearing my mother doing the same thing, years ago, when she was alone in the house one night. My father was off lecturing somewhere and she'd phoned because she was afraid. I had this image of her sitting on the stairs in the house I grew up in, crying, all small and lost. It broke my heart. I'd got on a train and gone to her.

Calm now, like it was all washing away from me, 'Is it over?'

'Yes.'

'Then you have to come over so we can say goodbye.'

As soon as I heard the words formed it was final and real. It *had* all gone. As the realization dawned on me I wondered why on earth I'd cried sooner because the pain that coursed through me right then was like none before and I felt suffocated and blinded and like suddenly I'd been pressed into the floor with wet sand. A whole beach of it.

He said then, 'When shall I come?'

'Soon.' Factual and quiet, like we were arranging a funeral.

'OK. I'll book the flight.'

I started to breathe again. 'Yes, book it now. Call me when you've done it. I'll meet you. Shall I meet you at the airport?'

'You don't want to schlep all that way.'

'I said I'll meet you. Do you want me to?'

'I'd love that.'

'Are you sure?'

'Yes, I'm sure. I feel relieved now, relieved to be coming.'

'Why?'

'Because you're right, you're right about everything. I'll book the flight now and I'll call you tomorrow.'

'No, today. Call me today.'

'OK.'

'I love you, Aedan.'

'You astound me.'

'How long will you stay?'

'Friday to Sunday.'

It didn't seem long enough at all. I wanted weeks and weeks. A year. I wasn't in a position to argue.

'Aedan, I can't bear this.'

'I'll see you on Friday. The thirtieth.'

'Tell me you love me.'

'I do.'

'Say it.'

'I love you, Ellie.'

'Change your mind.'

'I'm sorry, love.'

'So am I.'

'Friday, then.'

'Yes.'

'I'd better go. Leave you to your work.'

'Book the flight.'

'Bye, love.'

'Yes.' Small voice now. Phone down and the animal was really dead and I let out a wail. I was wracked with sobs as the pain engulfed me, and when I stopped screaming it struck me that we were never that hot on reproducing grief on the stage because when it was real it looked like it could only be a lie.

Chapter Thirteen

I set to work on the living room which was still overflowing with twenty-four years' worth of junk. I spent the best part of two days climbing in and out of boxes, dirtying rollers and brushes, cleaning them, dirtying them again. The sludge track suit became heavily splattered with County Cream paint. When I'd given the walls two coats and left them to dry for a few hours I heaved the carpet out of its plastic covering and grunting and wheezing I lugged it around the room. Some of the boxes got squashed in the process; ornaments got broken, glasses were smashed. I put everything into the hall to prevent further destruction and slashed the carpet in all the appropriate places till eventually it was laid and I collapsed into a heap in the middle of the floor and wept for an hour. When eventually I stopped and started work again I found there wasn't enough carpet left to do the hall and the bathroom so I made a phonecall and ordered more of the same. They said it would be delivered in two to nine weeks.

'Can't you be more specific?'

'No. Two to nine weeks.'

'Am I supposed to wait in for you?' I gave up. I put books on the bookcases. When they were filled I was still stuck with about seventeen boxes of homeless books so I went out and bought pine shelves for the walls which were looking bare. Spending so much money in such a short space of time made me feel almost alive again.

By the time I'd lugged the shelves home on the tube my interest in DIY had waned and anyway I couldn't locate one of the drill bits so I left the pine propped up in a corner to be dealt with another time. I rearranged the remaining boxes in a neat tower by the window and set about throwing away the rest of my belongings; old cards and letters, useless bits of paper, presents people had brought back from holidays that had never seen daylight. I was ruthless and without care. I put half my clothes into bin-liners and rolled them to the charity shop; I wanted no debris in my life, it was already far too cluttered. I took nine pairs of shoes to Barnardo's. My head ached.

In the grip of the shopping virus I bought two huge mirrors from a little man on the Old Kent Road. He gave me the pair for a hundred and seventy quid and delivered them and me back home for nothing. Alice said it looked like I was feathering my nest. Lottie said I should wait for Aedan to come home so we could do it together. Fat chance. I asked if I could borrow her Pentax because in actual fact *this was it*, he was only coming home to say goodbye. If I could just borrow the Pentax I would take a hundred photographs of the pair of us in our very temporary bliss. I would have a picture of every contour of his body and years from now I would show such a picture to my children and say *That man I loved beyond dreams*. Lottie looked disgusted and made a retching noise and said she wasn't convinced, but I didn't believe her at all. Sometimes I think it is the sole purpose of girlfriends to give you false hope. She laughed at me and said I was being over dramatic. I tried to tell her I'd faced it now, that this was the end, but she only laughed more.

I bought a bright orange jumper; a big happy looking thing made of chenille. At least he wouldn't forget me in a hurry;

it was so bright he'd probably have nightmares about it for months, and even if he did forget me he would never be able to forget the blaze of orange he spent a wild weekend with; an orange so orange you could almost taste its sweetness.

I hoovered and cleaned like a woman possessed. I washed the track suit and flung it to the back of the cupboard out of sight. I was cold all the time so I turned the heating up full and raced around maniacally in T-shirt and shorts. Lottie came over with the camera and some film and wished me luck. 'Maybe you could turn the heating down, Ellie?' she'd said as we sat sweating on the kitchen floor.

'But I'm so *cold*!' I said, fainting from the heat.

'Do you want him to *die*?' she said. 'This heat!' I was smiling rather brightly and felt proud of the disguise and then she asked me how I was coping and I couldn't answer. I couldn't speak. I was sick. She asked was I looking after myself? Well who else was going to do it? I said. Of course I was, I was just feeling a bit sick. It was probably the excitement.

When she'd gone I felt abandoned. I felt like the reality I'd been hiding from was now coming too close. Tonight; Aedan would be here, in my home. What rules would I have to adhere to? What would we be allowed to talk about? Was I just going to weep the whole time he was with me? Would I be sick again? Would I weaken? Would I lose control? I put on some warm clothes and killed time buying croissants and juice and some marmalade for Aedan. I found some orange-ish carnations and bought a dozen and about ten pounds of disappointing English winter-type fruit. I put the flowers in a jar by the bed, had a long bath and got into the orange jumper. I tied apricot silk in my hair and got out some mascara which was nearly dried to dust with neglect. Ready. Four hours early. How would I live through the time? I lit a cigarette and opened all the windows and waited till it was time to leave. When eventually the clock said six forty-five I tore out of the building as though it was on fire.

Chapter Fourteen

Heathrow was a swarm of people and baggage and nasal announcements. I went straight to domestic arrivals and bought coffee and smoked. I'd been quite calm on the tube, watching the stops, humming to myself, but now I began to feel fidgety and sick and I couldn't concentrate on being sane (and I needed to) and I was lighting one cigarette from another and swallowing a menthol sweet every five minutes so I didn't reek of tobacco. Would he kiss me anyway? Did it matter what I smelled of? Was kissing allowed? Would we be allowed to touch each other? Would we have sex when we got home? On the way home? In the restaurant? Would we have it *ever again*? I looked at an arrival screen and discovered that his plane was due in ten minutes later than I'd originally thought so I bought another coffee which tasted just vile after all the menthol and I smoked some more and waited.

His plane landed and I abandoned the coffee and stood by the luggage carousel and tried to look casual and thin. He would at least be able to spot me in the orange jumper; the crowd was grey. More menthol and then he was there and I felt a rush of adrenaline and nausea and relief and he seemed smaller than I remembered but more beautiful and more Irish. He was standing jammed on an overcrowded escalator that moved so slowly I kept thinking it had stopped. He was talking to some woman behind him who was all covered up with scarves and things like there was some sort of blizzard outside and who turned out to be a fairly famous actress called Kate, looking very beautiful and bruised beneath all her woollies.

Then he was there on the ground and coming through the crowd towards me with the actress following and I wrapped myself around him and held him for much longer than I'd intended and we neither of us spoke and then eventually he introduced me to the actress and we headed towards the underground talking about filming and generally being very polite and aware of Kate. She was not an idiot though and said she was in a hurry and would we mind if she went on ahead of us? Aedan stepped in front of me onto the moving walkway and I put my arms around his waist and clung on to him and breathed in the smell of him and wondered if such behaviour was permitted but then we were suddenly both laughing because we couldn't not and he handed me a bag with a bottle of Bushmill's in it which I knew we would have to drink together.

In the ticket queue he kissed me and I said, 'Is it allowed?' and he kissed me again, hard on my mouth and someone pushed in ahead of us and someone complained but still we kissed.

Much mauling and laughing on the tube and he said, 'It'll be all right, won't it?' like this was a surprise to him and I said I told you I told you. At Covent Garden we got out into the air and pondered restaurants, though he had eaten on the plane. He suggested Smith's but it was a Friday; I said we'd never get a seat and anyway it was too much, it'd be too busy and loud, so we opted for a quieter authentic-looking Italian place. It wasn't authentic at all and the food was muck so we left most of the meal on the plates and drank an inordinate amount of wine. There was a moment when I almost lost my resolve; something he said touched me so sharply I almost cried. But he saw what had happened and he looked so helpless and so full of guilt that I checked myself and pretended momentarily that I was not me and when the danger had passed I aimed to get fairly drunk and enjoy the safety of oblivion. We would have a perfect weekend. I would make sure of it. He would never be able to say goodbye to me at the end of it because of course it wasn't the end.

He was wearing a brown leather jacket. I remarked on its beauty and he offered to give it to me. I had never seen it before. So many things in his life I had never seen or touched. Poor Frances, I had said once. Poor Frances. *She* had seen the jacket. She had seen the pillows on his bed, his son, the walls of his bedroom. She would see them all again. Thinking this I remember having him kiss me all winey and garlicky and he paid the bill and took me outside and held me tightly like the wind was about to blow me away. In the cold and drizzle he pushed me into a doorway and pressed his face against mine, saying my name over and over. I can still smell that jacket, as though it were pressed against me this minute. Now I wish I'd taken it from him when it was offered. I think it went to a charity shop in the end.

We got back to Borough fairly early in the evening. At the station he took my hand and we walked back to my flat which was still too hot to breathe in even though all the windows were open. I turned the heating right off and we lit a candle in the bedroom because there was no lamp in there and we sat on the floor drinking the whiskey. We talked about our weeks. What about Her? Would he stay with her now, now that he wouldn't stay with me? He said he'd seen her. They'd fought a lot. I had ruined her life, she said. He had seen Frances and he would see her again no doubt. The relationship was not dead. I remember making a lot of flippant remarks and regretting each one before it was even out of my mouth. But he was humbled. He had hurt me, he said. Such regret. More whiskey and I got drunk enough to read him a poem, the memory of which I wince at even now. I said we've no need to have regrets. Turn back, it would be such a mistake to let go now, and then we were somehow in bed and touching and in spite of the weariness in us and pain, we made love and simply didn't stop, and as we were fucking he breathed For ever For ever For ever and I spat Yes, yes, *always*, and hours later we fell asleep. We were on top of each other, wet from fucking and sweat, and we stayed that way till about ten o'clock the next day when we seemed to wake in the same minute. I dragged myself out of bed and brought us a bottle of water and crept back under the quilt as if any sudden movement might wake me to find he'd never been there at all.

But he was smiling in drowsy contentment and I pressed my hands out flat on his chest to feel the reality of him, breathing in the smell of him and we drank the water and he ate me for breakfast and we had a very tired fuck and laughed a lot and I came a lot and much later we dragged our bodies into clothes and went out to shout all over our London streets and I thought *I cannot lose this man*. We cannot lose each other. I thought we would never be able to say goodbye properly, this weekend or ever and I thought that such fatigue and pain and confusion and love and grief would end up killing us both.

We looked at clothes in Covent Garden. We looked at clothes and candles and books and each other. We finished the film in Lottie's camera so he bought us another one and we clicked away in wine-bars, shops, in the streets, in doorways. We photographed each other all over London. It was a happy time. I felt we were under no threat. We ate a particularly good meal at the Café Pelican and later we watched *Husbands and Wives* at The Lumiére and laughed at all the rotting relationships. Smug. Sated from the comedy we wandered through town to the Embankment. I felt a bit dizzy, so we stopped at the Europa and then we headed home. The flat was too hot again. We opened all the windows and stripped off and took photographs of the two of us standing naked and hot in front of the new mirrors.

'Aedan . . .' Talking to his reflection I found strength. 'Don't leave. Come back to me soon.'

He said he was selling the flat in Belfast. He would be in London for the new year. He would not be away from me for long. And what about Frances? He didn't seem to be able to leave her either.

'I'm not in love with her any more. Not for a long time, now.'

'Will you still see her?'

'I have to. We're linked. She's a friend. We're best friends.'

I wasn't altogether happy with the best friend bit but it seemed a minor consideration if he was actually coming home.

'Will I meet her?'

But he didn't answer and we stopped talking about her and he took me into the bathroom and fucked me over the bath and then again in the hall against the wall. My knees bled.

It was about four o'clock when he fell asleep. I watched him in my bed. For two hours or more I sat looking at him until without waking he opened his arms towards me and I crept into them and fell asleep myself.

We went on a river boat; an old, apparently rotting vessel called *Fantasia*. It started to spit with rain and all the passengers went down to the sheltered seats and we were left alone on the deck. We didn't move into the dry cabin area because it was so warm – such bright, warm sunshine for October – or was it November now? We took advantage of the absence of the other passengers and he started to get into my jeans and I opened his shirt and his trousers and he pulled the jeans to my ankles and said, 'How could I leave you, love?' The jeans got stuck over my shoes. 'Leave them,'

I said, 'I'll do it.' I got one shoe off and he said, 'I can't wait any more,' so with the jeans hanging from one foot he pulled my knickers down to my knees and came into me with such force I shouted out and he put his hand over my mouth and pushed me backwards onto the seat. We came very quietly and he got up and walked away. I said, 'Come back, Aedan, don't go yet!' and a little girl appeared from the other side of the boat; a beautiful little girl with soft looking curly red hair and navy blue eyes. She said, 'How could you do this? I'm *so* embarrassed.'

'He's only gone to get us a drink,' I said. 'He'll be back soon.'

'Have you no shame?' she said, throwing Aedan's leather jacket over my legs.

'I'm sorry,' I said, 'but I love that man.'

'You're a fool,' the child said, and I watched as she slid through the railings into the water. I leaned over and shouted to her, 'I can't swim!' and she yelled back, 'It's too late now anyway. How could you *do* this to me?'

Aedan came back and I said, 'Help me! Quickly! There's a little girl in the water!'

'Where?'

'Over there!'

'I don't see anyone,' he said.

'She's there! She's drowning!'

'Where?'

Too late. Already dead.

Chapter Fifteen

I woke up alone. Late. The clock said ten-thirty but perhaps it was lying. I leapt out of bed into the kitchen, the hall, the bathroom. He was in the living room reading.

'I thought you'd gone.'

We sat and looked at the floor for a while.

'I have to go back this afternoon—'

'Not this evening?'

'Will we go to Camden first? Get you a lamp for the bedroom?'

'We don't have time.'

I made breakfast which we didn't eat. I took a photo of Aedan washing up the plates and glasses with no clothes on. We went back to bed. We tried to make love but couldn't. He phoned the airport to see if he could change his flight. It couldn't be done. We tried to make love again, went through all the motions, but it was a tragedy. We took more pictures. I got a heavy feeling like an iron bar on my chest. Then we got dressed and left the flat. At Heathrow we sat in the coffee shop and I cried. He cried. He looked terrible, defeated. He looked terrible but he still went. He still left. I watched him pass through the barriers and he watched me in my orange jumper as I cried and cried. I wrote a letter on the way home without him.

Beloved.

Darling lover.

*Thanks for such perfection. The weekend. Your love.
Such bliss I had. Such fear at the airport just now – I
wonder has your plane lifted off yet? I almost stopped
it leaving – I was so tempted; I pictured you coming
back through the barriers and me still sitting in that
coffee place drinking my cappuccino. I thought
perhaps a bomb scare would do the trick but don't you
need a special code word?*

*You'll probably reach Dublin before I reach home.
Bizarre isn't it? Such is the efficiency of London
Transport. We've just passed through South Ealing and
that busker's just got on – the one with the attitude
problem, remember?* HE'S SINGING THE SAME SONG!!! *God,
he really does hate his job, this guy. He's just told
someone to fuck off.*

*Aedan, Aedan, you cannot give up. This weekend
has surely proved that. We are happy here together.
You'll get better jobs here, you'll have a life – so many
of your friends live here and I'm here and you can do
better work here and have access to more actors. I
keep remembering Friday night, all drunk and still
fucking and never sleeping – we never do, do we? –
and your face all over me and candlelight and whiskey
and you. You can't just take it away one day and not
regret it for ever. After the last few days I can only
love you more. It would be so wrong to stop now. So
utterly wrong. You can't get out of my life now and I
cannot get out of yours. Please, Aedan, just remember.
Christ, we're at Piccadilly Circus already. The train's
going faster than I am. I keep stopping to reminisce.
Saturday night in the twenty-four-hour shop buying
pop and water. You in my home. You in Chelsea. The
two of us. I love you. I love you. My stop now. Take
care of yourself and for God's sake remember and*

*don't give up when everything we have is made of real
magic.*

All my love is yours,
Elle.

I pushed it in the postbox before I had time to think about
it. I called his house and left a jolly sounding message and
waited for him to call back. His machine was clogged with
messages. I imagined some of them would be Frances saying
'Where are you? Call me back, call me soon.' Just about
everything I'd said and more.

About an hour later he called. He sounded tired and
distant and somehow changed, as though the weekend had
happened ages ago or hadn't happened at all. He said he
needed to think.

'Aedan, don't just remember getting on and off planes.
Remember how we were.'

'It's just not as simple as that.'

'Why not? What's the problem? Is it her?'

'I just need to think.'

'Well, yes. Think of the weekend. It was perfect. Doesn't
that tell you something?'

'It tells me my life would be hideous if you weren't in it.'

'Then have me with you.' Really it seemed very simple.

'I'm really tired, Ellie. My ear's sore. I don't want to talk
anymore.'

And that was how we left it and the flat was empty of him
again and I faced another sleepless night haunted by him.
When I'd first got home that night he was still there; his hair
was all over the sheets and the whole place was covered in
his fingerprints. But now it was like this was someone else's
home and I was a visitor there. The whole place stank of his
absence. Perhaps I would follow him home; go over to
Ireland and stay there until he was persuaded. I would wait
on his doorstep if I had to. Perhaps I would howl up at the
moon.

Alice came over and said I looked tired. I told her about the weekend.

'Well, it sounds wonderful. So why do you look so pissed off?'

'He's still seeing Frances.'

'Are you sure?'

'Well, he says it's a doomed relationship, but I called him just now and he was all Dubliny with me, all distant. Says he needs time to think. If he has too much time she'll persuade him, I know she will. She phones him all the time, six or seven times a day. They live round the corner from each other. He helps her kids with their homework. They go wine-tasting together. I feel like a mistress.'

'Is he still fucking her?'

'He says not, but how can they not be? I couldn't be platonic with him. Why should she be any different?'

'Look, he has some say in all this. He might not want her any more.'

'I doubt that.'

'We *chose* this. We chose men with women and children in their lives. I knew all about Linda when I met David. And I knew he had a son. I accepted it. And now they're a part of my life whether I like it or not.'

'I know. But, y'know, I knew about Frances and Cara and I just thought it wouldn't matter, I thought I meant more to him than them.'

'You'll never mean more than his son.'

'No, but Frances. She sounds hideous. He says she's very short with straggly inky black hair. Poisonous little dwarf. He says he's not been in love with her for ages, if ever.'

'He sounds very weak, Ellie. Are you sure you want someone that weak? I mean what is he *doing* with this awful woman?'

'I don't know. Look, I know what you're thinking, but it's different with him. We're on another planet when we're together . . . I'm lost without him, without the idea of him. God, let's talk about something else. How's David?'

'He's not speaking to me. He's gone out.'

'Who's looking after Jack?'

'Sophie, our new nanny.'

'Alice! God, that's fabulous. When did you get her?'

'Yesterday. It *will* be fabulous, when David's got used to the idea. That's why he's not speaking to me. He doesn't think we should leave Jack with a stranger.'

'Well she won't *be* a stranger for very long.'

'Exactly. Dave will probably have fucked her by the end of the week.'

'Where's he gone tonight?'

'Fuck knows.'

'Are you worried?'

'Not really. He's in his track suit and that awful mustard top so he won't be with a woman.'

'When was the last time he messed around?'

'Eighteen months . . . I think. No-one since Fay. Now Jack's here he doesn't have the energy.'

'God, Alice, we're intelligent women. What are we doing?'

'Perhaps we're just pretending.'

'Pretending . . . ?'

'To be idiots.'

Chapter Sixteen

I took the films to Boots. The guy behind the counter charged me ninety pence and handed me two envelopes. On the first he'd scrawled FAILED in big red letters. The second one had two photos in it: one of Aedan with no clothes on doing the washing up and the other of him at the airport looking terrible.

'What went wrong?' I said.

'Could've been anything. Could've been the camera.'

'But it's a Pentax.'

'A freak accident then.'

On the phone that evening Aedan tried to make me better by saying there'd be many more opportunities to take pictures. Next time he'd bring his camera and buy me one of my own. I felt hollowed out by all his promises. I stared at the blank negatives for over an hour.

On Tuesday I was filming again and glad to be doing something other than living real life. Matthew Howard was mobbed by adoring women at the location. There was some fuss over how they'd found out where to find him but he was unruffled by it all. I think he was secretly enjoying the adulation. He'd made a film for the BBC and it had been released for cinema that weekend. The press was calling him the next Daniel Day-Lewis. Ian Turner who was attracting no attention even from his colleagues was quite clearly sick with jealousy and kept fluffing his lines and saying Fuck a lot. I was asked by some rakish-looking journalist if there was any truth in the rumour that Matthew and I had set up home together. I laughed in his face.

By mid-morning all the women and most of the paparazzi had been moved on by security which was a relief to everyone as it looked as though we were never going to get any filming done and daylight doesn't last too long in November.

'Chop, chop. Time is money!' the producer said, biting her nails.

At lunch, against all my better judgement, I called Aedan. He'd started work on the dwarf project and was ensconced in an office at a TV station in the centre of Dublin. We joked around a bit. We had two alter egos called Bryan and Brenda; they had cleft palates and thick North Country accents. They were very crude and stupid and made us laugh a lot. He sang to me. He sang Sting's 'Be Still my Beating Heart', though this wasn't anything unusual as he'd sung me songs right from the first day we met. He sang Madness songs and show-tunes and Steely Dan and The Beatles. We talked more and he sang more and then there was a slight pause before he said, 'I think we should leave it at the weekend,' and I said, 'It's Frances, isn't it?' and he said in a way it was; he'd been with her a long time now. They were fighting every day, he said. All the time. Over me. She said I'd ruined her life. He wanted to put things right with her. He felt he ought.

'You *ought*? You *ought*? What about me? You never fight with *me*. Aedan, she's married, she's got someone else's kids. Surely if it was worth it, if you loved her, wouldn't you already be with her? If you really loved her you'd never have even met me, you'd never have come to London in the first place.'

He said that he loved me still. In a few weeks he was going up to Belfast to try to sell his flat. He would be busy. We wouldn't see each other. Was she going to be there? He said she had relatives nearby and yes, she'd be there sometimes. I told him to think about the weekend, to think about what we were like with each other and then I got a signal from make-up and I had to go and have my face repaired for the next scene.

I understood Thérèse a bit more every minute. I understood now why she and Laurent had killed Camille. I thought of going over to Dublin or Belfast or wherever the fuck they were going to shack up together and stealing Frances' car and mowing her down with it. I would mow her down and then reverse over her. I heard her bones crunch under her own wheels. I saw her in the rear-view mirror lying helpless in the road as I drove away.

Kathy gave me a cup of tea but all I could taste was metal. Everything I drank tasted like battery fluid. At the end of the day when Matthew suggested we fuel the rumours by having dinner together I accepted, but when the food came I found I couldn't eat anything. I got the waiter to bring me boiled water and sipped at that instead. Matthew was apparently undisturbed by this and kept the conversation alive and ate my meal as well as his own. He was good company. At the end of the night he asked about my problems which he'd been tactful enough not to talk about all day. I guessed he was referring to my dying fiancé so I told him there wasn't much hope but, hey, I was doing fine and then I let him drive me to the tube.

Determined to stay calm and not behave like a lunatic I wrote Aedan a card which simply said, 'Life is just shite without you.' I thought it best to keep things simple and to the point and I would've left it at that but the phone rang at about two-thirty in the morning and an Irish woman said 'You've ruined my life.'

So I wrote a letter that wasn't simple at all.

Think of me. Think of the weekend – think of every fucking hour we've spent locked together. You said For ever for ever and for ever and that you loved me. She won't give you for ever. She won't give you children or joy. She won't give you for ever. Aedan, she's round the corner from you and she can poison you and tell you you're a fool and that it won't work and I'm a

*million fucking miles away and when we're together
you say Yes Yes and for ever and if she's any friend to
you at all she will see why you make love to someone
else and you can't cut me out of your life when the
time we spend together is perfect and when once we
spent six hours a day on the phone and we fucked
each other even with the sea between us.*

*If you'd been in love with her you could never have
fucked me and loved me and kissed me till the fucking
skin on my face was coming off, y'know, I looked in
the mirror this morning and I saw your absence and
my skin was literally flaking off from your kisses like
the very first weekend we got together my face was
blistered from your kiss and I cannot see how you
could take all that away from me and just disappear.*

*You were in London when I met you. Away from
her. You said she was on your shoulder. And then she
was not. That much you love her? We never fought
over her like you and she fight over me because we
never had the need to fight about anything and you
were happy in London and you'll be happy here again
and you're unhappy in Dublin because she won't let
you move on and if you're thinking of coming to
London then what possible gain is there in telling me
it's all gone when in one breath you say you love me
and in another you say For ever for ever and for ever
and when you know that as soon as you get back here
we'll be off again, living. We'll be back to square one.*

I left it at that. Short and sweet(?) I didn't even sign it.
The following day I sent him a piece of paper with a
painted daisy in the corner. On it I wrote:

*Set me as a seal upon thine heart, as a seal upon
thine arm. For love is strong as death.*

Chapter Seventeen

I found a card from him on the floor by the door. I'd had a long day filming. I wasn't in the mood for excuses. There were none. It simply said, 'Ever thine, Aedan,' and some kisses. How could I give up on him when he constantly sent me hope? I drank some boiled water and wondered where I could buy some fish. Instead of fantasizing about Aedan's momentous homecoming, or about murdering Frances, I was dreaming of fish all the time; raw fish, pickled fish, fish with heads and eyes. I had to have one. I cycled over to the Embankment in the middle of the night one night and bought some roll-mops from the twenty-four-hour shop. They were disappointing, they were only herrings, after all. They too tasted of metal. Perhaps it was the water. I complained to Alice.

'You're pregnant, aren't you?' she said, clearly horrified.

'What?' No, no I couldn't be. 'That's a ludicrous suggestion.' I was an intelligent woman; I wasn't a schoolgirl. But I looked in my filofax and found my period was late and, as I remembered our stupidity when we met and always after, it dawned on me that maybe this time my foolish bloody luck had run out. I took solace in the fact that eight days isn't exactly a long time and told Alice this, pointing out that it wasn't like I'd had any other symptoms. She questioned me on my metallic mouth and the number of times I'd thrown up in the last few weeks. I was shocked. Even as a teenager

I'd always been responsible and nowadays I always used condoms because of AIDS. But never with Aedan. What had I been thinking of? Had we regressed, the pair of us, into adolescence?

I thought about other things. I figured if I didn't think about it I would be relaxed and the problem would right itself, perhaps it wouldn't exist.

My friend Stevie came to stay. Her heart was broken. There was a lot of it about, it seemed. She wanted help; this man she'd been seeing had dumped her, not for the first time, and he always treated her badly but still she loved him. What should she do? I said I really couldn't advise as I had proved myself to be a total idiot. Stevie said perhaps I should send Aedan a letter. God, if only she knew. I was keeping the local post office in business; I'd sent him a letter every day. But each one of them said nothing except Come back to me, because that was all I had in my head. As far as Aedan was concerned that was the only problem I had and I found I couldn't tell him otherwise.

I put shelves up in the living room and unpacked the rest of my books. Alice said, 'Don't lift anything, don't move any furniture.'

'Who else is going to do it?' I snapped, sorry for myself. I bought a pregnancy test. LIAR I said when it said, *Yes there's a baby in there*. LIAR. And Lottie said, 'You're lying to yourself.' I read *Return of the Native* in a single sitting. I read *Brightness Falls*. I read *Madame Bovary* for about the jillionth time. I went to the cinema and wept at everything. I worked every day, all day, if not on the filming on the flat. At night I wandered around in a state of perpetual disbelief as still no period came. There was something odd in my character that almost wanted me to be pregnant just for the drama of it. My father used to say that I court drama, I woo it with my whole being; that without it I'm never fully alive. It would seem he had a point. So courting the drama I imagined that inside me a foetus lived that would grow into a little person and come out looking like Aedan and sounding like me and I would love this thing for ever, like mothers do. Drama and emotion aside I was actually quite worried about the practicalities of it all and I was angry with myself for years of decadent living. I had no money and the money from the film would be swallowed up in the abyss that was my overdraft. And how would I work to earn more money and look after a child at the same time? How would I live? I would be alone and poor and tethered to a child. I needed help. I had to tell him. I wrote him a letter but really I wanted him to guess. I wanted it to not be happening. I wanted him to come home before he found out. I wanted him to come back purely because he loved me.

Aedan,

I am sure, almost, that by the time you get this, any crisis either real or imagined will have blown away. I imagined that these were words I wouldn't have to send you because alone here since you've gone I've lived with disbelief at my own body and fear at all its messages and what can only be madness because I must be mad to want you as I do and it must be mad not to leave you drowning in your own mistakes but I am driven to haul you out each time you sink and hold you dripping in my arms.

I have not been able to share this thing with you because I was afraid it might break what fragile contact we still have left. So many times I've wanted to pick up the phone and say Help me, please. Tell me I'm not alone in this.

I think I might be pregnant.

I feel almost certain that I'm not though my friends tell me I'm hiding from reality, the reality being that I am now fourteen days late. I keep thinking that perhaps I've got some virus or that it's just stress or that my periods have stopped in grief at the loss of you; I mean, these things do happen to people. What just kills me is that I've been walking around the flat for days now, sleepless, and I'm going to the loo every five minutes and always I expect blood and it just isn't there and I feel so completely separate from every thing and every one. I'm telling you now in the hope that I might not feel so alone. A problem shared and all that crap. I shall probably come on any day now and we'll wonder what all the fuss was about.

This has forced me to think, properly, and although I long for you still, for something of you, I don't think I'm ready for a child. I don't know if I could look after one alone, nor do I have any desire to and I don't want you without your love and I am not Cara; unlike her I am not stupid enough to think that a baby would bring you home. But, Aedan, we were fools together you and I and I want to hear your voice and I miss you and I am so utterly wracked with such fucking sadness that we started with such hope and fervour and love and passion. What the hell happened to us both?

I was afraid to mention this to you, afraid that you'd send me the money for an abortion or something equally thoughtless, loveless.

Hey, maybe after all this angst I'm not pregnant at all. Maybe I've got a virus brought on by nights and nights without you, invariably hot and sleepless. I drown in sweat here. I am nauseous, but perhaps because of your absence, which I cannot bear. I love you. I love you. Please God don't tell me it is all lost.

I heard nothing. I thought perhaps the letter had got lost. My friends said Where *is* he? And I said *I am not pregnant.* And anyway, even if I was that's no reason for him to come back.

At night, curled up alone, I allowed myself my child. I imagined it was a girl, though secretly I craved a boy. I called her Daisy. I did another test and again it said, Yes, only this time I accepted its truth. Still he didn't phone.

Alice said, 'He's a cunt.' Lottie said maybe the letter had got lost. Maybe he's a bastard. I said Maybe he's dead and forgave his silence. Whatever, he was lost to me, and this sent me mad. I waited for blood and when it never came I waited for the phone and when it didn't ring I sat in the living room, champing away on avocados, washing them down with boiled water. I wondered what child could survive that but couldn't see any alternative. Sometimes I panicked and sometimes I was calm. In one such calm moment I picked up the phone resolved to tell him the news and he was actually there and it was so wonderful just to hear his voice, to find that he wasn't dead, that I didn't (couldn't) talk about Daisy or periods or abortions, the words would not come out.

And because I didn't mention it I think he assumed it had been a false alarm and that the crisis was over. The joy in my voice simply negated the whole letter I'd written. I am so stupid sometimes.

Lottie said that if I didn't call him and tell him soon she would do it for me. I begged her not to. I couldn't see what good it would do and threatening phonecalls from loyal friends would surely only send him further away.

'Well, fly out there, then,' she said. 'Tell him to his face.'

'I can't. I've just paid off a huge wodge to Visa. I haven't really got anything left.'

'What about the film money?'

'Well, it's fairly low budget and anyway it's disappearing into the black hole of debt.'

'Jesus, Madame Bovary's alive and well and living in Borough.'

'I'm a lunatic with money. You *know* that. I'm too extravagant.'

'Well you won't be able to be extravagant when the baby's born.'

'I won't be anything when the baby's born – *if* the baby's born – except a penniless drudge.'

My agent called and threw me into even greater confusion by asking if I'd be interested in doing *The Sugar Man* again. 'It'll be very easy, my darling,' she said. 'No lines to learn. They want to take it all over the place. They've offered three-fifty a week – in cash – and your hotels'll all be paid for and all your food. The only thing they won't pay for is alcohol.'

'Where is it touring?'

'Darling, you name it. Middle East, Far East. You'll love it. Think of it as a paid holiday.'

'The money's not good enough.' How could I fly? January, March – Jesus, I'd be enormous by then. I'd never get away with it. They'd never insure me. 'No. I can't do it.'

'Oh, Ellie, we can get you more money.' Plaintive. 'And there's nothing else going on. No-one's filming at the moment, it's too dark, the days are too short.'

'*I'm* filming.'

'Yes, well you're probably the only one.'

'No. Tell them no. I can't do it. And anyway it must clash with *Thérèse*, surely?'

'They overlap, slightly. You'd miss the first week of rehearsals, but as you've done the play so recently the director doesn't mind. He thinks you're fab. So do the producers. They'll even pay you for the week you miss. Think about it. You'll finish the filming, do a week of gentle rehearsal and then open in Dubai at the end of January – or is it the *middle*? – anyway, whatever, you'll spend a week or so in Dubai, a few days somewhere else, then Bahrain – wherever that is – then home for two days then off to the Far East. They're even going to China! Chance of a lifetime, sweetheart. All those fabulous places.'

'All those fabulous places and none of them are particularly politically correct. I'll have to hide my face and keep my mouth shut all the time. Some guy was flogged in Saudi last week for swearing. *Swearing.* Can you imagine?'

'Well think about it. Get a swear box or something. Sleep on it.'

I did think. I didn't sleep, but then that was nothing new. I thought of going to all those malarious places. I couldn't take a pill or have an injection. I'd be a sitting target for any hungry tsetse fly that passed my way.

I peeled an avocado and lay down on the living-room floor, just me, the avocado and Daisy. Where would her cot go? In here? What would happen if I gave birth to her and didn't buy anything, nothing at all, just arrived at the hospital completely unprepared? I imagined bringing her home wrapped in my orange jumper and lying her on my bed. She could sleep with me. She could live on breast milk. Thinking guiltily that I would have to give up smoking I lit a cigarette and apologized to my daughter, who would not be aborted. She would not be a burden to me or a struggle. Things would be different, very different, but certainly no worse than now.

Chapter Eighteen

I turned the job down. Everyone – *everyone* – thought I'd lost my marbles. My agent, Lottie, Alice, they all thought I was making a colossal mistake. Stevie even came over to the flat to persuade me to do it. She said people would kill for a job like that. She herself would die to do it. Her wanker boyfriend Tim had finally left her for good after several abortive attempts. For a long time we'd all wanted to tell her to leave him but what could we say? Your boyfriend's a twat? She would make her mistakes as easily as I had made mine. And now, of course, *he'd* left *her* and her self-esteem was in the toilet and her heart was smashed. He'd run away to Spain with some homoeopathic hippy artist and sent Stevie a letter saying it was all her fault. Mmmm. And so she wanted to run away on a foreign tour and forget. She asked me what she should do. How would she ever get over him? How could she get him back? I could give her no advice at all because I had met Aedan and loved him and got pregnant by him in an instant and was already without him and six months hadn't even passed. Now I'd been offered this stupid bloody tour and I was confused and it seemed I hadn't a rational cell left in my brain. Stevie said, 'Do the job, for Christ's sake. It'll help you forget.'

Forget. I did not want to.

Alice came to stay for a couple of days. A mission of mercy, I think, though she denied this. She was there to save me. We turned the phone off and played Black Jack and Rummy.

We went into Highgate where it was raining heavily and drank milky coffee in a pink and grey bistro-type place. We talked all day. The location, however, was probably a mistake because all day I could hear Aedan's voice saying, 'Will we live in Highgate, maybe?' At one point his voice was so loud I actually turned around and said, 'Aedan?' Alice was quite startled and held my hand and asked me if I was eating properly. She told me to take the job. Leave London behind for a couple of months and try to get myself better.

'What about Daisy?'

'Take her with you. Take her round the world.' I thought of the stories I could tell her when she was ten or eleven, stories like the ones my mum had told me. I could tell her I'd taken her to nine different countries before she was even born. The fantasy was crushed somewhat by her question, 'But who actually *is* my daddy? Was he the Irish one in that photo?' Good grief.

I could tell Alice was having difficulty remaining patient. I couldn't blame her. I droned on and on about Aedan and Aedan and Aedan, never reaching any conclusion, and suddenly I was not the woman she'd known for years and years. She wasn't used to it. I'd never behaved like this in my life.

I bought two pounds of smoked salmon and we went home. While Alice slept peacefully that night I sat on the floor of the living room making a papier mâché bowl and swallowing great fistfuls of salmon until there was nothing left of it. When she woke up the next day she looked down in absolute disgust at the one remaining thin strip of fish. She was impressed, however, by the bowl, which I had finished. I think she thought I was having a breakdown.

When she left I was bereft. My life seemed to deteriorate. Not that the past few weeks had been exactly wonderful, but suddenly I felt much, much worse, and physically I was feeling very odd and utterly exhausted. My agent called every day. They still wanted me for the tour and had offered five hundred. I accepted and cried for a whole day. I spoke to Aedan who was no help whatsoever as he had no idea of the reality of my life and I chose not to tell him.

I started to fall asleep at odd times of the day, frequently on the living-room floor and lying uncovered on the rough carpet I would dream of his voice on the end of a telephone saying, '*I'm coming home, love. Ellie . . . I'm coming back.*' In reality our phonecalls were light years from the truth. I heard his voice and was no longer pregnant and sad. We laughed and chatted and sang to each other and for the duration of each call I was me again. He always gave me such hope. If I was to get on with any sort of life that hope would either have to die or be realized. I said to him, 'Tell me you don't want me any more. Tell me you never want to fuck me again or touch me or kiss me. Let me be free again. Tell me it's all gone; that you lied and cheated and conned me. Tell me I'm a fool.'

He refused. He wouldn't tell me lies, he said. Bonfire night in London I called and asked if he and Louis would be having any fireworks. He reminded me that Guy Fawkes is something of a hero in Belfast and not a traitor at all. I felt English and stupid.

'What do you have then? Is it a special time for something else?'

'All souls,' he said. 'A bad time.'

All souls. It was indeed a bad time. Particularly if you were going silently mad in a corner of London with a baby you hadn't planned and a lover who's left you. Of course I didn't say any of that even though maybe it was time I did and so we went nowhere. Again. His voice got sadder on the end of the line and so again I asked him to let me go.

I went out to eat with an old friend but found I couldn't eat a thing and then found at the end of the evening that I couldn't work out how to get home. The tube had packed up for the night. I sat on a wall by The Angel for over an hour and then walked home. It took me half the night. I kept getting lost. The following day, at least I think it was the following day, I woke up and it was dark outside and the clock said it was ten o'clock at night. I'd missed a whole day. It worried me greatly that I'd slept so deeply and for so long. I couldn't even remember dreaming anything. What was even more worrying was that I pondered this curious fact for about a minute and then turned over and went straight back to sleep.

When I awoke the next morning there was a letter waiting by the door from Belfast.

My darling, darling Elle.
So many times you've asked me to write this, I figured it must be what you want. You ask me what happened.
I fell in love with you.
When we were in Holland Park, I saw you, I fancied you, I couldn't resist you. At the time I didn't think beyond that. I seem to have spent a lot of time trying not to be involved with anyone (Frances). With you it was different. I wanted you, all of you. It meant everything. I never lied to you.
When I got back to Ireland I changed. I was scared of leaving everything I am embroiled in here (Frances) scared of the consequences. It was more than a temptation, to come over and be with you, but I felt it would hurt so many people and I am a coward.
However, that's enough of the apologia pro vita sua. *Though I honestly believe I love you, that I never lied to you, I expect you think that at best it's self-delusion and at worst mere lies. You keep asking me to tell you that it was all lies but you must know as well as I do that that's not the case. I think of you every minute of*

every day. I regret what I've done every second. I've
made a mess of everything. My relationship with F. is
confounded. I think I have probably lost you both. I
only wanted to love you. Instead I hurt you and let you
down. I do love you still, though I am incredulous at
the extent of your love for me.

I don't think this is the letter you asked for, you said
you wanted to be released. I'm sorry. Decide for
yourself what the truth was and get on with your life.

I love you and will do always.
Ever thine,
Aedan.

As a result of all the sleep I was far more alert than I
would've liked, under the circumstances. I curled up in a
ball by the bed and sobbed till I made myself sick. I think by
the end of it I was dehydrated. Lottie drove over at
breakneck speed and took me shopping. We bought housey
things; rugs, china, prints. In the car we sang along loudly to
Lisa Stansfield. We drove through Chelsea and I cried and
Lottie sang louder. Later, when she dropped me at home she
said I looked almost relieved, that now, perhaps, I could get
on with the business of living.

But I was living in a toxic cloud of frustration and loss. I
was so firmly rooted in the centre of the cloud I could not
see the air around me. I didn't feel like I was in the same
atmosphere as everyone else. I had the idea, and it wouldn't
go away, that if only I could break my foot and get admitted
to hospital for six weeks then everything would be all right. I
went on a mission to Camden, where the traffic is especially
foot-breakingly hazardous, and stood on the pavement with
one toe in the road. After about ten minutes I was moved on
by police. Irritated, I meandered down to the market and
bought a silver Mayan ball with a tinkle inside it that was
supposed to help bring people out of trances and comas and
fits. I bought a silver chain for it and hung it around my

neck. The guy who sold it to me also said it had the power to soothe an unborn child. I tinkled it down the phone to Alice who called me Tinkerbell and said she was happy I was so much better. When I hung up I cried for an hour and stared at my breasts, so swollen and sore by now it hurt even to put my clothes on.

Alice phoned again and played the entire soundtrack to *The Bodyguard* down the line. She said it was just what I needed. It wasn't the sort of thing I would normally listen to but I went out and bought it the next day. It was Whitney Houston being over-sentimental and a heap of people I'd never really heard of but it pained me to listen to anything I already knew. Sting and The Beatles were out of the question, Elgar made me want to open my wrists, so good old Whitney filled the gap perfectly. I played the CD when I got home and there's a song on there by Lisa Stansfield that made me feel almost optimistic. As soon as it started I felt better. Whenever I hear that track it makes me feel light inside, even now.

I played this music twenty-four hours of every day. My friends started to rally against Aedan with all the strength they had. Suddenly no-one was sitting on the fence anymore. It seemed I was doing absolutely nothing about being pregnant and I'd made no decisions one way or another. I told them about the letter but they said I had to phone him. Even if it *was* over I was still pregnant and in trouble and he should be told. I phoned him. I'd been persuaded by the mob, I told him I was sorry to bother him but my friends were worried.

'And what do they think of me, your friends? Do they hate me? Does Alice hate me?'

'She thinks you're a cunt.'

Long silence.

'Think about that. Think about what they say. I'm not a strong man.'

'No, I guessed.'

'What can you possibly want with me?'

'A life.'

But I did wonder. What was I doing throwing my time away on him? He was not there. At this terrible time in my life he was totally absent. Sure, we talked on the phone and he constantly told me he loved me, missed me, all that bollocks, but where was he? When would I ever accept that he had left me and move on? I have seen black-eyed women, salty tears cruising down their crushed, broken faces as they whine, 'But I love him!' I've looked deep into myself for advice for them and found words of concern to spout, have looked pityingly at the futility of such relationships. I urged them to have some self-respect. I had a violent encounter with a guy myself once but walked away from it as easily as I'd walked into it. I assumed that intelligent women didn't fall into these mires, which I now know to be a pretty dim assumption; intelligence has nothing to do with it. The women I'd despaired of were no more stupid than myself. Aedan might not have battered me physically but he was not there, and yet he would not go, he constantly fed me hope, and did he really have no idea I was pregnant? Could he really be that stupid?

Aedan,

Aedan, *make me hate you.*

We talked but said nothing.

And then he was silent again. Silent in that he did not phone. Days went by. The phone rang and rang, always someone for me, a friend, always I expected his voice but it never came. In a card I wrote while sitting in the doctor's waiting room I said

You said 'You have the key to life.'

I said I do, I do. At such a moment you ripped open my mouth to kiss the very inside of me and we made promises. For ever For ever For ever you said, and I said Yes.

And promises were made.
Alone today – God, so bloody alone – I'm given
choices – tear the cells of you from my gut. Alone,
deciding to bleed again without you. 'Promise me,' you
said, 'promise me you'll love me till we die' and I said
I will. I will. At such a moment you tore open my
heart and burnt out the very inside of me and now you
say
nothing
and I say
remember me.
Remember
Me.

    For ever For ever For ever you said and I said Yes.
    Aedan, where the fuck are you?

I asked the doctor which injections I could have for the
tour, in my present state.

None.

I wandered into the West End and pondered my next
move. An abortion? I decide on a CD instead. I bought some
Bach and some Bruch but it made me weep and so I went
back to Whitney.

Chapter Nineteen

I didn't send the card I'd written in the doctor's because his birthday was coming up and I didn't want to depress him. I sent him a batch of poems instead which were probably even more depressing. I put them in a huge brown envelope with a card inside saying, '*Remember Me*' on the front and something morose I'd written on the inside. I photocopied some of the letters he'd written to me and sent those too. I began to feel ill. I phoned the doctor and said, 'I feel *ill*,' and he suggested I go into the surgery for a check-up. I didn't go. While papier mâchéing I got incredible backache and stomach-ache and I lay down and prayed for morning to come. On the morning of the day before his birthday I felt so ill I went to bed and thought maybe I would die that day. At eight-thirty I phoned the doctor who was intolerant and busy. Shortly before 9 a.m. I was overtaken by cramp; all over my body it seized me. I crawled to the bathroom and found I was bleeding. I saw the red of the blood and said *No no no no no no no no. Daisy.* On the phone I said, 'I have to see a doctor. I'm bleeding. My child is rejecting me.' He said lie down in bed or come in and see me. How pregnant are you? *Ten weeks, two and a half months, days and days and nights.* I lay in bed as still as death. If I didn't move then maybe everything would stay in its place, maybe the blood would stop escaping. When, hours later, the pain would not let me be still, I got out of bed and lay on the floor and the sheets were black with the death of my child and I called the doctor and he said, 'It sounds too late now.'

Wrapped in wool I went out into the night because on the six o'clock news they told me the moon would be eclipsed that night. I went out into the cold of the street to witness this but found I couldn't cross the road to see over the buildings to view the moon because my body wouldn't straighten out properly and so I missed the eclipse and went home and lay down on the black sheets and closed my eyes.

On his birthday I slept. I slept on bloody sheets in bloody clothes. I woke at noon, my hands and face bloody, my womb stone-like inside of me, like someone had reached in and planted a dry rock in there and left it resting heavy and infertile as a judgement on me.

Chapter Twenty

'He must have a fuck of a lot on his fucking Catholic conscience now. Has he phoned?'

'No.'

'Bastard.'

'No! He doesn't know.'

'What?'

'I haven't told him. Alice, he didn't even know I was pregnant.' She looked at me, horrified.

'Phone him. Tell him now.' She lifted up the phone and waved it at me. 'God, the coward. How could he do this to you?'

'He didn't. Alice, put the phone down would you? What if someone's trying to get through?'

'Like him, you mean? Jesus, if only he had the *guts*. Well, someone's got to tell him so if you won't . . .' She picked up my filofax and opened it at O.

'Please. Please don't.' I started to cry. 'He's not as bad as you think. He was always honest with me. I can't help it if he doesn't love me back. Anyway, what's the point in telling him now? It's all over. It's all gone now. I'm back at work, I'm filming again. I'm alive, aren't I?'

She looked stricken and dropped the phone and the filo. 'God, Ellie, I'm sorry. I'm so sorry.'

'I miss him!' I wailed. 'I miss him so much I can't bear it. I can't do my job, I can't do anything – I can't do this stupid fucking tour. I'm *paralysed* without him and no-one understands, no-one *met* him, they didn't *see* him, they didn't see us *together*.'

'But we *knew*. We knew he was different.'

'You didn't! No-one did. Only me. And him. No-one else had any idea. I'm sorry, I shouldn't be so *weak* – it's just – I can't do it, I can't go on as if nothing happened. God, my home, my lovely home I made myself and it's not mine any more, it's not me it's all *him*, every corner reeks of his absence and I miss him. I keep thinking if he'd only phone and say he's coming home, then I'd be – and people keep saying, Have an abortion, he's a cunt, get rid of him, get rid of the kid, he's a bastard and I was all alone and scared with his child but at least it was *something*, and now I don't even have that any more, even that rejected me and he's still not here, and he doesn't even know what he's lost, I mean, I couldn't have looked after a child in this state, I can't even look after myself. Look at me! I'm a mess, I'm disgusting, it's just I love him, I really love him and I miss him and that time. I just want it back, I want September back, I want the clocks to go back and give me back those days.'

We carried on like that, the pair of us, and the next day we carried on our lives. Resilience. Alice went off to Heathrow on some business venture and I got on a train to Manchester for the last throes of *Thérèse*.

Chapter Twenty-one

Wherever I travel. How ever many miles I move away from you I cannot forget.

You are strapped to my back. Today I go to Manchester and bleed out the rest of our child on the train and no-one here has a painkiller strong enough.

A woman says, 'Where is the pain? What sort of a pill do you want?'

'The pain is all over me. I want a pill to bring my lover back.' And my child.

I notice a lot of people sitting around look at me like I'm an idiot. One man laughs with his mate. I turn and look at him. 'Yes, it's fucking hilarious, isn't it?' I say, a mad woman.

He stops laughing but I feel sure he'll start again as soon as I go back to my seat, assuming he remembers what he was laughing at in the first place.

In a few weeks I go across the world and stay away for months and you won't even know I've gone. I dream of possibilities. Perhaps you'll return when I'm away and wait for me in the flat with a basket or two of fruit.

Life is just shite without you, Aedan.

I listened to the charts today. You'd have been appalled. All those bloody love songs people listen to; all about breakdowns of some sort. I feel as though my whole body's broken down and I'm lying in the road waiting for rescue. The me that walks around and holds conversations is an impostor, a fake, a piece of someone else's imagination. People believe it's me because the hair's the same and she has the same face and clothes as me, but that woman has no soul; her soul is me, lying in the road, dreaming of rescue.

Another letter I decided not send.

In some river the locations manager decided was a Seine look-alike I floated and choked and almost froze to death. I had a wet suit on beneath the nineteenth-century corsets and skirts and found it difficult to breathe even on dry land. I could not swim at that time but felt it would be damaging to say so, and anyway I didn't much care if I sank. Liam Johnston stood on the banks of our makeshift Parisian river with the rest of the crew and shouted his directions through a megaphone. Someone had actually stuck leaves on one of the dead-looking trees. The scene's set in the middle of Autumn whereas in reality we were in the second week of December. Winter.

Before we got into the little rowing boat a meeting was held. I asked if we really needed the ridiculous stuck-on leaves; surely they would convince no-one and anyway would Zola really mind? I put it to Liam that Zola had probably washed his hands of the whole film by now and was probably spinning wildly in his grave and shouldn't we have the fake leaves taken down? He agreed and a big fuss was made by the designer, Claire, who found that the leaves were well and truly super-glued and had to leave them where they were.

It was a bright day, though the sky was white rather than blue and it was hideously cold. None of us was relishing the idea of throwing ourselves into the water. Ian Turner kept spouting on about Equity and the temperature of the water. I thought rather irrationally that if he doesn't stop twittering on soon I'll push him under the water and hold him there. Matthew had a fraction more patience, though this was obviously wearing thin. He pointed out that we'd all been made aware of what was involved in this scene when we'd signed our contracts and accepted our ludicrously high fees. Turner refused to listen to such reason and flounced off to talk to some of the extras, which was what he usually did. Matthew maintained this was because Turner actually felt successful next to a walk-on.

Eventually we were on the rowing boat in the middle of the water, the dinghy, carrying an extra camera operator and a diver, following close behind. Film rolling, Liam Johnston stood with his megaphone, shouting out enthusiastic directions. Every so often he'd dive under a coat and scan the monitor to see what we all looked like on camera. Turner started some serious overacting and Matthew and I corpsed loudly and without shame. He told us both to fuck off and Matthew said that if he didn't want us to laugh then maybe he should learn to act. This didn't go down too well at all and an argument ensued between the two men and the rowing boat had to be hauled back to the bank.

Fortunately the caterers had arrived so we all grabbed coffee and scrounged cigarettes from Henry, the first assistant, who looked cold and miserable. I gave him a hug and Liam Johnston came over and kissed my head.

'I'm so sorry about Turner, my darling. I even thought of re-casting but it would've been just too expensive. He'll be all right. Charles is the best editor around.'

'Well, we really shouldn't have laughed like we did. I'm sorry, I'm a terrible giggler.'

'I wouldn't worry about that. So was Olivier. Never did him any harm. I'll go and try to cool him down a bit. He's threatening not to do the scene. Where do we *find* these cretins?'

Matthew came over with more cigarettes and Liam disappeared into the crowd of walk-ons looking for Turner.

'At least this is the last we see of him; only our stuff left now. How are you, love?' He put his arm around my shoulders. 'Thought any more about that Far East thing?'

'I accepted. Think I may have made a huge mistake.'

'Nonsense, you'll have a ball. A friend of mine did one a couple of years ago, said he'd do another one at the drop of a hat. Good money?'

'I suppose so. Five hundred a week and all expenses paid.'

'Well, you can't go wrong.'

'I'm not convinced.'

I didn't want to sound quite so negative but I was having serious second thoughts about the trip. The cast list had arrived; I didn't know anyone at all and I wasn't relishing the idea of getting to know anyone new. My personality simply wasn't up to it. They would surely hate me.

'How is he? Do you mind me asking? Your fella . . . is he any better?'

'Actually, no. He's dead.'

What colour he had left in his face in the cold rapidly disappeared. I thought he might even cry. 'God. Fuck. Shit, Ellie, I'm so sorry.'

'Don't be, you didn't kill him.' God, sometimes I am the devil himself.

'I don't know what to say to you.'

'I'm sorry, Matthew. I shouldn't have said that. I'm really sorry.'

'No. No. Look, do you want to talk about it? Have you told anyone else? Have you told Liam?'

'What's the point? No, I'd rather be silent, and I'd rather no-one else knew.'

'Well, you know where I am. If you need me . . . for anything, OK?'

'Thanks. Look, don't worry about me, babe. I'm all right. Really I am.'

Liam came over at that moment so I didn't really have time to think about what I'd just said and drown in my own shame. Poor Matthew. We were packed into the boat again and the cameras started to roll. We did the scene with apparently no mistakes. It wasn't my most difficult scene. All I really had to do was look on in stupefied horror as the two men grapple with each other. Shortly before Camille tumbles over the side of the boat to his watery grave I burst into sobs and collapse unconscious in a twitching heap on the floor of the boat. I remain unconscious even when Laurent capsizes the boat and everyone falls into the water. We did it as it was written. In the water I gave myself over to the depths. Matthew held me tightly in his arms, keeping my head above the water while at the same time trying to keep hold of the side of the upturned vessel and shout for help. The whole rescue scene was filmed and then it was a wrap, much to everyone's relief, particularly the dripping wet actors who were fished out quickly and dried off in three separate winnybagoes. Henry wrapped me in a duvet and rubbed me down and fed me hot coffee and kissed the top of my shivering head. He was really very lovely. Had I not been so bogged down in the swamp that was Aedan I might have dragged him home with me and lived happily ever after.

We had time off after all the exertion, which was just as well as both Matthew and I caught terrible colds. I went to bed for two days and contemplated death. On the third day, feeling slightly better, I had what I thought was a fantastic idea. I climbed into the sludge track suit and went to Oxford Street and bought a blonde wig from John Lewis and then I went into Miss Selfridge, a trendy little hive of young fashion victims, and bought a very girlie dress and some platform shoes and a black silky bomber jacket. In the changing room I tried on the whole outfit with the wig. Had I not known it was me standing there I would not have recognized myself. Perfect. I went home satisfied and packed a little overnight bag of knickers and a pair of jeans and my orange jumper and locked the flat up, hoping as I left it that I wouldn't see it again for at least four days.

Chapter Twenty-two

It rains in Belfast. Relentlessly. When it isn't raining it looks as though it's about to. The daylight, such as it is, comes mainly from the people who live there who are peaceful and warm and kind and on the whole quite naïve, considering what they've lived with for so many years. Perhaps it's romanticism and not naïvety at all. For obvious reasons it's not a place popular with tourists, so few people are aware of the beauty of the place which, in spite of the rain, takes one's breath away. At least, it took away all of mine. Structurally the city centre is like any other; ugly shops, ugly houses. When I knew Belfast, and perhaps things have changed since then, there were two major things that set it apart from similar size places; one was the presence of the soldiers with their guns and lorries and armoured cars and the other was the group of mountains the place is perched on and which you can see from just about wherever you look. You can reach these mountains in about ten minutes from any part of the city. The concrete of the shops and houses and hospitals just sits on these gorgeous hills. And then of course, only five minutes away, there's the sea; hopelessly polluted but enchanting nonetheless because it is, after all, ocean. I fell in love with the place on my first visit. I got a job there for a couple of months in one of the theatres and found, when the job ended, that it was almost impossible to tear myself away. I was twenty-two then – two years from then and years and years from now. Could it only have been two years? I had not met Aedan. Never even heard of him.

In my wig I was a stranger to myself. I kept catching sight of myself in shop windows and being surprised every time. It was quite liberating; in this other woman's body I could do anything. Under the name of Miranda de Reuter I checked into the Regency hotel on Botanic Avenue, close to the theatre I'd worked in and only a short walk from Aedan's flat. My room was small with a view of a brick wall. I found the number of the studio he'd said he'd be working at and dialled; some woman said he'd gone home. 'Is that Frances?' she asked. I hung up. God, *wasn't she dead yet*? I clomped out into the street in my platforms, bought a salad bap from a kebab shop and clomped over to the botanical gardens to eat and think. A man and a woman were having a heated argument which rapidly turned into a fight. When he punched her in the face and knocked her over I dropped my bag and limped over to them.

'Are you OK?' I said to the battered girl.

'Do I look OK?' her boyfriend said to me.

'Not *you*. You – what about you?' I looked at the woman. 'Are you all right?'

'Keep out of it, love,' the man said, lurching towards me.

'I'm not your love.'

'Neither am I,' said the woman.

I backed away from both of them and said, 'If you hit her again I'll get the police.'

The two of them stood quite still and just stared at me like I was from Mars or something. Out of breath and very red in the face the woman pulled on his arm and said, 'Come on, let's go.'

'Where?'

'Out of here. We'll go back to Gerard's.'

And off they went. Perhaps they were enjoying themselves. I took my ludicrous new shoes off and rubbed my weary insteps. I'd given up wearing uncomfortable girl-shoes when I was about sixteen. If the pain got any worse I'd have to go and buy a pair of trainers.

I bought an A to Z and wandered round to Aedan's. There were two For Sale signs up in his garden. The house looked empty and cold. He should've left a light on. I settled down on the pavement about fifty yards away and waited, though what I would say to him if he found me there I really didn't know.

Six and a half mind-numbingly boring hours later he appeared. My stomach jolted so much I thought I might be sick. He looked in my direction but registered nothing as though in my wig I was invisible. He went into the house so I phoned him from a call box round the corner. We chatted until there was a loud hammering in the background and he said he'd have to go. Someone at the door. By the time I raced round to my original hiding place he was standing talking to a woman in a car. I could only see the back of her head. Her charcoal head. She was small; only just visible above the steering wheel. As she drove off he hit the back of her car with his hand and shouted God! Loudly enough for me to hear. Good; at least they weren't snogging on the doorstep. I stood up straight and walked in his direction. By now the shoes had given me blisters and I was hobbling. He watched the car move away from the street. I quickened my pace, which proved quite painful, tempting recognition but when I was within about ten yards of him he turned and went back into the house and something prevented me knocking on his door. I went back to the hotel and phoned again but his machine picked up so I rang off without leaving a message.

I sat in the hotel room and stared into space. I must have sat there for hours. I didn't actually have anything specific planned and now I was here I didn't quite know what to do. I looked in the mirror at the blonde stranger and thought perhaps I needed to see a doctor. I would probably be locked up. Maybe it would provoke some reaction in Aedan; maybe it wouldn't. At about midnight I went back to his house and stood watching it from the other side of the road. He was either out or asleep or sitting somewhere in a darkened room. I thought of writing him a note but decided against it and went for a walk around the city. It was full of revellers out on their Christmas yahoos. The thought of Christmas made me quite faint with dread; where would I go? My father had offered to pay my fare to Australia but he'd met some woman, a psychiatrist from Holland, and I figured they might rather be on their own. Stevie said she was thinking of staying in London but I wasn't sure we'd be very good for each other; two broken hearts in a one bedroom flat, trapped there for two days. Maybe I'd find a soup kitchen somewhere and go and do something altruistic. Maybe I'd take six sleeping pills and sleep till the end of the wretched bank holiday. Maybe I'd get myself run over by an army truck and spend the whole of Christmas in hospital. Maybe I'd *steal* an army truck and run Frances over and *she* could spend Christmas in hospital. I walked back to the hotel and lay awake all night, vaguely wondering if I would ever sleep properly again.

I spent the best part of the next two days limping round the streets trying to think of something to say to Aedan should I ever run into him. How should I word it? I lost our child? Our baby's dead? I miscarried? Miscarried *what*? He hadn't even known there was anything there to lose. I followed him to the theatre; I sat six rows behind him thinking surely he can *sense* me here. I thought I would certainly be found out before the end of the evening but as it turned out the play was dreadful and he didn't bother coming back for the second half. I didn't realize he'd gone until I was back in my seat in the middle of the row. When eventually I'd managed to squeeze my way past several fat old women he was nowhere to be found. I lost heart. I got cold sitting outside his house every night and apart from that I was extremely bored. What sort of a life was he living? I'd followed him around on several occasions and he did *nothing*, absolutely *nothing* of any interest whatsoever. He saw virtually no-one. I saw the sooty haired woman's car a few times but unfortunately she was never in it.

On Sunday I decided to give up and go home. I couldn't talk to him in my present state of mind, that much was obvious. I paid my bill at the Regency and stood outside waiting for a cab to take me to the airport. That was where he found me, standing in the street in my orange jumper, wigless, witless and humourless. I got into his car and simply said, 'I'm on my way home, Aedan. Could you take me to the airport?' He did. As I was going through the barriers I shouted, 'I lost our child. Aedan, I was pregnant. I lost a baby.'

He stared, speechless, and I was shunted through the gate to my plane. I thought I heard him say my name but there wasn't time to go back and see.

Chapter Twenty-three

I'd been at home for about three hours when he arrived. He looked dreadful; panicked.

'Why didn't you use your key?' I tried to smile but found I couldn't.

'I didn't know if . . . I didn't . . . '

'Whatever. You'd better come in.'

I followed him into the living room.

'It's changed.'

'It's been a long time.'

'Papier mâché?' He looked at the bucket of mulch and the pile of objects made from squelchy newspaper, stained from avocado and grief. I would throw it all away now.

'Christmas presents,' I said. 'Thought I'd be creative.'

'You could sell them.'

'Yeah, yeah. Drink? Coffee? Whiskey?' He didn't answer. He just stood there looking around the room like he'd never seen it before. 'I'll make us some coffee, then.'

'Thanks.' He looked at me with something like shame. 'Black, no sugar.'

'I know.'

In the kitchen hostility rose up into my mouth but I swallowed it down and hoped it didn't show in my eyes. He came in just as the kettle was boiling and put his hands on my cheeks.

'I'm so sorry, Elle.'

'Yes.'

'Why didn't you tell me?'

'I tried!' I started to cry and apologized and he made the coffee while I pulled myself together. We sat on the floor of the living room with the television on for some reason with the sound down. I couldn't remember if I'd put it on or he had. We didn't speak at all. I smoked a bit and every so often he took a drag of my cigarette or kissed the palm of my hand. Or he would knot my hair around his fingers or kiss my shoulder or my neck. I buried my head in his stomach and cried more. He hated such emotion but I couldn't stop, and anyway I didn't much care any more.

We went out to eat, though I left my food untouched and drank only water. We talked about everything but, though at one point he asked had there been any side effects. I laughed into my food. He carried on eating; his appetite unimpaired.

We went to bed like two virgins. He didn't look at me when I undressed and I didn't look at him. There was no candlelight as there had been the last time we'd been there together because I'd bought myself a lamp. We lay side by side in its glow.

'I'm shocked. When you said at the airport today . . . It was the biggest shock I've had in . . . years, three years.'

'It wasn't a good time for me. I wanted you here, but . . . well, it's gone now.'

'I've been offered a job in London.'

'What?'

'Starts in April.'

'Have you accepted it?'

'Not yet.'

'But you will, won't you?'

'I don't know. Probably. Would you want me to?'

'Will we be together?'

'Yes.'

'Aedan, you *have* to take it, you really have to.'

'You still want me? After all this?'

'Yes. Yes, of course I do. Shit, yes. Yes.'

'Are you going to do the tour, the foreign tour?'

'I am. Twelve weeks.'

'I could be here when you get back.'

'Oh, God, yes. Yes.'

'We could work together maybe. Find a project.'

'We could.'

'We could be a golden showbiz couple.'

I went to sleep with my face resting on his stomach. I was at peace. He was coming home. Things were going to be all right. We would not be put asunder. My last sight before I slept was his face over mine as he kissed me and the last words he said were *I'm home now, Ellie*.

The phone rang at 4 a.m. Frances had been hit by a car. She was nearly dead. He went back. He would phone as soon as he got there, let me know what was going on. He rang at ten o'clock that evening to say she was alive but still in danger. He would stay for a while, a day, a little more, he didn't know.

I thought evil thoughts. I dreamed evil dreams. I walked around the flat saying I'm a wicked woman I am I am. Why had she not died? I drank a bottle of red wine and then another and another. I fell asleep on the kitchen floor. The phone kept ringing and waking me up but I was afraid to answer; afraid that if I spoke words that had any meaning at all I would wake to find that life was not a dream but a nightmare and he was never coming back. I couldn't remember where he had gone. I couldn't remember why he'd been here and why he'd suddenly left. Ah! The Irishwoman, she'd thrown herself on the traffic. *Isn't she dead yet?* I dreamed of Covent Garden at night. 'I cannot let go,' I screamed in the kitchen. I heard the man downstairs banging on his ceiling saying shut the fuck up. I had to get out. I had to go to Kensington. I had to find the restaurant

121

that had poisoned us that time. I put a T-shirt on and some shorts and my trainers, grabbed a set of keys from the kitchen table and left. On the tube I found I had Aedan's keys in my hand, not my own. The keys I'd given him, the keys to my flat, he'd left them. 'No!' I shouted, and everyone on the train turned to look at me. I felt touched by more madness than ever before. Frances was beating me. She'd done it on purpose. *I will not give up. I cannot give up.* A woman in a big overcoat and hat asked me if I was all right. 'I cannot give up,' I said, wondering why she was dressed for winter. When I got out into the street I realized everyone else was dressed for winter too. Everyone except me. *I cannot give up. Whatever it takes I must keep on and on.* I wandered around Kensington and found myself heading for the Brompton Oratory. It occurred to me I should go in and light a Catholic candle for his soul. This was where he said we would be married. I got to the door and found it was locked so I went straight back to the tube and took myself off to Kensington High Street and walked where we had walked together the night we'd been poisoned. I am poisoned now, I thought, only this time I will not be able to laugh all night. I will not be able to laugh and fuck in my sickness. Frances would never let him go. He would never let himself go. I remembered the feeling in my gut when I'd first laid eyes on him, when I first realized he was the person I thought I'd never meet. 'I am sick in love of him,' I said. Nobody even blinked. Londoners.

Aedan. *Aedan.* When I met him I was whole and happy. My heart was whole and attached to the earth and reality. And now my heart is held by him, held in a fucking vice, held so tight it stopped. This man crashes into my life without warning and stops my heart, my heart he tore in two and tied to the fucking moon.

I spoke to him when I got home. It damaged me a little more because he did not wave a magic wand when I knew he had one in his possession. It was the lowest point I sank to when he told me he wouldn't be home for weeks and weeks. Not even for Christmas. I sank easily, too weak to force my will on him. I had no words even. All this time I'd had so many words and such force and determination and such resolve you wouldn't believe. But all the words had left me just then, all of them dead.

Chapter Twenty-four

Alone on Christmas Eve. I kept saying It's just another day, nothing special. Why does it hurt so much? Why is today more painful than any other day? Why am I more lost than ever? It surprises me not at all that the suicide rate increases dramatically at Christmas. Walking around Sainsbury's, squeezing through the millions of late shoppers, I nearly gave up what I was doing in favour of catatonia. I stopped shopping and sat on the floor by the satsumas. I was not avoided; several people actually stepped on me. All the trolleys had been taken so I was lugging round a basket of items I didn't really want. I felt slightly unsure of how long the shops would all be closed and couldn't work out how much milk I needed or bread or coffee. Days since I ate even a morsel of food it seemed pointless to stock up with anything.

But Stevie said she was coming over so I figured I would have to buy some sort of food, even if it was just some cheese and biscuits. I lost my breath a lot while walking around Sainsbury's, kicking the basket in front of me, too heavy now to carry. I lost my breath because I kept forgetting to breathe. In the queue to pay I pondered the idea of sleeping for a few days and wondered if Stevie would be bothered by this. I then pondered having her sleep as well, to solve all our problems. Perhaps I could grind some Tryptizol into some milky coffee and give it to her unawares. Would that be considered poisoning? Maybe both our livers would fail. I'd have to think of an alternative.

I've never been so alone in my life. Seriously alone. I worried that I'd be a danger to myself. I worried that I'd take the sleeping pills and accidentally kill myself. I hummed *Daisy, Daisy, give me your answer do*... and jingled the little silver ball and felt loss like a tumour in my heart. How did I end up like this? Was I paying the price for a happy childhood? Was there a price to pay for being a working actress? For each ambition realized was there an emotional fee? Aedan called; Frances would probably be let out for Christmas; he would have to go over to wherever the woman lived and see her. He said he was sorry. He'd phone on Christmas morning.

Aedan, I am as unhappy as you could ever have made me. Alone and scared and lost and you are so far from me now.

And still I love you.

We could spend New Year together, couldn't we?

No, he said, we could not. Frances could not use her arm. Her life was intolerable right now. She was dangerously depressed. *Let her die.* He couldn't be away for that long. *Let her be dead.* She had threatened to kill herself if he left her again.

And so he would stay.

I wished him dead. I wished us all dead. I wished that Christmas had never been invented. I put the television on and some choirboys wailed some dirge-like carol, invading my living room with their poisonous tune. I pulled the plug out of the wall and put Whitney on instead. It was enough to make even the most insensitive person weep.

Stevie came over in a black sequinned baseball cap. We got stoned and watched a single episode of *Absolutely Fabulous* eight times. I made mulled wine and we talked about Women and what we were doing sitting around on Christmas Eve waiting for the phone to ring. We did wait. We each of us looked longingly at the phone all night. When it did ring it was never who we wanted it to be. We ate chocolates and drank brandy and Stevie painted a picture; rather an abstract design which turned out to look something like a woman's body. And still we waited. It was against everything we believed in.

It seemed we had no choice.

Chapter Twenty-five

We opened our presents together; me, Aedan and Stevie.
I kept saying, 'I can't believe you're here!' and he kept
smiling and looking at Stevie and then at me again.
Stevie said she was going for a walk in the hope of finding
a shop that was open; we'd run out of cigarette papers.
Aedan pulled a knife out of the kitchen drawer and said,
laughing, 'Say that you're mine for ever,' and I said, 'Of
course! Of course!' and he took the knife and cut lines
into my face till the blood had made a pool on the kitchen
floor. I did not complain. It was enough that he was home
for Christmas.

Stoned on Christmas day.
He'd promised to phone.
I expected to be let down.
I stopped myself from calling him and waited. I hid the
phone to make temptation easier to resist. I waited.
Stevie was still in bed. She was under no illusion that
anyone would phone her.

The phone sang out and then he was there in the room
with me.

Happy Christmas! At least I could be honest, I could
say *I pine, I starve, I cannot breathe here without you.* We
laughed. He was alone in his flat. I was alone in London. I

said, 'I still dream of you; even after all this time. I still dream in the morning of you.' *It is every minute*, I wanted to say, *every minute, lost here, alone, lost baby, O to be pregnant again. You must come home, you must you must.*

Nothing breathes with you absent. Here it is all dried up. The things you set on fire have burnt to nothing. I need water but without you I cannot drink.

Stevie and I ate garlic mushrooms and played music and laughed at ourselves. It really was a day worthy of the dread its approach had instilled in us. It was as bad as our worst expectations and then some. We didn't even get drunk.

Chapter Twenty-six

I started work again the day after Boxing Day. I've never been more grateful for a job in my life. Everyone was on top form; Matthew had had a gruesome Christmas with his family and was ecstatic to be away from them all, as was Liam Johnston, who'd had problems with his in-laws. Champagne was served on the bus and we all broke personal rules and drank before the shoot was over. It was heaven. At the end of the day we all went out for a meal and banned the subject of Christmas from all conversations. Fine by me. I let Matthew stay at the flat because he was too drunk to drive home and we couldn't find a cab that would take him back to Twickenham; all the mini-cabs said it was too far and all the black cabs said he looked like he might chuck up at any moment and they weren't prepared to take the risk. We walked home from the West End. Crossing Waterloo Bridge he tried to hold my hand and I said, 'No, Matthew. Let's not get into that. I'll make up a bed for you on the floor. We can't sleep together.' He didn't argue, but put his arm around my shoulders and said he would be in love with me whatever. I told him he was pissed and by the morning I think we'd both forgotten what was said.

We finished the filming two days later, though Liam said it was more than likely we'd get together again in early April for some post-synching, and of course for the publicity later on in the year, perhaps when I got back from Hong Kong or wherever it was I was going. There was also talk of a huge party in May when all the editing was over but people tend to get sentimental at the end of shoots and it was more than likely none of us would get there or even if it would ever get organized. We had a company bash the day before New Year's Eve and I said a very fond farewell to Henry, who I would miss. Ian Turner turned up but spoke to hardly anyone and got pissed on all the free booze and ended up shagging one of the runners in the ladies toilet. Matthew got terribly maudlin and said he thought if we lost touch it would break his heart. I felt quite numb. I was starting back on *The Sugar Man* with the new company the next day and my mind was already clogged with the dread of that. Liam Johnston got very drunk and said he'd enjoyed this time more than any other of his career. I knew what he meant, if indeed he really meant it. It had been quite special for everyone. For me too, in spite of Aedan and all that had gone on outside of the work.

I doubted that *The Sugar Man* would be quite as enjoyable and I still felt as though I were in the middle of some sort of mental breakdown. I kept looking at my feet thinking I'd put odd shoes on and once I got as far as the tube before I realized I was still wearing my pyjamas. I felt I was reaching the end of my line of tolerance; that any strength I had was being zapped away each day. I went into the rehearsal room, a vile place about a hundred stops down the District line, impossible to travel to in less than an hour. It was New Year's Eve so no work was being done; we were really only there so I could meet the rest of the company. They seemed sweet enough, though not the sort of people you'd want to go on holiday with. The two women, Helen and Caroline, had manufactured some sort of relationship out of necessity. Victor Christie, an older guy seemed sort of alone and sad and slightly odd, but affable enough. Then there was Clive Nelligan who I couldn't make out at all; a very beautiful guy, probably about thirty-five, quite distant looking. He looked as though he didn't really want to be there but was making a supreme effort to enjoy it. There was talk of hotel swimming pools and the sea and I mentioned that I couldn't swim and Clive volunteered to teach me. I saw him as a possible friend for the tour though we both had so many barriers up I wondered if either of us was capable of real communication. Thankfully there wasn't a great deal of time to analyse or assess each other or the situation as we broke at one o'clock and weren't called again till the following Monday. I met the Stage Manager, Lionel, and Luke the director who I vaguely knew and then we all went our separate ways. I got home to an apologetic sounding message on the machine from Aedan, saying he was having a crisis in Belfast and would more than likely not be home till the middle of the following week. I called him back and we had a tetchy, brief talk that went round and round in circles and I begged him to let me go over there and see him; I said that I'd get on the next plane and at least then he would have some respite from all the drama out there. He said the shock would probably kill Frances off. I didn't say the words that sprang into my head; if he only knew what a temptation it was to go over there and literally frighten her to death he'd probably never speak to me again. I grew more ashamed of myself every minute. I thought more and more wicked thoughts with every second that passed. I must have planned her disappearance a thousand times. I opened the Bushmill's and started to drink. Why not? I thought, this is what everyone else is doing today, so why the fuck not? Jesus, when would these confounded celebrations come to an end? Stevie called and invited me to a party in Islington. I said maybe and toyed with the idea of getting on a plane and turning up on his doorstep. But what if he wasn't there? What if he was with her or his parents or out partying somewhere? Where would I stay when I had no money for a hotel? I got slightly drunk.

New Year's Eve. What a bastard, *bastard* year. Perhaps I *should* be celebrating its demise. It had started off with such brilliance; I'd left a man, terminated a hopeless relationship and there had followed such relief and freedom and lots of work, and lots of fabulous sex and fun and I'd got the flat and I was so happy being single and independent and then *Aedan*. My whole life had changed, everything I had ever wanted suddenly changed and now I was worrying about what shoes I had on and if they matched and getting drunk alone on New Year's Eve and about to go to a party full of strangers.

I looked in the mirror before I left for the party. I looked haggard. I didn't look as I had when I went to parties at fourteen and fifteen. I looked tired and sad. Damaged. People will notice, I thought, they will say *She is bruised*. And of course they'd be right. He has bruised me. What thoughts run across his mind when he sits alone in his flat? Does he know that I never sleep? That I am hollowed out by all this grief? That I went to meet my new colleagues this morning and cried all the way there on the tube? Does he know that it hurts to go out, that it hurts to eat and drink, that it hurts to see people, to even speak? Even the music I listen to. *I am wrecked*, I thought, *deserted. I am broken into pieces*. And when I finally decide to glue everything back together I wonder if all the pieces will still be there. I feel that at best some of them will be too broken to mend and some of them will be lost for ever. He teased me with a taste of perfection. He teased me with the promise that such perfection would last for ever, and now I am damaged because I *believed* him; I tasted that and when will I ever have perfection again? Surely everything else will be second best.

The party was a nightmare. Everyone was Italian and no-one spoke any English and I don't speak Italian and Stevie was in hyperactive mood and wanted to dance all night. I stayed till midnight and chose to walk home alone, anonymous amidst the drunks and the revellers. Outside one of the tube stations a guy was lying, seriously drunk, in a pool of sick. His friends – and really he didn't need any enemies – were standing around shouting, 'Fucking lightweight!' I walked on and thanked God I didn't know people like that any more.

Oddly, when I got home I was feeling slightly happier. I told myself that maybe all this was worth it for what I'd had in my life; my mother, Aedan. I would've done it all again, had I been given that chance. I am lucky, I am lucky, I said as I let 1993 into the flat. I am very lucky. My father phoned and we talked fondly over the miles and I felt optimistic for more than a moment. Things would be different, it was unavoidable, but things change all the time and that's no bad thing.

Chapter Twenty-seven

On the tube a couple of people stared as I started to cry. I was not enjoying rehearsals. I missed the film crew. I missed being driven to the location in a car. I missed the smell of bacon butties even though I don't eat meat. I missed the money. I missed Aedan. I *hated* the eternal journey to the depths of West London. This particular day seemed some-how worse than the others; perhaps because the New Year had been a focus of optimism for me and on this second or third day I felt like a drowned woman again. As soon as I saw the sign for Sloane Square I had started to feel volcanic and tears had spilled easily down my miserable face. It was a typically British carriageful of people so there was no noise at all and everyone was avoiding everyone else's eyes. I let out a loud gulp and once that was out I couldn't really stop and *still* no-one spoke.

I spent a nightmare day in the church hall we were working in. The cast were at the stage where they were buying biscuits for each other at break-time and explaining their lives to each other. I was only a week behind them all but thought at this rate I would never ever catch up; I would be a stranger to them all. Clive kept himself to himself and I don't remember him joining in the biscuit routine but I couldn't muster any conversation even for him. I expect they thought I was just shy or surly and I couldn't foresee a time when I'd be able to disprove that. Let them think what they like; I will get through this, I will tolerate this time and in a few months it will be over.

I phoned my agent and asked to be released from the job. She was on holiday. Piers, her partner, was horrified and told me to '*Stick with it!*' As he would, thinking of losing all that commission. '*It'll be fine!*' he said, but the prospect of sticking with it filled me with terror. If I had to make that tube journey one more time I would surely die. I couldn't even drink coffee in peace; one lunch-time I'd gone into Hammersmith and ordered cappuccino and the smell had made me weep. All the years of my life spent in coffee shops. I mean, it was a hobby for me, a way of life, and now even that had been blighted. I tried to haul myself out of the mire of depression but was too weak. I left two cappuccinos untouched. In a mad moment I ordered a bright yellow sofa bed from Habitat. If I had to do this godforsaken tour I could at least make sure I would be comfortable when I got back. I bought a matching chair as well and kissed goodbye a grand and a half. They said it would be all made up and finished and delivered to me by the end of March. Perfect timing, just as the tour ended.

The tube journeys were hilariously bad. Intolerable. It amazed me how I ever reached anywhere, how I didn't leap out of the train and escape back into the street. I made the decision again and again not to do the job. Lottie said I had to continue with it or how would I ever pay for the sofa? She had a point, though there were moments when a spell in prison seemed like a feasible alternative; I could get done for fraud, or debt or something – did they still put people away for things like that? Lottie said I was being ridiculous and dragged me round Mothercare, buying things for her child that wasn't even conceived yet. I worried about her; she looked as ill as I did, as maniacal, she spent hundreds of pounds on something that didn't exist. A ghost. *The ghost of my child, your child dead, does not give me respite*. I shouldn't have gone into the shop. I had no idea how much it would hurt. I was losing my mind. Lottie didn't notice anything and paid her bill and packed away all the useless bottles and clothes and toys and again I was confronted with the ghost of my child. Your child dead. The ghosts of words you once gave life to come to me to give me pain; breathe life into a loss that should be dead. Still. You torture me, the memory of you torments me. Bastard, *bastard*, your heart is full of nothing.

At home, making coffee for Lottie, I slid down the units by the sink. 'He might as well be dead. I love him like a dead man. I don't question. I just love and love, such deathless love, and I have a need that makes me only despise myself; a physiological need for this dead man.'

She said, 'Go. Get on a plane.' But I had rehearsals to go to. Maybe I could go into work and do half a day and then collapse and run away; I could go to Ireland. I could go there for an hour, just an hour, just to see him and touch him. Lottie said, 'How are you going to do this tour? Look at you. Look at how you are,' and I said I can't see anything except this deathless love. I look back so often, how can I avoid being turned into stone, into salt? I love a dead man.

'But Ellie, *you're* not dead.' I felt as though I was. *Adapt, adapt*, I told myself. Learn patience, learn tolerance, rebuild. *Rebuild.* He will return. He will. Blind again, the only way to survive.

Chapter Twenty-eight

Nine hours later than originally planned I sat on the 1900hr flight from Gatwick to Dubai. The flight from Heathrow had been overbooked and everyone started to wonder if this was the way things were going to be for the rest of the three months. We were each given five pounds for lunch and complimentary alcohol. Victor Christie started on the red wine at about 8 a.m. when we were still waiting at Heathrow. 'Shit. Oh, shit,' Caroline said. 'Don't let him be a fucking alcoholic,' and she started to chant for sobriety within the company. When eventually we boarded the plane I saw him pull out an Evian bottle. It was either full of whisky or piss. When he started to guzzle it down I guessed it was Scotch.

I was sitting at the opposite end of the plane to everyone else as I had opted to suffer the smoking section. I would rather have suffocated in the smog than have to make conversation with anyone.

I was not left in peace, however. I sat trapped in a window seat by two chain-smoking ex-pat types dripping in yellow gold and reeking of Cacharel. He was mercifully silent but she talked loudly about their forthcoming marriage in the Seychelles; his second marriage, her fourth. She had *nine* children. I mentally gave the marriage about three weeks and put my Walkman on. Even over Whitney Houston I could hear her rattling on about white beach-hogs in the

Seychelles and how if you stand on one your foot can go septic in minutes. I turned Whitney off in favour of Sting. When we reached Dubai several hours later, 'Be Still My Beating Heart' was playing for about the seventeenth time that day and I was quite drunk. Dubai is actually rather beautiful when you approach it from the sky in the middle of the night and your blood stream is full of Famous Grouse. It looks bejewelled. A bejewelled isle. A well-meaning Lionel appeared to say that they'd all meet up with me at customs. I watched in amusement as he tried to squeeze his way back through the crowd to the front of the plane just as everyone was trying to get their hand-luggage from the overhead lockers. I waited until the last possible minute before grabbing my bags and following everyone else down the stairs. I could see the rest of the company about half a mile away already, getting on one of the bendi-buses that were ferrying people over the tarmac to Arrivals. I held back and got on the second bus. Clive had obviously had the same thought and sat down opposite me. We eyed each other knowingly and he laughed. His smile, which had been as absent as mine during rehearsals, was as dazzling as the sun after rain. It was like a reward. We said nothing and soon after I caught him looking sadly out into the night and wondered if he regretted taking this job as much as I did. By the time we reached customs I felt sick with regret. What had possessed me? It was hardly a career move. Who was going to come and see a show in the Middle East? Peter Hall? We met up with the cast at passport control. They were oohing and aahing already and we hadn't even got to the hotel. I looked over at Clive who stifled a laugh and looked down at his shoes. They were very beautiful shoes, expensive Timberland things. He was a veritable clothes horse. Rather a beautiful one. I felt huge relief that he was gay, thinking that otherwise I would probably have tried to bed him at the first drunken opportunity and then regretted sullying myself for Aedan. Ah, Aedan.

Chapter Twenty-nine

For the first few days we lay about the hotel pool enjoying the sun and getting better acquainted with one another. It was pleasant and remarkably healing if a little like a wit competition. Clive and I discovered we had a very similar sense of humour. Sick and dark. The more comfortable we got, the sharper our wit became and as a result we got closer and closer until it was just the two of us and the others went their separate ways. The two women went in search of temples and souks and Clive lay next to me in the sun, worrying about the weight he imagined he'd gained. I called him Nellie, in honour of the elephant, and he called me pudding. Lionel hung around with us as well, though mainly he swam. He swam about a hundred lengths at a time. It amazed me he didn't drown in boredom, going up and down the pool like that for days on end. Every now and again he would join us for coffee before dropping back into the water and doing another hundred. He was also a bit of a watch-dog, keeping an eye out for Victor Christie, who neither Nellie nor I wanted to see. We'd nicknamed him Vera (amongst other things) and discussed his mental health which seemed to be withering rapidly in the sun. He walked around in a bizarre stalk-like manner and when he wasn't muttering inanities to himself he was shouting at the hotel staff. We also discovered very quickly that he had no capacity whatsoever for learning lines, which was slightly worrying for everyone and deeply frustrating. I had originally thought maybe he was just nervous and then I thought maybe he had Alzheimer's and took pity on him but after three weeks I just loathed him. He stood for hours and hours in the sun some days, until his back was blistered and charred and we were sure this couldn't be helping his pin-sized memory span. Nellie caught him taking photographs of my hotel-room door and twice he called me at four o'clock in the morning, hopelessly drunk, declaring his love for me and asking if I'd fuck him. Very sad, I mean he was *seventy-eight*. Looking back, I think he was clinically depressed, but he gave up the business not long afterwards or perhaps he even died and I never heard of him again. On our first press night in Dubai he forgot his lines about seventeen times. Lionel called him *Weirdfucker*, though soon after that no-one called him anything at all, except perhaps one time at breakfast when he grabbed a waitress by her skirt and screamed that his coffee was tepid, and on that occasion Nellie called him a twat and they would've had a huge row only I grabbed Nellie and whisked him off to the gym before anybody got violent.

Amusing ourselves, Nellie and I made a great show of smearing our factor-ten sun cream all over each other. It became a bit of a ritual and we were so safe with each other and it felt like it was the only physical pleasure I could allow myself. Helen and Caroline thought it all rather odd and Caroline asked me one evening if she'd been wrong about Clive. Was he really a heterosexual after all? I teased her with silence and we confused her further by snogging at the side of the stage. We had a million little jokes that made us howl with laughter and I think everyone grew to hate us, except Caroline, who couldn't hate anyone, but we didn't care; we had each found a soul mate and this was as big and beautiful a surprise as we could ever have hoped for. I felt like he'd been sent to heal me. I told him that he'd probably saved my life and he said that in actual fact I had saved his. I thought I was too infested with grief to be a tonic to anyone, but Nellie said

140

that I was and I loved him for making me feel worth more than nothing. We went everywhere together. Every morning he knocked on my door, every day he phoned me before breakfast and we'd sneak away somewhere to eat our breakfast alone and annoy people in restaurants with our laughter which was loud and continuous. We *looked* like lovers, but we were not.

He asked about Aedan but only on occasion and he could always tell when I didn't want to talk about it. In fact, most days we didn't talk about it at all; Aedan, Daisy, any of it. Nellie seemed to feel it was his duty to help me forget. I couldn't do it, didn't want to, but I did need respite and so during the days I tried hard not to think. As Nellie and I didn't sleep together, however, I still had the nights to contend with. I dreamt of him still. I wrote a lot of postcards and made calls to Belfast. I'd fall into my bed after some drunken Arabian binge in some dreadful hotel nightclub and write long, pathetic love-letters. A lost cause. On the phone to Aedan one night I remember him saying I sounded happy, which indeed I had been during the day, but the words brought me crashing back down to the reality which was far from happy and a million miles from him. A million miles away and still I could not forget. It's also very difficult, when you know you're being charged about twenty pounds a minute, to get down to any sort of serious, worthwhile discussion. We talked about the thousands of miles between us, about Louis, the Middle East mentality (albeit briefly), and at one point even the weather was mentioned. The future, such as it was, was not even touched upon. Our love, such as that was, was kept for the final seconds of each call when we would hastily say I love you and he would always apologize for everything and I would always say it didn't matter, which of course it did. On one occasion I asked him if he'd accepted the London job yet. We were cut off. A sand storm, the operator told me, had severed the connection. Ha. If only it were that simple.

Chapter Thirty

We went in search of sex. Looking for a lotus to eat. I didn't mean it at the time, it was like a joke, but we'd started to get slightly bored; when you've seen one camel/souk/palm tree you've seen them all. It was really just a game more than anything else. I wasn't seriously contemplating doing anything about my sexless existence, though it had to be said it had been weeks and weeks since I'd done it and I usually start to climb the walls without it. Some of my friends have said I'm just like a man. The only reason I'd survived this long was because my heart was so broken. After Daisy I couldn't even masturbate. As it happens, Dubai isn't an ideal place for a woman to look for sex so it was just as well I didn't really want to find any. The Arabs we met were only interested in Nellie's bottom, or so it seemed. He took one guy out for a drink and I went to bed with a sleeping pill so I wouldn't cramp his style. In the morning, it transpired that Ahmiri or whatever his name was had been most interested in '*The White Lady*' but he'd been unable to even look me in the eye, much less shake my hand or kiss me, because, he said, it was disrespectful. With a man, however, he could do whatever he wanted. They could have whatever contact they liked and would not get thrown in jail or flogged for it. Strange but true. Nellie had put him off and taken a sleeping pill himself. He said he'd been more attracted to the dish-dash than the man underneath. He said he'd rather have spent the evening with me. Perhaps we were after the same thing after all.

I suggested a nightclub. We could go with some of the expats we'd met on the opening night of the show. We had an arrangement that if either of us got an offer we didn't want to refuse (highly unlikely from my point of view) the other would either go to bed or get conveniently lost in the crowd. I found myself getting lost on a number of occasions, thinking Clive would be getting on or off with someone but I was usually mistaken and he would come and find me saying I was better company than anyone there. We went out a few times but we always stayed together and at the end of each night we always separated and I would go back to my room alone. One morning over breakfast Nellie caught me looking lost into my muesli and said, 'Ellie, do you really *want* to meet anyone else?'

'No. No, not yet. I can't even bear to think of it, though I guess I'll have to at some point.'

'Would you have sex with someone else?'

'I doubt it. Maybe. I don't fancy anyone any more. Except him.'

'You fancy me though.'

'Yes, but probably because I know I can't have you. Safe.'

'You're wasted on that bastard.'

'He's not a bastard.'

'I think you're beautiful.'

'Don't be ridiculous.'

'You *are*. You've got a stunning figure, you're sexy, you've got a beautiful, *really* beautiful face. If I were a straight man . . .'

'But you're not.'

'No.'

We thought about it.

'Maybe if we ever get *really* horny and neither of us finds anyone to have sex with . . .'

'Yes,' he said. 'We'll fuck each other when we get to Guam.'

In Al Ain, an oasis in the desert, we were finally separated by sex. Some Egyptian guy took a shine to Nellie and took over for a few days and I was left to my own devices. I lay by the pool and read a little and reacquired the art of masturbation. One day by the pool, after a furtive wank in the changing rooms, I was reading a book and listening to Fauré's Requiem on my Walkman when a throaty Irish voice called to me from the water, 'It's cool in here! Come on in!' I looked up and saw some businessman who'd been to see the show the night before.

'I can't swim,' I shouted, turning the music down.

'I'll hold you up.'

I would've liked to go in but the pool at the Al Ain Intercontinental was about eight feet deep and despite Nellie's patient coaching and coaxing I was still quite unable to swim.

The Irishman came dripping over.

'Can I get a drink for the actress?' *Lovely* voice. Always a sucker for an Irish accent, I asked for a cappuccino sort of semi-seductively (I was out of practice) over the top of my Ray-bans and moved slightly on the lounger so that my thighs didn't look too blobby. He waved to the waiter and mouthed, 'Coffee,' and stuck two fingers up.

'I loved your show.'

'Thank you.'

'Where's your friend today?'

'Clive? He's gone to a camel race. I think. He has a friend here from Egypt.'

'Ah!' he said, as though I'd just explained the theory of relativity to him. 'I really loved your show.'

'Yes, you said. Thanks.'

'Thought I might come and see it again.'

'Oh. I could, well, I think I could get you a ticket. Would

you really want to sit through it again?' Before I knew it I'd started to flirt with him and I didn't know if I wanted to. Oh God. The cappuccino arrived and we talked some more and I flirted some more and I felt half excited that I was still alive when I'd thought I was dead and half terrified at the idea of sleeping with someone. But then this was just an innocent chat and it wouldn't get that far, would it? If I did that would it all be over? Would it be real then? Would it mean that Aedan was never coming back? Maybe it wouldn't. A bit of sex might not hurt. Maybe it would cure me. How old was this man? Thirty-five? Forty?

'What part of Ireland are you from?'

'Ballymena.'

'I've been there!' I gave him a big, wide, actressy smile. Really if I analysed it I'd make myself sick.

'Did you like it there?'

'I did. I thought the Antrim coast was . . . well, I think it's one of the most beautiful coastlines in the world. I had a friend who took me round – he'd lived there – and he talked me through the scenery and the sand and Belfast. Maybe you'll have heard of him, he's quite famous over there, he's a writer. Billy Shane?'

'Ach, who in Belfast hasn't heard of him? Is he your boyfriend?' God. Subtle.

'No. Just my friend.'

Silence. I thought of Billy, which made me think of Belfast which of course made me think of Aedan. The coffee arrived.

'So. Ellie. May I call you Ellie? Are you . . . are you happy in your job?'

'Yes. Oh yes.' I wasn't thinking straight. It was his accent. Jesus, ten minutes with an Irishman and I'm on my knees. It never fails.

'Don't you miss your family?'

'They're all dead.' Bit cruel, I know, but people are always assuming they're alive.

'I'm sorry.'

'Don't be. You didn't kill them.' He almost visibly shrank away from me. 'I'm sorry . . . ?' God, what was his name, Tony? Tom? Terry? He'd introduced himself. What was his name? 'I'm sorry . . . John.'

'Michael.'

'I'm sorry, Michael. I'm very bruised.'

'Ah. Will we mend those bruises for you?' Jesus, it was that sort of Irish flannel that'd got me into this mess in the first place.

'I doubt it.'

'You're not sad though, are you, surely not?'

'I'm afraid I am,' I said.

'How can I help?'

'You can't.'

I stopped flirting with him and drank my coffee. He dived into the pool and splashed around a lot. I saw him swim to the other end and then he disappeared. Moments later he was at my feet.

'A length under water.' Was this meant to impress me? I ordered a beer from the waiter and went back to my book. If I pretended I wasn't actually there maybe he would go away.

'Is it a man that's bruised you?'

'Yes,' I said, instantly cross with myself for forgetting to ignore him.

'Tell me about him.'

'No. I can't.'

'What sort of magic did you have that made your heart break like that?' Jesus.

'I don't want to talk about it.'

'It might help.'

'It won't bring him back though, will it?' I snapped.

'I'm sorry.'

'You have no idea.'

'Why did it go wrong?'

'I've no idea.'

146

'Is there any hope left for you?'

'No idea about that either.'

Soon afterwards I made my excuses and raced back into the hotel. The Reuters machine was tapping out the news by the lift. About ten miles of paper was spilling out of it so that the whole lobby was drowned with information. I looked at it and wondered what in God's name it was there for; it would take several weeks to plough through all those words; who on earth would bother? In the shop I ran into Nellie and we walked round to the lift. A man and a woman were in there looking awkward with each other. Just before we got to the fifth floor Nellie suddenly clapped his hand to his mouth and horrified, said, 'Oh my God. Oh my God!'

'What?' I said, 'What is it? What's wrong?'

He looked at me really seriously. 'I forgot to look at the news!' I laughed so much I wet my knickers. The couple smiled at me laughing because once I'd started I couldn't stop and that set Nellie off who had not expected me to find it quite so funny. The awkward couple looked even more awkward and started to snigger. I could not stop now and neither could Nellie. Screaming with laughter in the lift, tears streaming down my face, wet knickers, a couple watching us envious of our ease, I looked at Nellie and loved him.

We went back to my room and got changed for tennis and later we went back to Nellie's room and ordered an obscene amount of food and wine and talked about sex and life and love and work and I knew we would always be friends, till we were old and fat and half-dead.

Two days later on a plane to Bahrain from Dubai I ran into Tony or Tom or Terry or whatever his name was.

'Ah. Destiny,' he said.

'I think not.' Dry little laugh. 'Business in Bahrain?'

'Well, sort of a holiday really. I'm staying at the Hilton.'

'So am I.'

'Bahrain is the pearl of the Gulf.'

147

'So I'm told.'

'Though of course, that was before you arrived.' Nauseating. 'Cigarette?' He offered me a Marlboro. Nice to have a lung-rippingly strong smoke after a month of Silk Cut.

'Thanks.' I took it and he whipped out a Zippo and lit it for me.

'Happy holiday, Ellie.'

'Well, it's work really.'

'We'll see.'

Chapter Thirty-one

Bahrain was not only *not* the pearl of the Gulf, as described by my Irish friend, but more like the plastic bead of nowhere. The weather was almost English in its uncertainty and compared to Al Ain's temperature of over a hundred degrees it was freezing cold at only sixty-five. I was also decidedly premenstrual which made the whole island seem like a piece of floating solidified vomit. Much as I tried I could see no beauty in the place whatsoever. It even made Helen feel premenstrual and she'd had the menopause. The hotel was vile and I was prevented from learning to swim in peace by the constant presence of about seventeen teenage yobs who splashed around maniacally, leaping in and out of the pool like demented seals.

Dejected at breakfast one morning, hideously hormonal, contemplating a plate of Turkish mushrooms which had started to congeal, I grunted a vague 'good morning' at Helen. She looked at me with an 'I've-been-around-longer-than-you-and-you-don't-know-you're-born' type look and said with a sweet smile, 'You can't judge Bahrain on the hotel alone, my darling. It's like judging Watford on Watford High Street.'

'Oh, my God. Watford *is* Watford High Street. And actually I wasn't judging this fly pit on the hotel alone. I've *been out*. I've seen the museum and the fucking souk. It's the same as all the other fucking souks we've been to only there are MORE FLIES,' at which point Nellie came in and

149

whisked me off to the bar before I lost the plot. We were drunk before they'd finished serving breakfast, which mercifully didn't matter as there was no show that night.

'Well the food's all right here,' said Nellie, placating me. 'We should be grateful for that at least. He was tucking into a plate of hammour, the local fish, which, it had to be said, was something else altogether.

'I suppose it makes the sick smell sweeter.' We fell about in fits and crashed our way over to the dessert table.

On the opening night of the show the Irishman turned up. He talked a little about his soon to be ex-wife. She'd just left him. A pair of rejects, I thought as he handed me a canapé and I felt about as low as I had before the tour began. No word from Aedan for over a week now. I would be alone for ever if I waited for him. The Irishman seemed safe enough. Terry or Tim or whatever his name was. At least I would never have to see him again. He talked till my ears were sore. I didn't mind. I found it almost therapeutic. On the second night he made a fully-fledged pass at me. I gave him my room number and got in the lift. I showered and tried not to think, not to change my mind. He might cure me. I might be healed. I might forget. I might wake up in the morning and find there's no longer a bar on my chest. I may find I can breathe again. I cleaned my teeth and tried to calm my hair down a bit. I would've liked to have listened to some lively music but there was a knock on the door so I guessed it would have to wait. He stood at the door, smiling. My stomach churned.

He had a towel round his neck.

'Going for a swim?' I asked.

'What? Oh, this. I thought . . . I mean . . .'

'Never mind,' I said, half dragging him into the room so no-one would see him. 'I've ordered some drink.'

'No need. I brought this.' He produced a bottle of Jameson's, instantly conjuring up Aedan and Oakley Street; the two of us draped over each other that first night we'd spent together. I phoned room service and cancelled the order.

'I nearly got us some coke,' he said.

'I prefer to drink it with a drop of water,' I said.

'No, sorry, I mean *coke*, cocaine.'

'Oh. I see. Well, I don't take drugs. A bit of spliff every now and again but nothing else.'

'Sorry.'

'No, don't worry about it. I've no objection to other people blowing their nostrils out.' I always get prickly if I know I'm on the verge of a terrible mistake.

'I'll get some glasses,' he said.

'They're in the bathroom.' He clunked around in there and came out trying to look casual and un-nervous. He had a lovely face. Physically at least, he was a very beautiful man. Great blue Irish eyes and jet black hair, slightly thin on top. He did have a suit on though which unless it's a really beautiful Armani or Versace or something usually really turns me right off. It was navy blue which made it even worse.

'I've thought about you every moment since I first saw you on stage in Al Ain.' Oh, *shit*. What had I done? What was I about to do to myself?

'Do you come to see all the shows out here?'

'Well, some of them are shite. *Who stole my Wife's knickers, Vicar?* that sort of thing. We only get about four a year though so I try to see them all. We're culturally deprived here.'

'Is there a cinema?'

'I don't know. Probably.'

'How do you live like that? How do you cope? What do you do with your evenings?'

'I work a lot. I work most of the time in fact . . . Judy – my wife – she left me last summer and went home. She hated it here. I don't mind it so much. At least it's hot.'

'Is it lonely?'

'It is.'

We didn't speak for a few minutes. I thought of Aedan. I

151

expect the Irishman was thinking about his wife. I hummed nervously to myself.

'Is it a nice life, then – being an actress?'

'It is. When I'm working. The hardest thing about being an actress is being unemployed. Not been there for a while though, thank God. Touch wood.' I hit the bed-head.

'So why are you sad?'

'I'm in love with someone who doesn't want me. I was jilted.'

'The actor? Your friend in the show?'

'Clive? No, no Clive and I are just great friends. No. Someone back home.'

'He must be mad. How could anyone not want you?'

There was an awkward pause. I tried to blank my mind; the stuff running through it was what nightmares are made of. He put his hand under my chin.

'Ellie . . .'

I looked at him. Lovely face. Not Aedan's though. Don't think, enjoy. Come alive again. He kissed me. I lost myself for a moment then remembered and pulled away.

'More whiskey?' I said, dry throat now, panic.

'I've had enough.'

Yes. So have I. Get out. Tell him to leave. Let yourself be defeated. Tell him to go. It's not too late. A mistake. He kissed me again and we fell backwards. God no, a mistake. Scream, push him away. His weight. Tell him you're a mad woman, a woman mad. It's not too late. I pushed his face off mine into the air above me.

'Condoms,' he said.

I reached over to the night table and pulled one out of the drawer. I watched him open it. I was horrified. Why couldn't I speak? Where was my voice? I felt as though someone was taking out one of my kidneys and the anaesthetic hadn't worked and so I was still awake only I couldn't scream and say, 'Mistake! Don't take my kidney – I'm awake! I'm still awake!'

He was undeterred. I drifted off into a panic-like dream. Where was I? What was I doing?

The Irishman, heavy on me.

Crawling over and away from each other not daring to reject or encourage. Moments where I would succumb to the smell or touch of him and imagine I was not me; I was a woman I had never met; a business woman or a holiday maker. Another man's wife. Any woman other than me.

But imagination dies when the force of loss decides to engulf and at once I was me again, suffocating in grief, lost and dying.

A great mistake.

Straight into the bath. Wash away all trace of anyone but me. Me. I could not live with me. I could not be in the same room as me.

Logic. Find some logic, some sense. Look at this with logical eyes. Detach yourself. Nothing lost. Nothing risked. The Irishman used a condom. We did not speak except my words of regret.

'A mistake. You and I here. We are a mistake.'

Stopped before either of us could come. I could not have carried on. I pushed him out and away – five minutes it must have taken. Less. I was reminded of Aedan by my utter lack of love. I made him leave before he was even fully dressed. And so at last I pushed water and soap into me and scrubbed my inside walls. I cleaned my ears and the roots of my hair, my scalp, the inside of my mouth, in between my fingers and toes and again I cleaned out the inside of me. I buried myself in the water to cleanse, to heal, to erase what was the present, remove the new skin, newly touched by strangers.

Damaged. I do not want to be embroiled in anyone else. I want no-one's pain on my conscience. I want nothing because I can give nothing and nothing is enough for no man. Beauty is not what I see in myself. Inside I am dead. Hollow. Empty hollow where once He lived.

Chapter Thirty-two

The Irishman phoned my room.

'Did you just call me a moment ago? I was in the bath. It stopped ringing just as I got to it.'

I was not swallowed up by this lie, having used the same ploy a couple of times myself as a teenager.

'Why would I call you?'

'Women play such games, don't they?'

I did not respond. I did not want to hurt him. But neither did I want to speak to him or think of him or see him. Ever.

He asked could he fuck me?

No. A terrible mistake we had made.

He disagreed.

Then he says, all male, his macho pride bleeding down the phone, 'We did not fuck last night, Ellen, not by my standards and not by yours.'

'You don't know what my standards are.' And he says, 'I like to do it for a long time. I'd like to fuck you to the death.'

'It's not a competition.' I wanted to end the conversation right there and get on the next plane out of the country but I couldn't stop myself spitting out, 'It doesn't always have to be a fucking marathon. Sometimes a short sweet fuck is just the ticket.'

'Well, have a short sweet fuck then.'

'Not with you. Don't call me again.' I threw the receiver down. It was my own fault. I'd walked right into this. I didn't want this man or his cock or his love. I had wanted to take him to bed because he was Irish. Because I was lonely. I'd wanted to fuck him just to see if I could still do it. I couldn't. The Irishman had melancholy on his breath. He stank of it and such a stench I could not bear from any stranger. A mid-lifer; hit forty and found his life dried up around him. A man who wants it all ahead of him again. The clocks can only go forward.

Nellie phoned.

'I haven't slept,' I said. 'I'm not well. I'm ill. I might die today.'

'Don't be ridiculous,' he said. 'I'm coming round.'

He was there in minutes. I opened the door and climbed back into bed between the bare blankets.

'Where are your sheets?'

'I ripped them off. Sent them to Laundry.'

'Are you sick?'

'Yes. In the head.'

'Oh, baby.' He got into bed with me and gave me a cuddle. 'The Irish guy?'

'Yes.'

'Perhaps it's the accent. Perhaps you're addicted to the Irish accent. He was very pretty.'

'He wasn't Aedan.'

'He wasn't.'

'I don't want to live my life with him not in it.'

'Maybe you'll have to.'

'Don't.'

'If I ever meet that bastard I'll kill him.'

'Don't.'

'He's a cunt.'

'No. He just doesn't want me.'

'Then he's a fool.'

He went out to get us some breakfast. Five minutes later the phone rang again. Thinking it was Nellie I picked it up.

'Ellen?' The Irishman. Desperation seeped down the line.

Alone with him I had felt lonelier still. I had wanted to be a stranger to myself. I had wanted it to be another day in another country.

'Ellie?'

'What? What do you want?'

'You.' God.

'Don't call me again. Ever.'

He did. About ten minutes later. Again I thought it would be Nellie. Before I hung up he said, 'You are an island to which I can swim.'

'Bollocks. Don't waste valuable breath on me. I'm only trouble for you. *That's* reality.'

Chapter Thirty-three

Scrubbed clean, though not as clean as I wanted, I walked about Bahrain. I went on a guided tour. People took my camera and photographed me, dressed in white. I look thin. A ghost. I still have the pictures. Sometimes I look at them and say It was me it was me, because I have to be reminded.

I missed my friends. There is always that feeling on a long tour that really there's no other life outside of it. It's quite a claustrophobic sensation. I particularly missed Alice and Lottie who were sending regular faxes and letters. I missed my sanity. In my room one night I phoned Room Service and begged hot milk and Nescafé. They arrived with warm cream and some exotic ground coffee so I sent them away with a piece of paper with NESCAFE AND BOILED MILK PLEASE printed on it. At about 4 a.m. the Nescafé arrived and I made milky coffee and thought of Alice. Milky coffee was a ritual with us. Years – how many? – gone by, me and her on the phone through the night, when Carlo had left. She'd had a broken heart, a bar on her chest, a bit like the one I was living under. She took boiled water instead of meals. We were nineteen. I was at college, secure in my ambition, and she was in Manchester working with people with whom she had nothing in common. Carlo had gone and she thought her life was over, like you do when you're only nineteen. She could never sleep at that time so we drank milky coffee over the phone which was one of the reasons she was so much on my mind that night in the Bahrain hotel. We were very young. My parents were both alive. I had not met Aedan and so I had not lost him. We'd had no idea about real grief then. I drank my coffee, drinking in some of the past with every sip.

I went out to the pool. Some security guy waved me away and called something out but I went in anyway. It was cold. I was not surprised. It was refreshing but I still couldn't stay afloat and went back to my room and lay in bed watching MTV. I ate the complimentary fruit and drank the bottle of complimentary wine and as soon as it was a decent enough time to do so I phoned Lionel. He came round with his free bottle and we drank that and went down to the most ludicrous of the twenty-seven restaurants, a wild-west style place, and I ate an enormous prawn (about eleven inches long) and got more pissed than I'd been for years and fell in and out of the lift and into my room again and collapsed, fully clothed, on my bed, till the day was over.

Not surprisingly I was ill the following day; my drunken nausea compounded by white-knuckle period pains. I phoned Lottie and asked her to send Nurofen as speedily as she could and then I moped around by the pool feeling slightly lonely and very pissed off that I had access to all this luxury but was too miserable to enjoy it. The day came and went and before I knew it it was 5 p.m. and I'd done nothing except wallow. But the yobs had disappeared and I was alone at least and almost without thinking I slid into the water, not even bothering to take off my shorts, and stood in it up to my neck. Shit, what did it matter if I drowned? I threw myself forward, too depressed to be scared and I found the water didn't engulf me and I wasn't afraid any more and if I swallowed some it didn't matter or if it went in my ears I wouldn't go deaf and if I sank, so what? And then I swam. Not a big deal to most people but when you've lived twenty-four years being totally unable to get the hang of it, it really feels like a miracle. Helen saw me and raced over with a camera to catch my first strokes on film and I shouted and spluttered and got out of the water once I realized it wasn't just a one off and I could do it again and again and I ran around telling anyone who could understand me.

I went back up to my room and put an orange bandanna in my hair and pulled on a newly laundered orange dress and some orange shoes and felt like a success but wondered how I would celebrate. We had a meal but it was disgusting and as soon as I could find a suitable moment I went to the toilet and chucked the whole thing up and felt ridiculous and orange, draped over a toilet pan a million miles from anywhere looking like some sort of mutant fruit. I scraped myself up from the tiles and went to phone Aedan. I still didn't know whether he'd taken the job in London. Should I start to hope again? Would he be in London when I got back? Was he coming home? He said maybe maybe maybe maybe; he would send another fax.

I took to my bed. There seemed no point in getting up. I ordered fruit from Room Service and lay in bed. It can safely be said that Bahrain was where I went out of my mind, assuming I hadn't already done that months before. Nellie was away with two gold dealers, seeking sex. I couldn't blame him. I too would have gone away.

But I am not free.

I couldn't even lie on the beach in peace because I am a woman.

At least I can swim now, I thought, so I will not drown.

A man arrived at the door with an envelope on a silver plate. I think he expected a tip. Had I known what was in the envelope I would have given him nothing. It was a typed-out fax from Dublin.

And so I am lost again, I thought, this time in Arabia. This time he chooses to send a fax. Sad that an envelope such as this could fill me with such hope. Sadder that I waited for his handwriting and he deprives me of that one small thing.

159

On impersonal paper, some typed words said

My darling Brenda,
Around the world in, what, ninety days is it?
No Arabian knights for you as yet? I hope the
tour is doing you the good you deserve. I hear
from the Gulf correspondent on GMTV that you
have run away with all the notices which
surprises me not at all. I expect everyone has
fallen in love with you. How could they
resist?
   I think that in six weeks I will be history
to you. That you will be cured. I have been a
bad disappointment. It looks unlikely that I
will be coming to London this year. You'll
probably thank me in the end.
   Love you for a thousand years. And more.
   Two lifetimes of kisses,
   Aedan.

He deprived me of his whole self. Again. He deprived me
of hope, his love, the child he gave to me only so she could
be taken away.

And so this time he really was gone from me. And when
would I listen? When would I hear?

When we got on the plane from Bahrain to London there
was no hope left and it was almost a relief, a hideous relief. I
stared into space and let the feeling wash over me. I was not
sorry to leave. I noticed the video on the plane was a
documentary on the beauty of Ireland. I put my headphones
on and thought *Am I never going to be allowed some peace
from this man?* I could not wait to get home. I put a
compilation tape I'd made into my Walkman to drown out
the announcement that Captain Bates had started to make.
Bates? Was his first name Norman? The Nolans started to
serenade me with 'Don't Make Waves' through my British

Airways headphones. Jesus, what had I been thinking of when I'd put together this tape? It reminded me of my childhood. I switched it off and put tissues in my ears instead and slept till we got home.

Lottie was waiting at the airport for me. I wanted to kiss her face off for being there. She whisked me home and cooked breakfast and we talked about the tour and the fax and the swimming and then she told me she was pregnant. She would have a September baby. She'd also been asked to sing the theme tune to a children's TV programme and they would even release it on CD.

I felt joyous that luck could change so quickly; that only four weeks ago Lottie had despaired as much as me. I felt I must give up now and start again anew. I must give up on Aedan and false hopes and rebuild my life. I wrote a Valentine's card and decided it would be the last thing I sent to him. It had to be. It had to stop. I had to stop and start all over.

We came together.
We were put asunder.
What was in between
Was but a dream;
Not to be forgot

161

Chapter Thirty-four

> He's never coming back.
> Let him die.
> Let him be dead.
> Wake up. Wake up.
> He's never coming back.

We travelled to Singapore on Valentine's day. It was the first time in ten years I hadn't received a card. I felt more than slightly rejected. I felt like a widow. If I could only let him die then maybe I would get better, maybe I would come alive again.

It was a delight to see Nellie. I felt as if I hadn't seen him for a whole month. As soon as we arrived we checked into our rooms and got changed and went up to the pool on the roof. Compared to the biting cold of London the heat was almost unbearable but still wondrous. We tried to lie down but had to keep plunging into the water to cool off. I learned how to float. We played. It was exhilarating enjoying the water and each other and having no fear. I learned to swim under water. I began to breathe again even on dry land.

I shut him from my mind. I sent nothing to him and heard nothing from him and pretended he was dead. It made the days easier to live in even though at night I had terrible dreams whether I slept or not. Some of them were so vile I could no longer sleep without a light. Nellie was also suffering from terrible dreams though he couldn't find a reason for any of his and they were so extreme and abstract we could never work out what any of them meant. Mine were mainly about dead men. No prizes for working out the meaning there. In the end we tried to compete for the most hideous nightmare. We wrote some of them down and compared notes and laughed at each other and tried to work out which one of us was the most twisted.

We drank a lot of beer. We ate a lot of terrible food. Most of it was free because of the job and the deal the producer had done with all the hotel managers; part of the deal was that we had to sign house-cheques as though we were members of the hotel staff. Initially it sounded like a great idea but we found that the more house-cheques we signed, the worse the service got. As soon as the waiters realized we weren't wealthy paying tourists they wouldn't even give us the time of day. It didn't bother us; we chose to be amused. We laughed at everything. We would be happy this week if it killed us; we had promised ourselves. We would go out and about and enjoy this tour as though it were a holiday.

We survived like this happily till Sunday. Not a favourite day for either of us. Sundays are so often depressing; a reminder of solitude wherever one lies, sleeps, wakes alone. London, Arabia, Singapore, wherever. Dreaming (a nightmare) of those couples sipping coffee and drinking in the news from a hundred Sunday papers in the warmth of a shared home. The same bloody couples who enjoy bank holidays. I woke alone looking out through open curtains, shivering from the air-conditioning; afraid of the dark from nights and nights of sour dreams. And other dreams; some dreams so sweet they made the waking sour. A woman dreaming of the dead. A woman dreaming of the safe love of her gay friend who does not dream of her. Alone in this country a sweet dream can only be a lie.

The fire alarm went off. I didn't move. I didn't even turn over in my bed. I lay and dreamed of the past. I wondered if eventually someone would come and haul me kicking from the room. Nellie would not have a happy tour without me. Perhaps he too was lying in bed dreaming of being burned alive. After about half an hour the alarm stopped bleeping. At noon I went up to the pool and spent a rare five minutes with Helen and Caroline until Nellie found me and whisked me off for lunch. The waiters were now wise to the fact we were paying for nothing and napkins were whipped from under us and our drinks were warm and late. We laughed loudly and the service deteriorated even further. If things got any worse we decided we'd find some toy money from somewhere to leave as tips.

We went to Raffles expecting everything we didn't get. It was like a shopping mall. It is not the Raffles Hotel Noel Coward dined in; they knocked it down and built a replica. They are proud of this fact. The people who run Singapore do not relish the past; they treasure the new and build and build over the old so it lies destroyed beneath offices and shops and more shops. Raffles is an arcade. Perhaps they had the right idea; perhaps it is better to let the dead sleep. We saw a sign for the Raffles museum and went in search of it. What we found was a tiny room hidden at the top of a couple of flights of stairs with barely a hundred exhibits. These small remnants of history sit at the top of the hotel neglected. They are all that is left of the Raffles people travel miles to see, apart from the veranda which was apparently saved from restoration. I looked in the souvenir shop and bought old-style postcards to remind me of what I'd wanted to see. We took a couple of photos of each other and feeling slightly dispirited, got on the tube back to the Hilton where High Tea was being served in the lounge. We decided to have some and hoped they wouldn't recognize us as The Actors. We were too afraid to say, 'House-cheque' in case they took our cutlery away.

We went back to my room together, though I can't remember why; it seemed quite difficult to separate. I offered up my star-fruit and looked out of the window. We were almost awkward. When I turned around I saw Nellie rooting around in my mini-bar; when he saw I'd eaten all the chocolate he howled and called me fatty and we roared with laughter and he confessed he'd eaten all his as well and really was there no hope for us? We called each other names, silly names, like children might, and like a child I pretended to hit him and hysterically we had this mock fight and somehow I ended up on the floor, my legs in his grip, my back scraping along the carpet, and then the mock fight became a mockery of sex as crying with laughter he dragged me along the floor and my dress ripped which made us laugh so much we could hardly breathe because my breasts were exposed and Nellie screamed and then laughing he left, and in separate rooms we came alone, still laughing. I still holding a mocking memory in my fingers.

I fantasized about him and felt no guilt. He was my beloved Nellie, my Clive. Safe and adoring and adored. I did not feel like I was betraying the memory of a dead man because it felt like a game, a game between two soul mates, two kids. Clive was a gay man; I was safe from him. Safe from myself. But we played on. Such games. Toying with violence, real violence, my fantasies were brutal; I could not be hurt or battered enough; I couldn't make myself come if I wasn't hurt. Toying with my imaginary partners I learned something old of myself. Years ago a gentle man couldn't give me an orgasm. I had wanted nothing gentle or kind. Until Aedan. Until him I had had to be bruised. I wanted evidence; marks all over me as proof of the act. I never learned why. I asked myself but never found a reason. I thought all that had gone from me a long time ago. Nellie said he had no violence in him and found it all disturbing; he hated it. That only made me worse. I told him what I dreamt of knowing it could only confuse him. I teased him. I drew no lines between fantasy and the games we played together. The mock fight we had in my room that Sunday became something we found ourselves going back to again and again. I teased and provoked until I knew he was half aroused by it and the man without violence raised his hand to me and then I had won. He never hit me of course, he said he never could and never would, but I made him lift his hand to my taunts and teasing I'd say, wicked, 'Come on then! Come on! Do it!' and I would laugh, a wicked laugh that he said almost frightened him and then the mock fight became a prelude to something quite different from before, something dangerous, far away from any safety. And so perhaps from the day of the star-fruit, perhaps a little later, we were no longer safe from each other and we were half excited and aroused by this and half terrified. Lines had been crossed. He wanted sex, quite desperately, though not with me with a man. I wanted sex with Aedan. We neither of us wanted to spend our lives masturbating. The heat sent us mad. There was no respite from it. We drank much beer in the hotel lounge and sat on the street, on Orchard Road on a bench, game playing. Flirtation. Each time I made him lift his hand, each time we made the other forget who we really were, each time he had to stop himself either striking me or fucking me I would laugh. Triumphant. And afraid now, he would smile and acknowledge that I had scored another point, that things had changed, that the heat was making us crazy. At the end of a particularly hot, desperate evening when I thought that if I didn't get fucked soon I would die, he said, 'God . . . Ellie . . . I feel . . .'

'What do you feel?'

'You can't do that . . . You're teasing me, you're flaunting . . .'

'What am I flaunting?' and we had a locked moment of seeing clearly how things could go before the blinds were drawn again. We would not sleep together that very night but it was good to pretend we might. Sometimes he looked at me with such a look I felt like I'd been given a prize; such a look that made me feel that what was impossible only days ago was no longer so; that perhaps I wasn't dead at all.

Satisfied with pretence we went to a club that was loud and young, a club that in London we wouldn't be seen dead in. We found a huge Australian and toyed with the idea of the three of us in bed. We toyed and then we made a move on him but he was too tight, too young, too straight to want the both of us so we stuck to each other. We danced. I felt alive and we were able to touch and hold and sweat all over each other without the danger of reality rearing its not so pretty head. He said I looked beautiful, really beautiful. I thought I would remember the song we danced to for years, I felt it was a moment of profound significance but I was playing games even in my own head. The words, the tune, even the rhythm left me as soon as we stepped away from each other.

Touring is very rarely about reality. Things happen to actors on tour that they might not even dream of at home; leading women fall in love with leading men; husbands forget their wives and vice versa; safe people become dangerous. You might adore a person in Peking and despise them in London. People change when they aren't at home, when they're staying in hotels, when their responsibilities are in another country. Nellie and I were aware of all this but the heat had sent us mad and we loved each other. I couldn't injure him, whatever I did, and he couldn't injure me and with every day that passed things were changing, and what was unfamiliar became less so.

In Kuala Lumpur we went to a nightclub with a sign above the door saying, *The management does not accept liability for death on the premises.* Inside there were strange looking dancers in crinolines doing show-tunes. Young men cruised the eating areas. I left Nellie to it and wandered around by myself. In the toilet a woman in a silver sequinned hat slithered past me and stroked my breasts. Brain-dead with alcohol I watched her hand as it moved down my body and then she was gone. I clung to a sink and stared in the mirror at the stranger I'd become. The sequinned woman came back only this time she put her hand right between my legs and felt

167

my cunt before wandering off. In my stupor I contemplated following her into a quiet corner and having her fuck me but my reflexes were too slow or maybe I was just feeling too straight and by the time my body worked out my brain was telling it to move the woman was out of sight. I found Nellie and told him and he called me a cottage queen and said that surely that was his territory and what was I thinking of?

We parasailed in Penang and went on an inflatable banana, dragged across the ocean by a maniacal Penangian who took great pleasure in taking corners so fast we were tipped into the sea. It was liberating to be so devoid of fear. We sank into the sea together, unafraid of its depth, its hostility, afraid of nothing. We played volleyball in the pool with a whole crowd of people, all from different countries, different professions, all with apparently nothing in common. Communication, we found, was not difficult at all.

People assumed we were married and we felt like we were. We might have had sex, had we stayed in the heat of Penang, but we were there for only four days and then suddenly we were in China and our sun-tans were falling off in the cold chill of Beijing, and instead of gliding over ocean waves we cycled around Tiananmen Square and made a personal silent protest. There was no sign there, no plaque, no memorial stone; there was nothing to say how many students had died there only a few years before, or how they had died or for what. It was as though the massacre had never happened. We tried to talk about that and other politics with some Western business people who came to see the show but they refused, saying they didn't want their businesses whipped from under their feet and they'd seen it happen to others who'd opened their mouths. Their advice to us was to keep quiet. It was nauseating. In the minibus that ferried the actors to the Great Wall, the driver had a picture of Chairman Mao hanging on the mirror (all the drivers had them) and Nellie said, 'That doesn't look anything like him,' meaning the driver. We all laughed, even Helen and Caroline, but the tour guide said we really shouldn't crack jokes like that, that the people of China have been brought up with fear and that they're encouraged to report even their close family to the police. It was not uncommon to shop your mother. It all seemed very sad and filthy to me, though not as filthy as the streets themselves; I've never been to such a dirty city. It would take a million years to clean it up. Some of the public toilets were literally just a pile of shit on the floor and if you were very lucky there might be a door or a curtain dividing you from the street outside.

We went to the silk markets, because you can't really go to Beijing and avoid them, and Nellie bought me a pair of pure silk short dungarees. I nearly cried. He said, 'Don't get emotional and don't get affectionate. Just wear the fucking things and look beautiful in them.'

Some members of the Communist Party apparently tried to stop our show on the last night there. It appeared they thought we were a Brazilian band and were distressed to discover we were not. I expect half the audience felt the same way as no-one seemed to understand a word we said. We were unbothered, content to absorb the whole place which was like nowhere either of us had ever been. Before we left for Guam we cycled all round the city, past the Summer Palace and back to the hotel. I felt happy and well travelled, but relieved that we were heading for the Pacific later on that day, and that in only twelve days or so I'd be home in London. Three months is a long time to be away. Aedan came crashing into my head but I sent him away. I wondered if he would be at home waiting for me when I got back, but remembered I'd killed him off in Singapore and quickly tried to turn my thoughts to something else. It wasn't easy. If I closed my eyes his face would haunt me. If I kept them open, eventually he would walk into the room; I would look over and his name would rise up in my throat and I would try to speak, to beckon him over, I might say his name two or three times before I realized he wasn't there at all, before I realized it was only a ghost, and a man-made one at that.

Chapter Thirty-five

Of all the places we went to on the tour I would choose to go back to Guam. A tiny Micronesian island, slap bang in the middle of the Pacific, it felt about as near to Paradise as I could ever get. It's inhabited mainly by lunatics, which I guess is part of the attraction. There are people living there you might choose to know for the rest of your life. I imagine the number of crazy people living there is largely due to the fact that it takes a particular type of personality to uproot everything, leave mainland America or Australia to go to live on an island only four miles wide and thirty miles long; an island from where it takes several hours on a plane to get to any other country and an island where, I am told by people who know, they have several typhoons a year, typhoons that destroy buildings and frequently leave the island without power for anything up to six weeks at a time. Someone told me the other day that the hotel I stayed in has actually been blown away.

We arrived in the middle of the night, greeted at the airport by some sort of Guamanian ambassadors who hung leis around our necks and carried our luggage into limos. We were whisked off to the hotel after a slight hiccup at the visa desk and shown our rooms, which were pretty much the same as the other jillion hotel rooms we'd seen so far.

Nellie phoned and said, 'There's a fucking lizard in here. This place is a fucking dump.' It was our joke. We'd said the same about all the other places we'd visited; most five star hotels are virtually identical. It had to be said also that until we saw the island the next day we thought perhaps it really was a dump. The only thing we knew about the place was that it was a military base and that didn't exactly inspire enthusiasm, though Nellie pointed out that the uniforms might be rather nice.

In the morning all our doubts were quashed. We walked around and gazed at the coral reef and the clear water everywhere and the nearly-white sands. We checked out the shops, which were just like any other shops only massively over-priced, apart from alcohol which was duty free. We got about a gallon of gin each and several gallons of tonic water and sat on the beach. We did a TV interview and filled our faces with some rather glorious food and spent the night wandering around, wondering if there was any sort of night-club there. The barman at the hotel had suggested a place called The Jungle but we couldn't find it so we sat by the pool and got drunk.

As usual after the first show we were invited to a VIP drinks party. Those things are invariably more boring than watching paint dry; people hover around asking questions like, 'How *do* you learn all those lines?' and 'Don't you get *nervous* in front of all those people?' Like, we're *actors* for fuck's sake; that's what we *do*. We went all round the fucking world and the VIPs asked the same questions from Leeds to Penang. Another commonly used conversation killer is, 'Oh, of course *I* could've been an actor. Everybody's always said . . . y'know, I do a lot of work for the local operatic society . . .' Yeah, yeah. By the time we reached Guam we'd had nine weeks of this crap and Nellie and I had given up being polite and pretending to be interested and had found a table in a corner and sat down away from the group with two bottles of champagne and a plate of crudités.

'Oh, my God,' Nellie said, looking over my shoulder.

'What?'

'The guy behind you. Oh, God.'

I looked round and the most beautiful man we'd seen in twelve weeks stood looking completely out of place in the midst of a small group of VIPs. He had a suit on which looked like he'd never worn it before in his life and probably never would again, and a boot-lace tie. An absolute stunner. He looked quite uncomfortable but amused.

'He's gay,' said Nellie.

'He's mine.'

And then a small, beautiful woman pulled on his arm and pointed to us and Nellie laughed and said, 'He's hers. Tough.' They came over and we all introduced ourselves and smiled a lot. She gushed out praise of the show and our performances and the beautiful man smirked at her side. He was to die for. It was all we could do not to sit with our mouths hanging open.

They turned out to be healthily irreverent and very amusing. She was a teacher on the island. She'd been born there and lived there all her life. He was a pharmacist and had come over from Utah about eight years before. They were a couple; apparently very happy together. Bill and Landé. I tried not to think about him sexually because she was so lovely but it was quite impossible.

I held on to the fact that a simple thought can't do any damage and we arranged to go to The Jungle with them the following night and Nellie and I made our way back to our rooms. In the foyer we found them loitering by the lift and invited them to my room to drink the gin we'd bought. We talked all night. Landé stayed sober because she was driving while Nellie and Bill and I drank a bottle and a half of gin. They were quite taken with us, though I think Bill would've liked anyone or anything because by five o'clock we'd drunk him under the table.

When the alcohol was all finished they left quite reluctantly and Nellie and I were left to die peacefully pissed on my bed.

'Alone on a tropical island,' he said.

'Dreaming of married men.'

'They aren't married.'

'They're as good as.'

'Better keep your hands off then.'

'You too.'

'He wouldn't want us anyway. We're too fat.'

'Speak for yourself.'

'Oh yeah? What's this then?' He pinched my stomach and I pinched his. I was so drunk I fell onto the floor and dragged him with me. He landed half on top of me.

'Do you want me to move?'

'I want you to love me.'

'I do.'

'I want you to fuck me.'

'Now?'

'This minute.'

'Are you sure?'

'Yes.'

'Are you really sure?'

'I am.'

'You're my best friend.'

I kissed him and we had a little snog and burst into peals of laughter.

'OK.'

'What?' I started to laugh again and he took his shirt off. 'Are you serious?'

'Only if you are.'

'And it won't spoil anything?'

He undid my shorts and snorted with laughter. We actually laughed all the way through it. I even laughed as I came and laughed even more when he came because it all happened very quickly and afterwards we lay in hysterics on the floor and he wailed, 'Oh my God! My God! She raped me!' and he crawled onto my bed and held out his hand to me and said, 'My beautiful pudding, my beautiful fat pudding.' I laughed till my eyes streamed and crawled onto the bed next to him. We fell asleep in a paralytic stupor, on the top of the bed with the empty gin bottle at our feet.

'No regrets,' he said, before he closed his eyes and I said, 'None. Never.'

We spent the next day playing kids' water sports with a group of teenagers in another hotel. Bill and Landé turned up after the show that night and took us to The Jungle. Bill was looking infinitely more comfortable than he had the night before, wearing shorts and flip-flops and a T-shirt. We were glad we hadn't bothered to dress up; it was one of the roughest, dirtiest places I've ever been to. Within five minutes there was a fight at the door between two military guys and two islanders. Bill said this went on all the time, it was a way of life. People frequently got shot or stabbed. I went to the toilet and found there wasn't even a door on the cubicle. A woman kindly stood in front of it while I went to the loo. It was strangely exciting. I think because it was so different from anywhere I'd been and because it felt dangerous to be there and because despite the violent outbursts nobody seemed to care, nobody seemed at all hostile; everyone just drank beer and danced to loud, out of date pop music. We all drank tequila which tasted like poison and we danced and shouted to each other over the noise. Nellie said he hated the place, that it really wasn't his scene, but I loved it. Perhaps I was truly mad. We went on to a pub called The Tower of London, which amused us, and Bill and I knocked a load of pool balls around; it could hardly be considered a game as I'd never played before and Bill was too entertained to care. We drank Budweiser and Bill took Landé home. They lived separately. Nellie said maybe they weren't such a happy couple after all but I wasn't convinced. Bill took us to his apartment and we drank some more and then Nellie said he wanted to get back, it was four o'clock by this stage, so the three of us drove back to the hotel. Nellie got out and said, 'Go for a drive or something.'

He was trying to push us together. After he'd gone I asked if I could drive the car round the island. Bill's brand new car; he'd only got it the day before. He let me. I couldn't believe it. I didn't drive at that time, I hadn't even taken a test, I had never learned how. I drove past jungle and along the road by the sea. I sped down the road that led to the beach and screeched to a halt before we hit the sand. I felt like a fourteen year old. I felt healed. Bill said something about his mum, said that she'd died the year before and I said, 'Then you'll *understand*,' because no-one knows what it's like to lose your mother until it happens to them, no-one understands that sort of pain until it's their own. 'Maybe they're hanging out together,' he said, when I explained. 'Your mom and mine. Maybe they're looking down at us right now.' I liked the idea of our dead mothers being friends somewhere. We went onto the beach and ran around a bit. Later he took me back to the hotel and asked questions about home, I told him about Aedan. He called him a crazy bastard for leaving me and we hugged each other and said goodbye quite reluctantly. Instead of kissing him I thought of Landé and how much I liked her. Bill asked after Nellie.

'He's saved my life. He's my friend.'

'Are you two sleeping together?'

'No. We're best friends.'

'I hope I know you for the rest of my life.' I hoped he would too. We said goodbye again and hugged again and I went into the hotel.

We went out together again the following night though we kept out of The Jungle because it was even more overcrowded than it had been the night before. We went for a quick beer in The Tower of London and then we all went skinny-dipping. I kept thinking *The Pacific! I'm skinny dipping in the Pacific ocean and life can be good, it really can*. I thought of all the stories I would have for my children. I would be able to say, 'I lived, I really lived. I was wild and happy and outrageous. I survived.' Nellie got a lift home with Landé who had work in the morning and Bill and I went to a bar and drank a drink called Dr Pepper, only the alcoholic version which we set alight. I spilled some and set fire to my legs and burned off half my body hair. I met a friend of Bill's called Raoul and the three of us drank our way around the island. I stayed at Raoul's house instead of the hotel and once again felt like life was smacking me round the face with its promise. I started to burn with hope again. In the middle of the night we heard gunshots outside and Raoul took a shotgun from the side of his bed and went outside and fired it into the darkness and I thought how totally different from England this all was and how far away from it all I felt. I felt far away from Aedan and glad of the distance. This was more exciting and inspiring than anything he knew, or would know. I felt as irresponsible as I had when I was adolescent, when I thought I could do everything and more and still live to see my twentieth birthday.

In the morning after about three hours sleep the guys took me round the island. I swam through a cave that had only inches between its ceiling and the top of the water, a tunnel that was so narrow there was only enough room to hold my arms outstretched in front of me rather than actually swim and the only way I could propel myself forward was by kicking my legs. I think I would've tried anything; if they'd said we were all going swimming on the coral reef I probably would've agreed to it. I felt infallible. We went back to Bill's in the afternoon and he cancelled a flight to another island because I was there and we didn't have much time left. He told me Landé had been jealous of this and I felt flattered, but sort of glad we were only friends. They took me to a bar for lunch, though I was too elated to eat, and Bill bought me a disposable camera so we wouldn't have to go all the way back to the hotel to get mine. They talked about the Hash Run, which sounded like some sort of wild running expedition that culminated in a huge drunken party. Bill found me running shoes and I thought I couldn't do it, I had a show to do that evening at nine and I hadn't run anywhere for years and years. I was daunted, but they were enthusiastic and took it for granted that I would do this Hash thing as it was a really big deal to them and apparently thousands of Hash House Harriers worldwide. Before I could do anything about it I was standing with about thirty or forty islanders, learning the rules of the hash. It's a sort of hare and hounds principle; two runners (the hares) set off running ten minutes in advance of everyone else and leave a trail of stones and ribbons and strange codes and it's the job of the rest of the pack (the hounds) to seek them out and catch them before they reach their destination, which is only known to the two hares setting the trail. At the end there is a bonfire and an initiation ceremony and a lot of beer is consumed. I felt tired and hot but thought *What the hell? I'm alive, I've got legs, I can run, I can do anything.*

We ran through jungle and farm land and through streams and along roads. It was eighty degrees or thereabouts and I hadn't eaten or slept for more than a day but I ran with the hounds, and two or three hours later, dripping with sweat but feeling like I'd achieved some dream I hadn't even known I'd had, I finished the run. The bonfire was already alight and cars and trucks had arrived loaded with chilled beer. The initiation ceremony involved all the runners standing around the bonfire and the new people – there were only three of us who'd never done it before – had to introduce themselves to the group, crack a joke or sing a song and drink a bed-pan full of Bud. I did my bit and was introduced as the Thespian and everyone cheered and said how great it was that I ran the hash and it was such a big thing and half of them had seen the show and if they hadn't they'd seen the TV interview and all of them thought it was a thrill having an actress amongst them, celebrating her mother hash. I got the round of applause to beat all others and as it got dark round the fire I ran to Bill and hugged him so tightly and I said, 'I love you, I really do, we must *never* lose touch. Never.'

I did the show that night with jungle grass still between my toes. It seemed appropriate that it was the very last show of the tour, that I hadn't had any sleep for days and days, that I had met these wonderful crazy people who had shown me their fantastic island and breathed hope into me and life and joy. I was joyous. I was ready to face the fact that when I went home Aedan would not be there. I was ready for anything.

Chapter Thirty-six

A small tin of Heinz baked beans
An orange fruit bowl
Two passport photographs
A vase
A blue shirt
A burgundy belt
A cream linen jacket
A blue T-shirt
Jif pump dispenser cleaning fluid
A bag of French coffee
Beloved by Toni Morrison
Some tapes
A Joanna Trollope novel
A heap of letters and cards

All the things he ever gave me. I put everything into the middle of the living-room floor. I had intended throwing the lot into the bin but found when it came down to it I just couldn't do it. Another day perhaps. Perhaps not. I put everything bar the tapes, the books, the fruit bowl and the shirt into a box and locked the box away in a cupboard. Later on I rescued the Jif pump dispenser and put it back in the kitchen even though it was now quite bereft of cleaning fluid. Later still I rescued the photographs and put them at the bottom of a drawer. It wouldn't hurt me if I didn't do it all at once. I sat down on my new sofa bed in my new and beautiful living room that was the same but different and thought only of the future. There was some wallpaper paste on the chest of drawers by the TV from long nights of papier mâchéing. But I was a different person then and it was a million hours from now.

I worked out. I tried to do it every day. Some days I was too busy as I'd made a lot of plans and was sticking to them but I did it often enough to get fit. My legs changed shape. I got a radio play and then another and another so the wolf was kept from the door and I was kept even busier which was just as I wanted it. I slept the whole night through; every night I slept. I ate regular meals. _____

I threw his toothbrush away.

I had a nightmare.

I dreamt I had a dream, and in the dream a man was lying old and dejected in a bed. He said to me, 'Why didn't you wait? Why didn't you come back to me? Now I am dying and it's too late, it's too late,' and I said, 'I thought you were already dead,' and he said, 'But we promised we'd do it together, and now I am old and without you and alone and you are a million miles away from me, and you are happy when I am sad and this wasn't what we promised. Don't you remember? Had you forgotten?' And then I dreamt I woke up and there was dead fruit in my bed and dead flowers, and a woman came in and said, 'There's a dead man in your kitchen.'

Awake I went out to the bins and climbed into one of them looking for the toothbrush. I realized that when I'd thrown it away I hadn't meant to rid myself, I had meant only to replace it with a new one. I was thinking that it was old and unused, that when he came home we would have to get him a new one. The bins had been emptied. I asked the caretaker where all the rubbish went but he said he really couldn't be sure. He looked at me as though I was a lunatic as I climbed out of the skip.

And I had thought I was cured.

I put my behaviour down to nothing more than the growing claustrophobia I'd felt since I returned from Guam. I put it down to the drop in temperature. I put it down to too many workouts and not enough sugar in my diet. I wanted to forget. I wanted to go back to paradise. I didn't want to ever feel so alone again, so desperate. I wanted to be me again, I wanted to be normal. Bill telephoned from Guam. We talked for three hours. I wished he lived closer so we could go and drink a crate of Budweiser together. We talked of getting together at Christmas time, but we weren't really serious. It was a long way off and anyway it would cost thousands of dollars we neither of us possessed. I went back to my workouts. I did the second of three radio plays. I went post-synching with Matthew who said he'd missed me and asked a lot of questions about the tour. We went to a studio in Soho and added dialogue to our own faces. They mocked me from the screen. Matthew asked me out to dinner and I accepted. Why not? If the dead man wouldn't leave my head I could always take him with me. During dinner I decided to have a party; a very small gathering of lovely people. I would celebrate ridding my system of the Irishman. Or at least beginning to. I could only try. Maybe I would flush him out with new people.

Matthew said, 'What's it for then, this party?' and I said, 'To celebrate the living and to say goodbye to the dead.' I expect he assumed I was talking of my dead fiancé. In actual fact I was talking about myself, dead for far too long now, desperate to breathe again.

Smoking a joint in the bathroom Nellie asked me what I was playing at.

'I don't know what you mean.'

'Bullshit. You and Mattie. What's going on?'

'Nothing.'

'What's he doing here then?'

'He's a friend.'

'He's in love with you.'

'Maybe.'

'What does he think about Aedan?'

'Not a lot. He thinks he's dead.'

'Why?'

'Because that's what I told him. Leukaemia.'

'It's a bit extreme isn't it? Got any biscuits in here?'

'Next to the toilet roll. It was ages ago, I told him ages ago. What should I do? Tell him I lied?'

'Will you have a relationship with this guy?'

'I've not even thought about it. I'm not up for a relationship. I'm ruined. Aedan ruined me.'

'And have you told Mattie this?'

'Many times. He doesn't listen.'

'Have you fucked him?'

'No. But I think I might.'

'And then what?'

'And then nothing. I just want some sex.'

'Come on. He likes you. You can't treat people like that.'

'I wouldn't. I'm fond of him. He's been good to me.'

Matthew walked in.

'Speak of the devil,' I said.

'Sorry . . . I thought . . .'

'No!' Nellie said. 'Come on in. I was just going.'

'Do you want some of this?' I said, handing him what was left of the joint. He took it and inhaled.

'I think I'll be going soon,' he said. This threw me slightly; it wasn't what I'd expected. 'I mean, I'd like to stay but . . . I think I should leave.'

'Why?'

'I'd like to sleep with you.'

'No harm in that.' I burst into laughter.

'You're stoned.'

'You're right.'

'I like your friends.'

'Stay then. No-one's leaving yet.'

In the hall a couple of people sat slamming tequila on the carpet. In the living room Mark and Clare were watching an episode of *Prisoner Cell Block H* and laughing at every line. Lottie was draped over Tom who was hanging off the edge of the sofa. Alice, who was now lying flat out at Mark and Clare's feet, said, very seriously, 'Did you like being an only child, Ellie, or have you ever hankered after a sibling?'

'I always wanted a brother so I could fuck him.'

'God, you're gross sometimes.'

'Well, it's the truth! I always did. Didn't you?'

'God, I wouldn't even contemplate going to bed with my brother. Not even for money. He's hideous.'

'Mine isn't,' said Matthew, who was looking decidedly stoned at this point.

'Have you ever fucked him?'

'Alice!' Lottie looked at us all, appalled. 'I can't believe we're even discussing this.'

'I slept with my sister.' Everyone turned to look at Matthew.

'Was she good?' I asked.

'She was quiet.' We both howled. I couldn't decide if he was joking or not. Mark and Clare continued to watch the TV; Lottie, newly sensible from pregnancy and so the only person in the room who wasn't stoned or drunk, got up to make coffee for everyone. Alice started to roll another spliff. Nellie quite suddenly kissed me and took his leave, crashing into the door frame as he went. I could hear him laughing long after he'd gone. I finished the last Jaffa Cake and Matthew's hand brushed against mine. I grabbed it and looked at his palm.

'It says you'll meet a wild woman with curly red hair and a history. Says she'll do you no good.'

'She'll do me no harm.'

'She might.'

'What else does it say?'

'It says I'm too pissed now to care.'

'Can I see you again?'

'Again when?'

'When you're not stoned.'

'Take me as you find me or don't take me at all.'

'I'll wait.'

'Till when?'

'The morning.'

'Did you really fuck your sister?'

'Don't tell the tabloids.'

'What did she look like?'

'You.'

'You're more fucked up than I am.'

'Maybe.'

Lottie fell into the room with a cafetiere full of coffee and another twin packet of Jaffa Cakes. 'I found chocolate!' Definitely a cause for celebration. Everybody sprang back to life. When the Jaffa Cakes were all gone people started to make moves home. Alice wheeled off into the night on a bike she'd found just outside the door and the others tried to work out how many they could squeeze into a car.

'You can stay if you like,' I said to Matthew.

'Are you sure?'

'Not really, but you can't get in the same cab as that lot. Five's too many as it is and Lottie's as big as a horse.' When everyone else had gone I poured two enormous glasses of whiskey. 'There's another bottle in the kitchen.'

'I think I've had enough.' He took both the glasses from me and kissed me. Too gently. I pulled away and took a gulp of Bushmill's.

'Come on. Bed,' he said.

'What?'

'Sleep. We're going to sleep.'

I wanted to sleep. I followed him and collapsed on top of the duvet. 'Either you get undressed or I do it for you,' he said. 'The choice is yours.' I let him do it. I enjoyed it. I enjoyed every sensation. I looked around the room for Aedan but in the drunken haze I couldn't see him. I felt no guilt. I kissed him. Matthew. Not Aedan. They weren't even similar. I lay on the bed in my knickers and T-shirt.

'Now you,' I said, undoing his jeans.

'You're too drunk.'

'No, I'm not, I'm not. Let me.' I put the whole length of him into my mouth but he pulled away and said, 'No, you're too drunk,' but he pulled off my knickers anyway and I took off the T-shirt and he put two fingers inside me and I said, 'More, get more in,' and he did until he nearly had his whole fist in me and I said, 'Well you may as well fuck me now,' so we looked around the bed for a condom and he found one in the pocket of his jeans and put it on him and we fucked and fucked and at one point I said, 'Am I as good as your sister?' and he laughed and we nearly lost our rhythm and I thought, I'm happy, I'm all right, I'm not dead any more and I really like this man and maybe I'll get over that Irish bastard after all and I am fond of this man I really am.

I fell asleep by his side. Matthew. Not Aedan. Not even similar. I fell asleep happy that maybe I wasn't dead at all. Only sleeping.

Someone said, 'A man has just collapsed!' and I ignored all the fuss because that's what people in London do; we get used to everything. When someone says there's a person under the train, the tourist says, 'Oh God, how *awful*, what were they thinking of? How terribly sad, etc., etc.' and the Londoner says, 'Fucking hell, there'll be delays for ever now.' And so when they said a man had collapsed I didn't even look round, until the collapsed man said, 'It's me, Ellie, it's me. Have you forgotten me so soon? Didn't we make promises? Ellie, it's me!' And so at last I turned around and there he was, in the dirt, his hands wet in a pool of muddy water in front of him. His hair was greyer than I remembered. His face had more wrinkles. He was smaller, but more Irish and more beautiful. I pushed my way past the people who were only there to see blood. 'Aedan?' He looked so different I couldn't even be sure it was him; he wore different clothes. He wore clothes I'd never seen before. He was the man they were all talking about, the man who'd collapsed.

'You didn't wait,' he said. 'Why did you forget me?' I knelt down in front of him as he sank lower and lower and someone behind me said, 'He's gone, he's dead,' and I said, 'But I will not let him die. We made promises,' and they said, 'Love, you're too late for that.'

I could not picture his face. In my memory I looked for his features but they were my own features or Matthew's or my father's. Where are you? Are you gone for ever now? Because I left you for an hour or more are you gone for ever? Even the memory is slain. Where were you while I was happy? Sick fear in me that is guilt that is the loss but not the loss of you. Why did you not die? I would that you were not alive without me. Would I at least have some peace then? I would that the silence of a dead heart did not mock me. I fell asleep without you. I slept with a man. You were not forgot but I was without you. Out of my head. I fell asleep without you but woke and you'd been there all night, racing around a dream on your knees. On your knees, on my back, face in the dirt, whatever, you were there and you wore clothes I'd never seen and some of your hair had gone and new lines on your face had grown. I am changed but still the same. The baggage I would deny is wrapped around my neck. Ruined. Be not a stranger to me. Be not a memory. We were put asunder and that was for ever. Now I believe it. In my fondness I believe you are gone from me. You went. Ripped away from me by your own hand. I did nothing. Once I wept, but now I do nothing, except last night I fell asleep with a man and woke to find that even the memory is slain.

Five a.m. The ceiling was slowly moving down to meet the floor. We would be crushed. Pressed to death. What sin warranted such an end? Women used to die like this by order. For adultery. Debt. I am guilty of both. My heart was not sounding its normal beat. It was louder than usual, a bang rather than a thump. The more I listened and worried, the more it banged until I could see it move in my wrists. The room got smaller and smaller until I could step out of bed right into the kitchen. Matthew slept on. I wondered that my heart did not wake him. How could he sleep through such a noise? Was he not disturbed by the sinking roof? Or the walls? I prayed that he would leave as soon as he woke; that he would get away from me and never come back.

The other rooms, I found, were also shrinking. I opened the window in the kitchen and leaned out. But it was not peaceful as I had hoped. I wanted to be calmed by the open sky but the cars were too loud, too fast, and the air too cold. I felt the wind wrap itself around my neck. A choker. A noose. I couldn't breathe. Even over the cars I could still hear my heart, going so fast now it seemed like one long thunderous boom. I would have to wake him. I needed help.

'Matthew!' Nothing. Alone still, in the kitchen. I went back into the bedroom, the size of a small cupboard by now, and shook him. 'Mattie! I think there's something wrong with me.' He moaned gently; morning noises, calm and sleepy and content. 'Matthew, wake up. Wake up, you must wake up. Something's happening to the flat.'

'What?'

'I'm having a heart attack.' I grabbed his hand and put it on my neck. 'Feel!'

'What is it? What's wrong?'

'Help me!' He put his arms around me. 'No! I don't need affection! I need a fucking ambulance!'

'Sshhh. You're all right. You've been dreaming.'

'Do something! Can't you hear it?'

'What?'

'My heart! My fucking heart!'

'Ellie . . .'

'Oh, for fuck's sake . . .' I grabbed a coat and stormed out of the flat. He followed me into the street and dragged me out of the road away from the traffic.

'Fuck off, would you?'

'Ellie—'

'Don't call me that, just go.'

'I'm getting a doctor.'

'Why? Are you ill?'

'Ellie, come inside. I'll call somebody. A friend or something. I'll get an ambulance if you want.'

'Don't be ridiculous.'

'I want to help.'

'Well you can't.'

He let go of me and I was instantly ashamed.

'I'm sorry. God, Mattie, I'm so sorry. I don't know . . . I didn't feel well in there. I'm not usually like this.'

'I think you probably are.'

'Oh, what the fuck do you know? What the fuck do you know about fucking anything?'

'I'll go then, if that's what you want.'

'It is! Fuck off. Just fuck off and leave me. I'm ruined. I'm fucking ruined.'

'OK then. Whatever you want.'

He walked off. I stood in the street and looked at my bare feet on the pavement. It seemed a couple of years had passed when eventually I went back into the flat which was, thankfully, no longer shrinking, but quite still and sad and without life. A bit like me, I thought, and went back to bed.

Chapter Thirty-seven

I started the last of the radio plays. On the second day of recording I had an offer of a small part in a TV series. I told my agent I didn't want to do it but she said it wouldn't hurt and it would only take two days and I'd probably get about a grand for doing not a lot of work. I thought wistfully of *Thérèse*. I thought of Guam. I thought of Aedan and pushed him to the back of my head again but he always came back. If I didn't think of him during the day he would only haunt me at night. The phone rang a few times and nobody spoke. I started to get cross. I didn't need a heavy breather as well as everything else. The phone rang again and again and still no-one spoke. I left the machine on for a whole night. On the fourth recording day I was up and awake at dawn. I made coffee and looked over the script and remembered. I could not forget. I didn't really try. I tried to conjure up his smell, his touch, the way his hands felt on my back. I wanted to cry but my body was too dry. And then as though he'd heard what was in my head he was suddenly there on the other end of the phone and I realized I'd known all along it had been him, silent. I stopped breathing. I felt like someone had shot me in the back. He said, 'Aedan O'Brien,' and I said, 'I know. I know.' I would've known even if he'd stayed silent; I would've recognized his breath.

'I'm in London.'

189

But you're a dead man. A dead man. I do not talk to the dead any more because I'm no longer dead myself.

'Can we meet?'

'I don't know,' I said. *He's dead. He's dead.* Hang up. Don't talk to him. 'Where?' I had no willpower. What was the use in pretending?

'A little bird tells me you're doing a radio for the BBC.'

'I can't meet you there.' People I knew would see us together. They would watch me as I turned to dust at his feet. I would be dust again, and someone might blow me away. How could he sound so casual?

'At the Dome then?'

'Nostalgic.' How many times had we been there before? Five? Ten? I wouldn't be able to sit with him there without fainting or disintegrating or shrinking to nothing.

'OK,' I said. 'What time and when?'

'Tomorrow? Five-thirty?'

'Fine.'

'We've a lot to talk about.'

'Too much.'

I would tell no-one. They would think I was mad. They would worry.

The phone rang again.

'What are you doing right now? Could we meet today instead?' Oh, my God, too soon. He's a dead man. He's dead. What did he want from me? Did he want to finally finish me off?

'What's wrong with tomorrow?'

'It isn't soon enough.'

'Five-thirty then. Today.'

I put the silk dungarees on, the ones from Nellie, and an apricot silk shirt, and my orange clogs. I went into work and recorded some of my bits and chatted to everyone and had lunch with them all and we did a few scenes in the afternoon and then I raced across Regent Street to meet him. I was in the Dome by five-twenty. A busy time at Oxford

Circus. I expected to have to wait for a seat, but our usual table was free, as though in the time gone by no-one had dared sit there. I ordered two beers. I drank the first quickly, without even breathing, and as I began gulping down the second the months started to drip away. He wasn't dead at all. In minutes he'd be right there in front of me.

At five twenty-nine he came through the door looking directly at the table, at me. He looked quite scared. I stood up and a big child-like grin spread from deep inside me to my face. We clung to each other. I don't know who trembled the most.

'It's good to see you,' he said. Soft, Belfasty tones, hard to forget.

We looked. It seemed it was all we were capable of. Eventually we sat down. A waiter came over with vague recognition in his eyes and asked us what we would like. He had coffee and I had beer. I couldn't stop smiling. I wanted to say, 'Why did you let me let you die?' But he was so obviously alive it seemed inappropriate and so I just smiled and smiled. He held my hand over the table. We discussed the play I was doing. We talked about the director, who had met Aedan on a couple of occasions years before. We talked about the weather here, the weather abroad. I was so hideously excited, so utterly on fire with the excitement of having a dead man alive and in front of me, only inches away from me and no longer lost to me, I hardly had anything to say. He looked exhilarated himself, as though it was a shock to him as well, and his smile was as broad and unstoppable as mine. We ordered more drinks and I wondered where we would go from there. Was it just to be the one drink? Were we just friends now? What next? I felt it was entirely his choice; I would've done whatever he wanted. Would he choose to take off again and breathe someone else's air? I should be strong and say, 'It's not enough, I need all of you.' I said nothing.

He asked if we would go and eat something but we did not

191

move. I said, 'I have to touch you. I can't sit here and watch you and not touch you,' and he took hold of my hand and said, 'I'm so sorry,' and kissed my hair and my face and my arms and the back of my neck. We talked for some time and then left. I almost expected it to be dark outside until I remembered it wasn't winter anymore. We walked to Leicester Square and ate a baguette in a wine bar. Later, much later, when I had enough liquor in me to ask, I said, 'Where's Frances? Are you here for ever? Are you here for me?'

He answered with apology in his eyes. I ordered coffee and tried to sober up and remember how I had coped before. Who had I killed? Who was the dead man?

'She's still with you, isn't she?'

'I want to explain . . . It isn't how it seems . . . I never wanted you to wait in case it took months . . . Frances is . . . well, she's ill . . . she's—'

'She's still with you, isn't she?'

'In a way she is. But not for ever. Not for much longer now.'

'How long is that? A year? Six years? I can't wait for you. I can't do it any more. My life was shite when I waited for you, I was ruined. I *am* ruined. You've ruined me.'

'I'm here. I said I'd come back and I have.'

'You also said you'd disappoint me.'

I picked up my bag and tried to walk away but he took hold of my arm so tightly I couldn't get away. He led me out into the street.

Still clinging to my arm he said, 'I'm dead without you.'

'I know that. I killed you. I let you die.'

'No. I'm here in London. I'm here now. I'm not dead now.'

We fell back onto the door of a twenty-four-hour emergency doctor's surgery down a narrow street near Leicester Square. He started to kiss me. I could only kiss him back. Voices screamed inside me saying, 'Don't do this,' but I ignored them all. I heard my dungarees ripping, I heard his clothes ripping under my own fingers, I felt his skin under my fingernails and then his fingers inside me and then his cock and instead of pushing him away and saving myself I pulled him closer and tighter with my thighs and gripped half the breath from him. We might have killed each other, but we didn't. We might have said goodbye, had I had the strength, but we didn't.

I said, 'You'll kill me. Just knowing you will kill me, y'know?'

'It'll kill us both.' A shop-owner who'd obviously watched the whole scene shouted threats in our direction; boiling water and the police if we didn't move along and be disgusting somewhere else. We ignored her and he rocked me in his arms. Still holding me he asked when we'd meet again. I said probably at breakfast. He came home with me. The flat was a surprise to him. He liked it. He liked everything I'd done. I'd done it on my own. I could not stop the thought. Everything I'd done I had done on my own. He said he was sad he'd missed it all being put together. He told me again the next morning, guilt in his face.

'You did it all on your own. I should've been here.'

'Tell me about it,' I said as I left to go to work.

'When will we meet? Tonight?'

I suggested Friday, by which time I would've had time to think about things. I asked him to call. He said he would, but that he'd be at Oakley Street if there was anything I needed, anything at all. If I needed anything that night, he would be at his friend Mark's in Belgravia. I didn't suggest my flat again and neither did he. After all, I'd thrown away his toothbrush.

He telephoned on Friday morning to say he was going back to Belfast for a few days or more, he wasn't sure. He didn't have much choice. He mentioned something about Frances but I was too numb to hear. The ache in my thighs from a

193

couple of nights before mocked me. My face, blistered again from his kisses, mocked me. My reflection in the mirror mocked me. His apology echoed around my head; it lived with me for days and days. He called me again and left messages. I ignored him. He wrote me letters which I put unopened into the box in the cupboard. Matthew called, asking how I was. I said I was sorry, really sorry about the other week. He said it didn't matter and I said it did. He offered me dinner. I turned him down. He offered me lunch, but I said, 'No. I'm ruined, I really am. Remember last time?'

Chapter Thirty-eight

Matthew came back. Poor, poor Matthew. I was ashamed. I felt unworthy. He turned up one night, quite drunk and bleary-eyed, and I had to let him in. What could I have done? Put him in a taxi? I made him a mug of hot Vimto which he scalded his mouth on. I laughed and sat next to him. Together with him I laughed at my aloneness. He laughed as well, thinking I was sharing some joke with him. But I was quite alone. I tried to be serious, to tell him to leave. I even picked up the phone to call him a cab but he knocked it out of my hand. I would hurt him if he loved me and I didn't want that. He would be as ruined as me.

'I'm in love with you,' he said, sadly. 'That's why I had to come back. I'm sorry.'

'No, Mattie. You're not in love at all. You're pissed.'

'I think of you.'

'I think of me too.'

'I dream of you.'

'I dream of the dead.'

'I could make you happy, Ellen.'

'Never.'

'I'll do anything you want.'

'Be someone else then.'

Fortunately for both of us, but mainly for him, he fell asleep. I hoped he wouldn't remember when he woke up how unkind I'd been.

In the morning I shunted him out of the flat without even giving him coffee, but then felt guilty and took him to the café by the tube. We had a rather pleasant breakfast, though he ate his food very fast and very loudly, smacking his lips and squelching a lot and I'm a bit anal about that sort of thing and found it intolerable. I felt less irritable once he'd finished and we ordered more coffee and talked about work. He'd just started filming a couple of episodes of some series up in Yorkshire; a bloody long thing about miners with no women in it. He invited me to his rented cottage in Ottley.

'Matthew, you've got to be mad to even think of that.'

'Look, I know you don't want to be with me. I know it's too soon, I mean, when did Aedan die? But we can be friends, can't we? It's not too soon for that?'

'I've been so horrible to you.'

'You have. But at least you've been honest, I mean, no-one can say you've led me on.'

'I'm really sorry.'

'No, I understand, I really do.'

'Really?'

'Well, maybe not completely, but a bit. I can imagine, that's all. I can only imagine. Come up to Leeds. Have a holiday. The cottage is wonderful. Breathe some air, there's no air in this fucking city.'

'It doesn't seem right, y'know?'

'A holiday. No strings.'

'There are always strings.'

'Bring some scissors with you then.'

I did a terrible thing.

I went to Leeds. Unforgivable. I don't know what drove me to go there. Perhaps it was lust. Perhaps I was kidding myself I was ready for lust. The prospect of no sex ever again, certainly if I stayed in London. Unforgivable. I went there to fuck him. Poor Mattie. On the train I thought, This libido will surely hang me. I felt vicious and cruel. I had no heart left.

Mattie's ridiculous pleasure at my arrival at the cottage nearly made me turn right back round again. The guilt I felt was enormous. I reasoned with myself that he would probably derive as much satisfaction from some vigorous sex in the countryside as I would. Hadn't he begged me to go up there to see him? Hadn't he said he understood?

In his bed however, I found I couldn't do anything. I lay beside him like a corpse thinking vaguely that if I couldn't bring myself to sleep with Matthew, of whom I was really very fond, and actually found very attractive, then I'd more than likely never be able to sleep with anyone ever again. When he rolled over and kissed me clumsily on my neck, I saw Aedan just above my face. I let out a moan of grief which I imagine Mattie took to be a moan of ecstasy or thereabouts. He put his hand between my legs and the next moment he said, 'You have such a beautiful cunt, Elle,' and that was it for me, it was all over. No more. I couldn't cope with a description along with everything else. I rolled off the bed and found my way to the bathroom where I collapsed heaving over the toilet. Some time later I felt a hand on my head and I threw up. The hand pressed firmer until the fingers actually got tangled up in my hair so that when I tried to move the hand away I pulled my own head back with it and retched even more. I think he thought I was being affectionate or grateful or something because he held on even tighter after that and a minor fight ensued, a bizarre fight, since only one of us knew it was happening. Eventually I stopped retching and knelt down on the floor, my hair released at last. I begged solitude, which he gave me.

My agent called and said Get Back Home and I felt saved. Some young shit-hot director wanted to see me for a low-budget film about a lunatic. She said the part might have been written for me and I should get home as soon as I possibly could. Mattie offered to drive me. I refused but he said he would've gone home anyway had I not turned up out of the blue as he had a few days off. He came back home with me. I'd invited him and he'd accepted. It wasn't such a bad thing in the end, he was quite easy to be with when we weren't trying to have sex. I kept thinking that at some point I'd be able to do it again without Aedan and rather Matthew than anyone else.

The script was fantastic. I was up for the part of a deranged sculptor, Elizabeth. There was lots of brooding and grieving to be done which I'd grown rather adept at. Elizabeth makes lots of phonecalls to a dead man's answering machine, sitting listening to the same message several times a night. The death of her lover dries up all her creativity and she gives up clay and becomes a cartoon artist for a children's comic. She cannot get over this dead man, Daniel, until her best friend introduces her to a choreographer who falls in love with her. We discover that Elizabeth is actually totally mad and that Daniel died several years ago. He too was a sculptor and they had as near to perfect a relationship as one can get. Lots of flashbacks to it. Lots of scenes of lunacy from her rented flat in North London, as she phones the flat she shared with Daniel in which she's unable to live without him. Several wild mad scenes in restaurants, in the street, in her home. Eventually Lucas, the choreographer, gets through to her (or so he thinks) and they finally have sex after a drunken evening discussing life and death. Later on, while Lucas is sleeping, she drives away and attempts to drown herself. She is rescued from the suburban pond by a doctor who takes her home to Lucas. But basically after that she's even more mad and thus we see her steady decline. Lots of humour in spite of the subject matter and also some poignant moments and some hilarious ones and some seriously dodgy schmaltz, but really a rather moving account of a woman having a nervous breakdown. I wanted the part so badly I figured I would never in a million years get offered it. I would go to the interview and be so eager to please them all they would think I was too desperate and give the part to someone else.

Matthew left me alone for my interview. If he hadn't I would've kicked him out and I suspect he knew this. In the morning I was doing what I usually do on such occasions; reading anything relevant to the job, listening to music, thinking about the part, the money and smoking too much and guzzling far too much coffee. On about the seventh cup the phone rang. I knew before I even picked it up who it would be. I'd dreamt of him; a nice dream without complication. Ignoring his messages and leaving his letters unopened had had little effect on either my nightmares or my dreams. I welcomed the sound of his voice but resolved to be strong and brusque. He asked if we could meet that morning. I told him I had an interview at one o'clock and what was so urgent? He said, 'You. I have to see you, love. Will you come?' I couldn't refuse. The reality of his voice was too persuasive. I dressed in too much of a hurry and felt uncomfortable with what I'd chosen. I didn't have time to rake the lugs out of my hair so I looked dishevelled and my eyes were clogged with three-day-old mascara. I couldn't find my orange clogs and put on an old pair of yellow espadrilles instead. When I got to the tube I realised the sole was coming off one of them and an ink cartridge had leaked onto the back of the other leaving a big bluey-green ink spot. I thought, well it's too bloody late now to go back and change and made a mental note to pick up a pair of clogs or something if I passed a shoe shop.

He was waiting for me on a bench in Soho Square. He looked older, greyer. His eyes were red and he hadn't shaved. He saw me coming towards him and literally ran into me almost knocking me over.

'What is it? What's happened?'

'Nothing . . . I just needed to see you. I had to see you. How are you?'

'I'm busy. I have an interview.'

'I know. I'm sorry. Should we meet later instead? I'll wait for you somewhere if you like.'

'No. I'm here now.'

'Thank you.'

'Aedan, what's up? This isn't about nothing. What's happened?'

'You stopped waiting, didn't you?'

'I did. For the sake of my mental health.'

'Didn't you get my letters?'

'I didn't open them. They're in a cupboard, locked away.'

'I've tried to explain. I never lied to you.'

'You're not here to talk about letters though, are you? What is it?'

'Frances.'

'You dragged me out to talk about *her*?' I got up to go. He pulled me down onto the bench. 'OW! Aedan!'

'Ellie . . . what am I going to do?' He started to cry and pulled me to him. I tried not to respond, not to comfort him but I couldn't be cold to him, this man I dreamed of virtually every night, this man I loved more than my own self. It was all I could do not to break down myself as he choked wet tears into my chest.

'Frances . . .'

'Tell me.'

'She's in hospital again.'

'Did she jump in front of another car?'

'She cut her wrists. One of her kids found her. She was carried off half dead. I mean, her *kids* . . . Her husband phoned me and told me to get over there right away, he said it was my fault.'

'He *knows*?'

'He's always known. She looked so small when I saw her. She just cried. She just lay there and cried. She said she'd do it again. Even if they locked her up somewhere she'd find a way and do it again.'

'She's blackmailing you.'

'I know and I'm allowing it but I couldn't live with that. If it was just *her* . . . y'know, her kids were meant to be away for the night . . . I mean, she'd packed them off to friends, only Caitlin, the wee one, came home early . . . I don't know why, whatever, and she found her. Caitlin's *eight* . . . Jesus, what did I do? I feel guilt *all the time*, because I think only of ways to get out of this and she says it's my fault she's sick and we have mutual friends who phone me every day and say it's my fault, why can't I just be with her? I never meant to get involved with you while she was still hassling me, while we were still attached, but you . . . it was inevitable, us, wasn't it? And I felt . . . and I knew you felt the same as me and you gave everything and it knocked me backwards, your love, your certainty . . .'

'I thought you felt the same, I thought you were certain too.'

'I did. I do, I mean, I am. Only . . . in Dublin no-one has anything to say about it except how can I do it to Frances? How can I leave her when she's so ill? Is it my fault she's sick? What did I do?' I thought about it. I couldn't deny he held some responsibility for the whole mess. He had never said no, not properly, and that was his crime, that's what he'd done, and the fucking relationship had gone on for years and years and the woman loved him and was ill. However much I hated her by this stage I could understand her despair. I stood up.

'Why don't you go to her? Give her what she wants? Why don't you do it?'

'I can't.'

'But you can't leave her either.'

'I want to. She won't let me. She'll kill herself and I can't live with that. But I want to go, I want to be away from her.'

'Let her die then.' I looked at my watch. I was starting to

201

feel sick watching him. I wanted to hate him but the longer I was near him the more I remembered. My hope. My love for him.

'If she dies . . . I couldn't live with that . . . I'd be useless to you. I'm weak. I know I'm weak and I should get on with life, with you, I'm weak for letting you get this hurt when I only ever wanted to be with you and love you and make you happy.' He started to cry again. It was the most emotional I'd ever seen him. I felt I knew a bit more about what mothers must feel when they see their children in pain. I wanted to be able to walk away and say, Make your decision without me. But I couldn't let him have that pain on his own, I couldn't walk away from him when he was so lost.

'I think of you, y'know?' he said. 'When we're not together you're everything I think about.'

'Don't. Aedan, I can't bear it . . .'

'We might never be together . . .'

'Don't.'

'And if that were the case I might as well be dead myself.'

'Aedan . . .'

'It should have been me in that bed with fucking tubes coming out of my arms . . . Not Frances. She looked so small . . .'

'Aedan, I have to go . . . the interview . . .'

'Ellie . . .' He grabbed my arm as I moved away.

'Let go.'

'No, never.' He pulled me down onto the ground, gripping my neck so tightly I started to cough. He pulled my hair back roughly. 'I hate you for making me love you like this . . . the guilt . . . I should be with you now, I know I should . . . It's ruined my life, meeting you, fucking you, loving you—'

'And leaving me! What do you think it's done to me? What do you think leaving me did to me? Do you think I have a normal life since I met you? I don't eat, I don't sleep, I can't think properly any more, I can't do anything because of you.' People turned to stare at us. A man came over and asked if I was all right. 'Fuck off! Just fuck off and mind someone else's fucking business!' Aedan let go of my neck and I fell back onto the grass. He knelt down and tried to rub my neck and my face but I hit his hand away and he fell onto the corner of my shirt. I tried to crawl away and the shirt ripped underneath him. 'Look at me! Just look at what you've done to me! And all I ever did was love you. I'm supposed to be in a fucking interview! This is my *career* I could be fucking up, I'm allowing you to fuck up the one thing I can still love, the one thing that still makes me happy. Are you satisfied? Are you proud? I hope Frances dies! I hope she fucking dies in front of you so you remember it and have to live with it, because I have to live with what you did to me, every day of my fucking life I live with the fact you promised me the fucking moon and more and then you took it away and left me nothing, nothing at all of you except a fucking bastard shirt and few fucking letters because you were too bloody weak to do what you said you wanted to do.' I pulled myself to my feet, holding on to the side of the bench for balance. I looked down at him, still and silent.

'I'm going,' I said. 'It's not healthy all this shit. I loved you too much, I still do, only it's not healthy.' He looked up at me, still silent.

As I walked away he said, 'I'm sorry. I'm *so sorry*, love.' I didn't even turn around. I thought of pillars of salt and kept looking in the one direction away from him.

I caught sight of myself in a shop window. I'd got grass stains and a long tear in my trousers and my shirt was ripped. My hair looked like I hadn't brushed it for a month. My nose may have started to bleed slightly as well but it might have been a trick of the light in the reflection. I looked like I'd just escaped a secure mental hospital.

I got the job.

Chapter Thirty-nine

'I've made cauliflower cheese.'

'Oh.'

'Comfort food.'

'Oh. For you?'

'No. For you. You've got to eat.'

'I do.'

'Wine?'

'OK. Red.'

'That's all we've got.' *We?* Who had asked him to move in? It seemed to have happened so suddenly. How? When did it happen? When I was asleep? He clunked around in the kitchen and came back with four bottles of wine on a tray and two mugs.

'Are we aiming to get drunk?'

'I think we should.'

'Oh, Matthew.' I opened one of the bottles. I wanted to be on my own. I was exhausted. The filming was exhausting because there was no real routine and the hours were all over the place so my body clock didn't know where to set itself. They weren't doing any of the scenes in chronological order either so there was no typical day. I'd gone in one day and filmed two scenes in a mental hospital, one in a supermarket and a scene in the office of the editor of a children's comic, *Bunty* or *Jinty* or something. The following day I'd had to run through Finsbury Park about eighteen times wearing only a

T-shirt. The only constant thing about the schedule was that it usually started bloody early and invariably went on till bloody late virtually every night of the week. If I'd been going home to a quiet, empty flat for a peaceful evening alone, I would've been quite content, I love working long hours, I always have, but Matthew was always waiting for me. He cooked meals for me and watched me move the food around the plate as he asked a thousand questions about things I had no desire to discuss. I found messages on my answering machine for him and mail started to arrive for him. I kept thinking, *But this isn't his address, this isn't his telephone number; why doesn't he go home?* It felt like he'd lived there for months and months, like he'd sort of grown into the flat like ivy and I hadn't even noticed until it was too late and he'd climbed all the walls and made it more his home than mine. How long was it since I'd gone up to Leeds? It couldn't have been more than a few weeks. I'd got the job and had costume fittings and rehearsals and when I hadn't been doing that I'd gone on long walks alone and spent time with Alice and also Lottie, who looked about eleven months pregnant at that time. My body clock went insane; up at five some days for the filming and sometimes asleep at midnight for a couple of hours, or sometimes in bed at five and awake at noon. Some days I didn't sleep at all. The director of the film thought I was some sort of method actress, as with every day that passed I looked more and more like some long-term psychiatric in-patient. Colette, my make-up artist, said she had less and less work to do on my face with every scene we shot. I remarked on her tact and diplomacy.

Matthew, on the other hand, looked settled and happy. I was irritated. I couldn't sleep properly with him next to me; I got angry whenever his friends phoned up, but every time I tried to say anything, every time I tried to explain why I was so uncomfortable, I sounded like a mad witch and he would go silent and look wounded for the rest of the evening but the next day he would still be there, like he thought I needed him. Perhaps he needed me. I fucked him. It made him happy. It made me feel like a lunatic. I despaired of myself. He thought my problems were all from outside my home, and so, to help me in some way, he brought a lot of food and a lot of wine into the flat and every few days he'd open a few bottles and try to get me drunk.

'Is it the filming?'

'Is what the filming?'

'You're unhappy.'

'I'm tired.'

'Why don't you get an early night? Have a bath and a spliff and get in bed.'

'Going to bed does not necessarily mean I'm going to sleep. Going to bed earlier just means I'll be lying there going out of my mind with frustration for a few hours longer than I normally do.'

'Why don't you take a sleeping pill?'

'They make me groggy in the morning.'

'What about hot milk?'

'What about it?' I snapped.

'I don't know what else to suggest.'

'Then don't suggest anything.'

'Sorry.'

'You're always sorry. Stop being so fucking apologetic all the time.'

'Sorry.'

It would be unfair to say we fought, because he never said a bad word to me, even when I screamed myself hoarse trying to get a rise out of him. If I had loved him only half as much as Aedan I would've thrown him out of the flat.

I got home one night to find a note saying, '*Gone to Birmingham for the washing-powder voice-over. There's pasta sauce in the fridge. Messages on the machine from Alice and your father and Nellie and two from Lottie. I'll be back tomorrow afternoon. Thought we might go and see* Jurassic Park *if you're still free. Love you. Please eat some-*

thing. Mattie.' I tore it into tiny pieces and threw them all on the kitchen floor. Why did he have to write me a note every time he went anywhere? I wasn't his mother. I didn't care if he wasn't coming back for a night. I didn't care if he never came back. I put some Michael Nyman on and opened a can of Budweiser and enjoyed the space of his absence. I listened to the messages on the machine. There was one from Aedan right at the end of the tape saying, 'I love you. Could you phone me?' I couldn't work out if it was one from ages and ages ago or if it was fresh. I chose to ignore it and drank another can and then another and another and then finished the rest of the crate till I was swaying around the flat quite drunk and rather content, all things considered. Only eleven o'clock and I felt able to sleep. Relieved by the prospect of oblivion I got into bed without even bothering to undress.

I dreamt I was being carried through a swamp. Matthew was holding my head out of the mud, squelching through the mire. I said, 'It doesn't matter if I go under. Save yourself.' He didn't hear me because I was unable to speak properly. I dreamt I told him about Aedan and he kept saying, I love you, I love you, I don't care about Aedan and I said, 'But I do,' and he started to cry and I flung my arms around his neck and begged him to stop and he begged me to stop sending him away but of course I could not do that and I felt my head sink into the mud again.

I left at ten the next morning with a hangover from hell and a decidedly furry mouth. I thought I'd been burgled in the night because all the Budweiser cans had been put into a bin-liner and the mountain of washing I'd left in the machine had been folded into neat little piles. Either they were very domestically orientated thieves or I had been drunker than I thought. I couldn't remember being so organized the night before.

I didn't feel very well at all. Fortunately I was only needed for a couple of hours and all I was required to do was lie on the floor of a hospital room with a broken piece of sculpture clutched to my breast. I thought of Matthew and felt relief at not having him there when I'd woken up. I thought of going round to Lottie's so I'd be out when he got back from Birmingham. Maybe I would stay away for a few days and work up the courage to say we should not be living together. Lottie, in her bigness, was a joy to be around. Tom was doing a lot of work at home and they were enjoying a new lease of love for each other. I changed my mind about going over there and opted for home instead; perhaps Matthew wouldn't come straight over after all. I phoned Lottie to say I'd probably pop over to see her during the week and as soon as I lifted the receiver I heard the key in the door and my stomach turned over. What on earth had possessed me to let him have a key? But then how was I to know he'd move in so quickly, so freely? How was I to know my spine had disintegrated? I was allowing all these things to happen so it was even more my fault than his.

'Hi, babe,' he said. He popped his head round the door. He looked tired.

'I'm on the phone.'

'Fancy a take-away? Pizza? Chinese?'

'No.'

'Indian? Thai?'

'Nothing.'

'Has he moved in for good?' Lottie sounded confused on the other end of the phone.

'Not if I can help it.'

'What?' said Matthew from the hall.

'I'm talking to Lottie.'

'Give her my love.' *Why? She's my friend, not yours.* 'If you don't fancy a take-away I think I'll just have beans on toast or something.'

'Have what you want,' I snapped.

'Is everything OK?' Lottie said.

'Absolutely fucking wonderful.'

'What?' said Matthew.

'Fuck off!'

'Ellie, what's going on there?'

'Sorry, Lottie. It's Matthew.'

'Aren't you getting on?'

'Not really. He's too bloody nice. He cooks for me. He's driving me mad. I'm driving myself mad.' He walked in.

'Ellie, when was the last time you ate anything?'

'Just a minute, Lott. Matthew, I'm on the phone.'

'Yes, I can see that, but tell me when you last ate.'

'No. Now would you let me talk to Lottie in peace, please?'

He went back into the kitchen and came back with his beans on toast.

'Which beans did you use?'

'Well . . . we only had one tin . . .'

'*We?*'

'What's going on?' Lottie, more confused than ever.

'Lott, I'm really sorry, can I call you back?' I slammed the phone down.

'Where did you find them?'

'What?'

'The beans. Where did you find the beans?'

'In the cupboard—'

'Which cupboard?'

He looked bewildered. 'The one in the . . . they were in a box . . . I thought—'

'What did you think?'

'I don't—'

'Matthew!' I started to cry and walked out. He followed me into the bedroom.

'I'm sorry.'

'Oh, you're always fucking sorry. You can't *help* me, you know? I don't *want* to be helped, I don't need it. I'm *ruined*. How many fucking times do I have to tell you I'm fucking useless at this? I'm useless for you! I don't want *anyone*, OK? *Not anyone*.' I screamed abuse at him but he did not hear. I had been screaming abuse at him, one way or another, ever since he'd moved in on me, on my home, my bed. I screamed abuse at myself for allowing it. I had tried to treat him well. I liked him. He was a good man. I had thought that allowing him in was a kind thing to do, but it would've been kinder rejecting him outright, right from the start; it would've been kinder had I kicked him as far away from me and my life as I possibly could.

I pushed past him and went to find the empty bean tin.

'Where is it?'

'What?'

'The tin. The bean tin.'

'In the bin.'

'Oh, Matthew, *why*?' I sat on the floor and hated him. 'Why didn't you die? Why didn't I?' I spat bitter, all-engulfing loss-induced anger, regret. Such Loss. Half a soul missing; half my head, my brain, my guts. Halved. He'd eaten the beans. He had stolen something of Aedan and eaten it. I spat like an animal who knows no better. He stood in the doorway and looked pained and I hated him even more. His eyes took in each ounce of anger and resentment. He looked like he was going to cry and still I carried on and on. He'd eaten the beans.

'Ellen. I'm sorry. I don't know what I've done. I just know . . . I think we need each other . . . It'll get better, I know it will.'

'No it won't! Don't kid yourself. I don't need you or anyone. I need nothing. I expect nothing. It's all lost. I'm lost. Broken. I'll ruin you — well I would if you weren't already on your fucking knees. Don't give me your love. I don't want it.' He stood and stared at me. 'I DON'T WANT IT! It *suffocates* me, I can't *breathe*. I hate it. It reminds me . . . it reminds me of my inability, my complete inability to love you or myself or anyone that isn't him.'

'The dead man.'

'Yes the fucking dead man.'

Chapter Forty

He didn't leave.

We had sex; sterile, rough sex, like we were both angry. He said he found it difficult to be so angry. He said his roughness was manufactured, said he was afraid of hurting me. I told him it was the only way I could do it these days; I was in mourning.

The filming took me to Germany for four days. I thought I would be glad to be away; out of the flat and away from Mattie but anyone who has ever been to Leverkusen will understand what a tragedy it is to be closeted in a hotel there for four days and five nights. The only restaurant open on our first day there was a McDonald's so I didn't eat. The following day we filmed all day on an industrial estate near the Rhein and the German catering wagon served only ham, cheese and more ham. I put in a request for a vegetarian meal to stave off death and got a parcel of cheese and some Bavarian bread. I figured death was preferable. Both Colette and her equally dense assistant fainted from hunger on the third day and the production assistant spent three hours trying to get through to London on her mobile phone in order to find some extra help and some decent food. I met David Lewis who was playing my dead lover and indeed he really was quite dead. He spoke to no-one. I wondered how on earth he'd got the job because although it was a dead man he was playing, there were a lot of flashbacks that were supposedly there to highlight the electricity between the two of us; lots of fighting and an inordinate amount of sex. I tried to communicate with him when we were off camera, just for the sake of an easy life, but he made no effort at all. I would've probably been quite annoyed but someone told me it was a broken heart he was suffering from; he'd lost his girlfriend to another man and I instantly forgave him and kept well away. We went to a beer cellar and poured apfel schnapps down our necks. David stayed for only one while the rest of us talked and drank the night away. It seemed rather unwise, going back to the hotel on his own like that, particularly when he was already so obviously depressed. The hotel was on another industrial estate and the rooms were like prison cells. I had a single bed in mine which sort of stuck out of the wall like a shelf and was covered by a tissue-like duvet, so thin it frequently floated off in the night. They didn't even do room service and there was nowhere around to buy food or drink so once you'd got to your room you were trapped in there without facilities till morning. One night I got back and found David sitting at the deserted reception desk. He still had his coat on and his script under his arm and he'd finished filming hours and hours ago. When I asked him if he was all right he said he was quite simply desperate for coffee so I took him into the kitchen and we found an espresso machine and drank coffee together in silence for about two hours. At the end of it he thanked me for being damaged enough to understand him. I got to my room wishing I understood nothing and could be happy with mediocrity. There was a message on the floor from Aedan and two from Mattie. Trapped in that place I lost my resolve and dialled Aedan's number in Ireland. He wasn't there. I tried Oakley Street but he wasn't there either. Perhaps it was fate giving me a second chance at strength. I called my flat to pick up my messages, hoping to get the answering machine. Matthew answered.

'Someone called Bryan phoned for you. Said he was your

uncle or something. He had a strange North Country accent. Sounded like he had a cleft palate.' Aedan.

'Did he leave a message?'

'He left his number.' I took it and rang off. I tried to go to sleep without phoning him but I kept opening my eyes and seeing the piece of paper by the bed and then I'd look at the phone and at the paper again and the indecision kept me awake. I really shouldn't do it, I kept telling myself, he's doing you harm, you're doing yourself harm.

The phone rang.

'Ellie?'

'Aedan.'

'Will we talk?'

'What is there to talk about?'

'You haven't answered my messages.'

'No.'

'How long are you in Germany?'

'Till tomorrow.'

'I could meet you at the airport.'

'No.'

'We need to talk.'

'I'm too busy.'

'Who's the guy staying at the flat?'

'An actor. Matthew Howard.'

'Is it his home?'

'It's my home.'

'Are you sleeping with him?'

'Not at this moment.'

'Can I see you when you get back to London?'

'I'll hardly be in London at all for a while. I'm filming in Hampshire.'

'Can I see you there?'

'No.'

'You still love me.'

'I've got to be up at six tomorrow. I've got to sleep now.'

'You still love me.'

'You're not wrong. But it does me no good. It's futile, like pouring water onto sand. I could pour and pour but the sand wouldn't change. You don't change. I'm wasting energy. It's like writing words on the surface of the water, the sea, a pool; it doesn't matter how hard I try I get nowhere. It seems the more I love you the less I get from you. You see more of Frances than you do of me and she's married to someone else.'

'She hounds me.'

'You allow her to.'

'I'll change that . . . I've tried . . .'

'But not hard enough. I'm going. I have to sleep.'

'I love you.'

'You make things so difficult for me. It might be better if you didn't contact me at all.'

'You don't want that.'

'I want you.'

'You've got me.'

'I haven't.'

'Elle . . .'

'I'm listening.'

'Will we get married?'

'Unlikely.'

'I'll book it. September?'

'I'm going now.'

'But you'd marry me?'

'I wouldn't break a promise.'

'Meet me next week.'

'No.'

'It'll be different . . . Frances is—'

'Don't talk to me about her.'

'Look, meet me. Please.'

'You don't know where I'll be and I won't tell you.'

'I'll find you. Meet me. Please, Ellie.'

'I don't know. I'm going now, I really am.'

'I'm sorry, your sleep.'

'Your phone bill.'

'I don't mind.'

I put the phone down and then took it off the hook. I would not be walked over any more and therefore I would not meet him next week or ever. If he was never going to be rid of Frances then I must not see him ever. It hurt too much. I should not allow it to happen. I must think about work and nothing else. At least the director was happy with me. The imbalance in my brain seemed to be lending unique qualities to my performance. I remembered a famous song-writer saying she was so happy with her husband she couldn't write anything any more and she would surely have to leave him before she wrote another great number. Sure enough, as soon as she was miserable again she had a hit and then another and another. Jesus.

And so, stuck in Leverkusen, jolted further by more contact with the dead man, we found the scenes came easily and we were doing it in fewer and fewer takes and people stopped making mistakes. My mind pulled itself from one thing to another like it was made of elastic. Before I could stop myself I was thinking of Aedan, alive and within reach of me and in only a moment he would be gone again and in my head I would be sitting in my flat again drinking boiled water and facing the loss of him. I felt I hadn't the strength to go through it all again. I felt the weight of Matthew on my shoulders. I felt I was approaching the end of both of them; how else would I repair my damaged self? It would finish soon, it would have to. I would make it finish and then I would go away and learn to breathe again and never make the same mistakes again and I would never hurt anyone and they would never hurt me.

I decided Mattie should be the first to be released and when I got back to England I invited him to the hotel in Hampshire with the intention of ending it with him. He thought I meant this as a romantic sort of reconciliatory gesture so I told him we could have a meal together and a long talk and then I really must be left alone for the rest of the job. I'd have to think of some way of telling him it was all over, that he'd have to move out of the flat. Maybe I would plant the seeds in his mind and then wait a couple of weeks before actually kicking him out. Maybe he'd just know and leave early of his own accord; pack his things and never come back.

The evening was not a success. We had an argument in the restaurant about something trivial and went to bed angry and half drunk on empty stomachs. I got a terrible headache and took two Nurofen, half expecting to collapse from the hole that had surely been burnt in my stomach by the painkiller. Matthew fell asleep with his back to me. I turned the ringer on the phone down to low and tried to sleep myself. Impossible. Hours later the phone purred at me. I listened to it for a few seconds, shocked at the strange sound it made. Matthew didn't move. I picked it up, careful not to move around too much in case Sleeping Beauty came round.

'I'm in a phone box by a pub called The Fox. It's near a pond, about ten minutes away from you.'

'By car?'

'On foot.' I put the phone down and crawled out of bed. I picked some shorts up from the floor and a jumper and went to the bathroom to put them on. Matthew turned over in his sleep. I looked at him, worried for a moment that he'd woken. He hadn't. With any luck he'd sleep through till ten and go straight home. I looked at my watch. Midnight. I put my trainers on without socks, since I couldn't see any lying around, and left the room without making a sound.

He was sitting on the pavement by an olde-worlde-type post office about fifty yards from The Fox. He had his head in his hands. I walked around the duck pond to get to him and wondered where all the ducks went to at night. The water was still and yellow from the glow of the street lamp.

'Aedan.'

'I thought you wouldn't come. Thank you.'

'I shouldn't have. Matthew's at the hotel. I left him in the room.'

'Matthew?'

'The guy you spoke to at the flat. He's staying with me here.'

'Why?'

'Long story.'

'We've got all night.'

'Why are you here?'

'I can't be without you.'

'Liar.'

'It's true. I can't.'

'You can. You proved that. You left me.'

'I came back.'

'It's too late.'

'It isn't.'

'What about her? She run into any traffic recently?'

'It's over with Frances. It's been over for months. I've left messages for you. I tried to tell you.' I wanted to believe this but couldn't.

'You've told me all this before. You come back and you talk and love me and fuck me and then she does something and you're away again. It hurts more and more each time you do it.'

'I never wanted to hurt you.'

'But you did. You do.'

I felt a bit strange, like I'd had too much to drink. I felt my judgement was impaired. I felt confused; leaving Matthew lying in the bed and now standing in an unfamiliar village street with this man who'd been haunting me for so long. Whenever I saw him now it was like I was in some sort of dream or film. I sat down on the ground next to him.

'You don't look well,' he said.

'I don't feel it. I'm stressed. I think there's a hole in my stomach. I think I might be making myself ill, but I never

217

have enough time to think about it properly. Maybe I already am.'

'You look thin.'

'So do you.'

'You're still beautiful.' He kissed me. I thought I should not do this, I should walk away and leave him and then leave Matthew. But his kiss was familiar. It tasted of fruit. His fingers tasted of fruit. His body, when I took his clothes away, tasted like some dream I'd had every night for a year. We fucked like two ghosts, each knowing we were the only people we could ever really touch, knowing that even together we were still dead. It had been too long. A car wound its way round the lane past the deserted pub. Its headlights settled on us for a second or two as we lay by the water. We didn't move.

'Come away with me.' What was I saying? Ah, the truth. I could not walk away alone. Hadn't I proved that already?

'I will.'

'Now. Do it now.'

'Soon.' I moved away from him and knelt in the dirt.

'Soon isn't enough. I'm worth more than that. Aedan, I need you now, not soon, not when you're ready. You'll *never* be ready. She'll always come back and drag you away and you'll always allow it and that's not enough. I deserve more.' I went dizzy and then felt everything suddenly crystallize in my head and I wanted to shout out but I stood up and said, quite calmly, 'I've had enough,' and then I wasn't calm at all and I backed away from him and turned to the pond and waded into the water and said, 'I've had enough, enough. I've had enough.' He followed me in and pulled at my jumper, torn from the fucking, now wet and heavy on me and I turned around and screamed at him and pulled him by his hair into the water until we were both underneath and he pulled me more to release himself but only made us sink deeper and the floor of the pond was soft so that our feet sank deep into the mud. He managed to get

218

our heads out into the air and drag us nearer to the bank and he said, 'I'll marry you, we'll get married, we'll do it tomorrow. We'll be married, I promise you we'll be married.'

'NO!' I screamed, half choking on the water and the word and the promises. 'NO, NO, NO, never, never, never, never, never!' Dripping wet he watched me scream and took a step back and lost his balance slightly and tried to turn round and drag himself to the bank and I rugby-tackled him and we were both under the water again, pulling each other away from the air. And then I let go of him and spent a moment beneath the water choosing breath or suffocation. Without much effort I chose to bring my head up and breathe and crawl out to the dry land. Behind me I heard him spitting and coughing.

'Ellen, wait.'

'No,' I said, picking up my shorts and walking away.

'Wait.'

'I've already waited too long. Can't do it any more. Too tired. Too fucked. I've lost it, babe.'

Matthew was sitting up fully dressed. I dripped into the room. I saw a glimpse of myself in the wardrobe mirror; black with mud and grass, my hair hanging wet through, the water from me dripping all over the carpet.

'Don't ask.'

He stared at me, utterly shocked, as I peeled off my clothes and got into bed still wet and filthy.

'Ellie—'

'Don't ask.' I ignored him completely as he said my name over and over again. He sounded like he was crying. I slept. Really quite peacefully. Like a dead woman.

Chapter Forty-one

I got indigestion. I wondered how this was possible as I hardly ate anything. I worked and slept, though there wasn't a great deal of time for sleep, it seemed like a great feat. Matthew kept saying I would kill myself if I carried on the way I was. I told him it was more likely I would kill him and why didn't he just leave me alone.

I was called on to do an enormous number of mad scenes which was no problem for me at all. I felt on the verge of flu or something and didn't want to hold the filming up by getting ill so I took Nurofen to stop my bones aching. I took vitamins and oil of evening primrose and I drank a lot of milk. I got headaches and thought perhaps I had a slight gas leak in the flat and was being slowly poisoned by it but Matthew said he felt fine and perhaps I was overworked and maybe I shouldn't be drinking all the milk.

The end of the filming loomed and fear crept into me. Mattie started work on another TV job and my agent phoned to say the publicity for *Thérèse* was starting with a vengeance and arranged about thirty meetings and interviews with the press. She also told me that a rather large and prestigious company were doing *Romeo and Juliet* and the director wanted to see me. I looked in the mirror and thought he would have to be retarded or blind to cast me as Juliet looking as I did. There were blue lines under my eyes and my face was drawn and I felt about a thousand years old. I was given two days to familiarize myself with the play and they would interview me during my lunch break on the final day on location. I knew the play back to front anyway, it's one of my favourites, so I didn't bother learning anything from it, I simply went to meet the director and hoped I didn't look too grey and jaded. He looked slightly taken aback by my appearance so I explained I was playing a lunatic in a film and that in reality I was really quite young and pretty. I read a speech from the play and felt moved by poor Juliet, who really never stood a chance against such opposition and such blundering mistakes. I shook the director's hand when I'd finished and assumed I'd never see him again and on the tube on the way home I felt the loss of the job, both the jobs. Only a miracle would get me Juliet and the film had finished. I wished I'd been in a better frame of mind for the Shakespeare interview because it was a long tour and a wonderful part and I knew I could do it. Back at home I took three sleeping pills and thought I'd sleep away the end-of-job blues. After only six hours or so I woke up with a dreadful headache and took more Nurofen and two more sleeping pills and hoped to sleep for a day or more. I found, however, when I got back to bed that I was dying from thirst. There wasn't anything in the fridge and I wanted Coca-Cola or Lemonade or Lucozade. I wanted something fizzy and sugary and cold. I wanted it so badly I put some clothes on and went to the 7-eleven. I bought Lucozade and drank it outside the shop on the pavement, which was where the ambulance picked me up when I collapsed.

I ran through a house from room to room looking for a bed. I found one and ran to it and pulled away the duvet and my mother leapt out and said 'NO! You can't come in, *I'm* in here!' and so exhausted I went about the house in search of sleep again. I found my father in a corridor phoning the coroner. I said, 'But she isn't dead yet!' and he said, 'She will be by the time he gets here – the traffic's terrible. You'll be going with her if you pursue this particular line of thought. Don't be an eejit.'

I woke up in a cubicle of the Accident and Emergency department of St Thomas' Hospital. A woman said, 'We pumped your stomach but we need to know what you've taken and why.' I said I didn't know what I'd taken but really I was fine and could I please go home. She said that wasn't wise; I might have died from whatever it was I'd done to myself and they wanted to keep me in for a few days for observation.

'There's nothing to observe,' I said and asked where I could discharge myself. A big fat ginger-haired man came in and said he was a psychiatrist.

'Oh, that's all I need, a fucking shrink.' I found reception and filled in a form releasing the hospital from responsibility. I asked them if they'd phone me a cab but they gave me such grief about leaving I ended up wobbling out on my jelly legs and flagging one down in the street. I wasn't completely sure what my actual address was so I told him to drop me at the Borough tube and I would hopefully find my way from there.

Chapter Forty-two

'Elle ... Ellie ... ?'

'Let me sleep. Please let me sleep.'

'Can I get in with you?'

'Do whatever you want. Just let me go back to sleep.'

He clambered in next to me and seemed to fall asleep almost instantly; where did he find such apparent tranquillity? I lay awake listening to his easy breathing. I debated whether to make coffee and accept the fact I wasn't going to have an easy night, or lie there in silence all night and escape in the morning.

He slept beside me with a faint glimmer of childlike peace on his face. I sat up and smoked, resenting his ability to make himself apparently blind to what was going on right under his nose. I saw a packet of Marlboros peeping out from his jacket pocket on the floor by the bed. He told me he'd stopped smoking about a week ago but he'd been lying. I'd smelled smoke on him every day. I resented the pretence because I didn't care one way or another. I resented him lying in my bed. My bed, in my flat. Nothing belonged to him there. His happiness suffocated me; I was suffocated by the guilt of knowing I was partly responsible for it. Now I was unable to continue doling out hope. I respected him too much to let it go on any more.

I coughed loudly on purpose and moved around in the bed in the hope he would waken and find me crying next to him and realize without being told that this was the end. He didn't move a muscle.

I am gutless, I thought. I cannot tell him the truth. I don't have the guts to wake him and tell him to leave.

I got out of bed and went to sit in the living room. I stared into space for a while and then, with a view to writing a poem or something equally indulgent, I got out the type-writer. No poetry left in me so I typed some gibberish onto a piece of yellow paper. It was quite relaxing. Some time later – an hour? – he walked in and stood in the doorway watching me smoke.

'Put some clothes on, would you, Mattie?' I couldn't talk to him seriously if he was naked.

He looked at me with what could've been vague realiza-tion and disappeared into the bathroom. I heard him peeing and then running the taps. Then he was silent. *Hurry up.* Was he taking his time deliberately to make it even more difficult for me? He came back wearing a bathrobe I'd forgotten I possessed; a red and black Noel Cowardy thing that looked like it needed a wash.

'I'd forgotten I had that.'

'I've worn it before. Put it on last night in fact.'

'Oh.'

I lit another cigarette. He took it from me and sucked in a lungful of smoke.

'God, I miss it already,' he said as he exhaled and handed it back. I looked at the floor hoping he had guessed what I was about to say.

'Stevie Smith,' he said.

'What?'

'Your yellow paper. *Novel on yellow paper.*'

'Oh, yes. Only thing I could find to write on.'

He sat down next to me and took hold of my hand. Neither of us spoke. Eventually he got up and sighed.

'I'll make some coffee.'

'Have we got any Bushmill's left?'

'I think so.'

He came back with a bottle of Jameson's and two glasses.

'May as well skip the coffee.' He poured and we drank in silence.

'How are you feeling?'

I looked away from him. What did he expect me to say? I obviously wasn't all right.

'Look,' I said. 'I know what it must've looked like but I wasn't trying to injure myself or anything. It was an accident. I fainted. Everyone overreacted. I was all right.'

'I wasn't.'

'What?'

'There's a message on the machine when I get home from rehearsals, from St Thomas' hospital, for one Aedan O'Brien. Your dead man.'

'Aedan?'

'I call the hospital and I say, "I'm Mr O'Brien, what's the problem?" and some nurse tells me she's just admitted Ellen Millar, unconscious, with a suspected overdose of tranquillizers or something similar. She says to me, "As you're her next of kin, it's our duty to contact you as she may be in some danger at the moment and could you tell us if she's on any sort of medication?"'

'I'm sorry.'

'Aedan O'Brien. The dead man.'

'Look, my passport was in my bag . . . I went to the shop to get some pop and . . . his name's in the back of my passport. I put it there when we were together.'

'When he was alive?' I said nothing.

'He isn't dead though, is he?'

'What does it matter?'

'It matters that I thought I was going to lose you, I mean I thought you were going to *die*. I thought you'd tried to do yourself in.'

'I didn't. I'm fine.'

'I stole a car.'

'What?'

'The Northern line was all fucked up . . . I needed to get to you.'

'You're not serious?' Jesus, you don't realize the lengths people will go to for you till they're given a crisis to deal with.

'I thought you were dead or dying. I had to get to you.'

'So you just took someone's car? From off the street?'

'Well, what else could I do?' I had to stop myself laughing. He looked deadly serious. 'What would you have done?'

'I don't know.' I thought of Aedan.

'When I got there they said you'd gone. I thought they meant you'd died.'

'What about a taxi?'

'What?'

'Instead of the car, nicking the car.'

'I had no choice. There wasn't any time.'

It all seemed quite ludicrous. He was obviously as mad as I was. I tried to remember what it was I'd taken that had caused this whole drama. My mind was spinning. My brain ached.

'Where is it now? The car, where is it?'

'Just outside.'

'In the car park?'

'I drove back in it.'

Good grief. I took this in, at least I tried to. Any minute now we'd have the police hammering on the door looking for the thief.

'Ellen . . .'

'I'm really sorry.'

'Why didn't you tell me about Aedan?'

'I thought I had.' Lies. Sometimes I even believed them myself.

I got up to go to bed, feeling suddenly very tired and cowardly. It was all too much. I would have to get the keys back from him and take his knickers out of the drawers and

226

pack up his toothbrush and his razors and tell him the truth, but not yet; it would have to wait till morning, when I had some strength. He grabbed me before I got through the door.

'Elle . . .'

'Let go.'

'Where are you going?'

'Get off me.' He softened the grip he had on my arm. 'I need a walk.'

'God, show me some respect. Please.'

'I'm sorry.'

'Tell me about him.'

'Mattie, do we have to go through all this?'

'What happened between you two?'

'I'm surprised no-one told you.'

'I'm surprised you didn't.'

'Can I have a cigarette? I think I've run out.'

He sighed. 'Can't hide anything from you can I?'

He got a packet of Marlboro Lights out of the pocket of the bathrobe. 'I managed to stop for a couple of days . . . but . . . well, you know.'

'I'm sorry. I made you smoke again.'

'I wouldn't have managed to stop, anyway.'

'I'm held hostage by cigarettes.'

'Yeah, me too.'

'I'm a fucking hostage to cigarettes and fear and the telephone – so fucking *silent* – I wait for him to call, you know? I keep thinking . . . perhaps . . . I'll forget him, that I'll get better, but . . .' He'd started to cry. 'I'm sorry, Matthew. I never meant to hurt you.'

'He abused you.'

'I allowed it.'

'He couldn't have loved you.'

'He did.'

'I love you.'

'I know.'

'And I'm *here* for you. I'll do anything for you.'

'Find someone worthy of all that.'

'You are.'

'Don't waste your time on me. I've told you I'm ruined for anyone else. He ruined me. I'd rather you left. You'll thank me for it, I promise you.'

'Why did you tell me he was dead?'

'It was easier than trying to explain. And anyway, I couldn't bear the idea of him breathing somewhere without me. Sometimes I even believed it myself.'

'I found out weeks ago. Before Germany.'

'How?' I wasn't surprised. Messages on the machine. Notes. My friends. Perhaps Lottie had told him. Anyway, Aedan was a director and Matthew was an actor; maybe Aedan had interviewed him. Ha. That'd be just the sort of thing Aedan would find amusing.

'I came back here once when you thought I was in Birmingham. I thought I'd surprise you.'

'When was this?'

'Two or three weeks ago. Four. Don't really remember. I got back and found you outside in the car park. You were all curled up on the floor by the benches. You were just crunched up in a ball, crying, and I lifted you up and brought you back in here. You don't remember?'

'No.' I didn't. I remembered dreaming of him carrying me through a swamp. Was it then?

'You felt so thin. I said, "You're tiny, aren't you?" and I put you into bed and told you I loved you.'

'Where did you go?'

'I got in beside you and smoothed your hair – it was all in your eyes. You said you loved me and I asked you if you really meant it.'

'What did I say?'

'"Hollow. Empty hollow between tomorrow and now." And you had black eyes – your mascara had run. You said, "I'm haunted," and then, "he's not dead at all. I am."'

'Was I drunk?'

'Yes. I think so.' We didn't look at each other. 'I stayed with you all night.'

'I would've remembered.'

'You were dead to the world.'

'Yeah. That'd be right.'

'I can't let you do this to yourself.'

'You can't stop me. I feel like I've been poisoned.'

'Fight it.'

'I love him.'

'He's gone.'

'He'll come back.'

'You don't believe that.'

'I'm just going to hurt you. I already have and I never wanted that.'

'I could stay and just . . . be a friend to you. Help you.'

'I'm not that selfish. I couldn't do it to you.'

'Let me stay.'

'No. It isn't fair to you.'

'Give me a few days.'

What could I say? No? 'I'm not sure it'll do any good.'

'More alcohol?'

'Yes please. I'd like to be drunk.'

The following morning we were both too ill to regret or discuss or even think. I was sick into a carrier bag in the kitchen. If anything was going to make him leave it was the grossness of me. He came out of the bathroom and walked in as I was hiding the bag at the bottom of the rubbish.

'I'll take that out to the bins,' he said, forcing a smile.

'Go back to sleep for a while if you like. You look awful.'

'So do you. You have sick in your hair.' God, he didn't miss a trick.

'I'm going to get some Lucozade. Want anything?'

'Twenty Marlboro. Take some money out of my jacket.'

'No, no. It's my fault you're smoking again, it seems only fair I should pay.'

He kissed me as I was leaving. Had I not felt so ill I

would've grabbed some belongings and left that minute, just got on a train and travelled for miles and miles and not come back. Propelled by guilt. But I couldn't think quickly enough for any of that so ten minutes later I was back with a four pack of Lucozade and forty cigarettes. He was dressed and shaved.

'I'm going.'

'Oh.'

'It's what you wanted, isn't it? I can always come back . . . if you change your mind . . .'

'Matthew . . .' I didn't know what to say to him. I hoped he didn't love me as much as he claimed. I felt I would drown in guilt at any moment. 'I'm sorry. I'm so sorry.'

'Don't be. *Mea culpa*. I had my eyes open.'

'No. I should've been more honest with you.'

'You were.'

'God, you're so bloody nice.'

'If you change your mind . . .'

'Don't hold your breath.'

'Well, you know where I am. If there's anything you need . . . a chat . . . anything. Just call.'

When he left I felt as though I'd poisoned my own brother and watched him choke.

Chapter Forty-three

I was interviewed by women's magazines and TV listings papers and national newspapers. I did a daytime chat show interview for a husband and wife team. Lottie said, 'Isn't it a hassle?' But it never was. Not then. It made me feel important. I felt like an actress. I was even asked to model some clothes for one of the tabloids, which seemed utterly ludicrous as I am not model material at all, but I didn't refuse. I ran into Matthew at one point, at an interview for an arts magazine programme. He looked pained and asked me if I'd like to go to dinner with him. I said no. My mind was unchanged. Aedan sent a card saying he'd seen a poster for *Thérèse* on the tube and would I meet him. I sent the card back saying, *'Call me when Frances has gone.'* I was completely alone but unbothered by this. I felt my whole body needed repairing. I would cleanse myself with solitude. Some of the interviewers asked about my private life. I said, 'I live alone,' and nothing more. Matthew was less reticent and frequently declared that he was desperately in love with me but unfortunately his love was unrequited. After that I played wicked tricks on all the various presenters and told them I was a widow, or that my fiancé had died three years ago. I gave him a different death each time. The one that worked the best was when I told some guy my fiancé had been killed in a canoeing accident somewhere off the coast of southern Spain. He had almost laughed and I'd said, 'Go ahead. I know it's funny. I always resented his comedy death.' I took pleasure in the discomfort this caused.

In the midst of all the publicity work I was offered Juliet. I accepted. The job was due to start on the seventh of September. Perfect timing. I could go away and forget; immerse myself in new people. The cast and crew preview of *Thérèse*, to which some press were invited, was scheduled for September the first. Mattie phoned to ask if we could go together. Perhaps we could meet for breakfast first? I said I would meet him there at one forty-five. I didn't want to walk in there alone but if I wasn't going to have Aedan on my arm I wouldn't have anyone.

It might not have mattered so much were it not for the date. It was our anniversary. Getting dressed in the morning I thought only of the good moments of the year. I put on an orange dress and some orange tights and some orange clogs. I tied the apricot silk in my hair and remembered a moment not so good when I'd waited for the moment to say goodbye. I looked in the mirror and laughed at myself. Van Gogh apparently said that orange is the colour of insanity. Then I am truly mad I thought, as I put on an orange jacket. On the way to the tube a little boy shouted, 'You know when you've been tangoed!' so I figured I must look like a fizzy drink and laughed again and wished He had phoned me. Perhaps he did not remember. Was it only one year ago? It felt like ten. I could not remember what it was like not to have him in my head. Did he see my face in his dreams as clearly as I saw his? Perhaps he did not dream of me at all.

I met up with Matthew and we played at happy couples. Liam Johnston, looking most out of character in a suit and tie, whisked us around the room introducing us to everyone and at five-to we found our seats dead centre of the screen.

I loved it. It is not often I can watch myself on screen without balking but Liam had photographed everything in such a way it was hard to look away and anyway I looked like a stranger, a ghost. I think even Zola might have been rather impressed. Even Ian Turner didn't come out of it too badly. We all cried. At the end there was a stunned sort of silence and then a thunderous eruption of cheers and applause and whistles. Everyone stood up. Liam grabbed me and hugged me and said, 'This is it for you, Ellie, this is it!' In the reception area champagne was sprayed everywhere and we all drank a toast to Liam and then he toasted the producers and they toasted me and Matthew, and so it went on and we thought perhaps it might never end. A couple of journos started asking me about my relationships and the way I lived and who I was shagging and it was while I was talking to them that I saw him. He was standing by a table of publicity photographs and soundtrack recordings. He mouthed, 'Will you marry me?' and I lost the thread of the conversation with the journos and had to excuse myself. I didn't go over to him. I stood on the edge of a group of guests and stared over in disbelief. He came to me.

'Happy anniversary.'

'You remembered.'

'How could I not?'

We looked at each other and he leaned over and kissed me. A few camera flashes went off and he said, 'Shall we go?'

'Where?'

'To get married. Have you got some ID?'

'Yes.'

'Will we get married then?'

'Aedan, what are you doing here? This isn't meant for the general public.'

'I'm a director. I said I knew you.'

'Why are you here? Why now?'

'You said you'd see me when it was finished with Frances. It's over now.'

'And?'

'Marry me.'

'What?'

233

'Marry me.'

'Oh, God, Aedan, don't do this to me.'

'Trust me.'

'Why?'

'We made promises.'

'You broke them all.'

'Never, I never broke a single one. I promise you now. We'll be all right, now, she'll not bother us again. Marry me.' He knelt down at my feet. 'I'm on my knees to you.'

'Oh, get up, for God's sake. What have you done with her? Is she dead?'

'No, but she won't get to us now.'

'Why not? Why now but never before?'

'She knows it's lost. We talked. We talked for two days. Ellie, remember the day we met.'

'I do.'

'Remember how we were. Remember those weeks we had. Perfection, you said.'

'It was. And you left me. More than once.'

'It wasn't simple . . . I did try. I tried not to hurt you by making you wait, but then you waited anyway and I thought we were both mad, I thought you were mad for not letting go, I still think it's mad and then I remember and it isn't crazy anymore, I remember what it was like when we met, when we were together and so I couldn't let go either. Do you remember the restaurant and the fish, the poisoned fish?'

'I do.'

His voice was getting louder and I could see a couple of people close by who were now beaming in on the conversation.

'Ellie . . . I can't forget. I don't want to. It's over with Frances. It took too long and I'm sorry, I'm sorry. But it's all finished now. Remember the first minute in the studio that time? You had a bar of chocolate for your breakfast. We shook hands and . . . do you remember all that?'

'Yes.'

He had not forgotten. His memories were the same as mine.

'Trust me. Marry me.'

Someone behind me said, 'What was that?'

'Yes,' I said. 'Now?'

'Yes.'

'This minute?'

'Yes. Yes. Now.'

We got in a taxi to Baker Street and managed to catch the Register Office minutes before it closed. It had been sorted, booked, paid for. While I was in Leverkusen he had booked our day for the day we met and unbroken a broken word. A little man with a speech impediment married us. He called me Eddie Bidder and when it came to Aedan he couldn't pronounce his name at all. Our witness wasn't the usual tramp, as is common in these scenarios, but a cleaner who'd just started her afternoon shift. She asked us where we were going for our honeymoon. Aedan said, 'Home,' and we went to Oakley Street. He carried me over the threshold and tripped on one of the steps nearly killing us both. He'd bought champagne and food. We put Michael Nyman's *Drowning by Numbers* on a loop and listened to it at full volume over and over again. He tore the orange outfit from me and shredded the tights. We fucked over the kitchen table and on the stairs in the hall till I had such a severe carpet burn on my back he had to lift me bleeding up the stairs to the bedroom. We rolled onto our newly baptised wedding bed and crushed a champagne glass in the process. The music was too loud but we couldn't be bothered turning it down. It carried on, relentlessly, even when at some point, something went wrong; there was a strange noise, three or four times the music was disturbed by loud bangs. I thought a bomb must have gone off nearby; I thought it must have gone off somewhere on Oakley Street because the noise was so intense I went dizzy. I went so dizzy that it was a moment or two before I realized I couldn't breathe and from the noise of the explosion there was a ringing in my head – is it the door, this ringing, is someone there? I couldn't breathe at all now and somehow Aedan wasn't moving any more and I wanted to shake him and say, 'Don't play games, something's gone wrong, don't play games today,' but I couldn't move my right arm and my leg was aching with something like cramp. I wanted even more to shake him when in the half light I saw that a woman stood in the doorway. It didn't occur to me that she shouldn't be there because she was so familiar, standing there with her lank hair and her bare feet. I went to speak but still I couldn't breathe. *Move! Why wouldn't he move?* The lank-haired woman turned around. I heard her crashing out of the house; she must have knocked some things over as she went. I could hear everything outside amplified and then it occurred to me she'd left the door open. I couldn't breathe still and Aedan wouldn't move and we were both wet from something, I don't know what, and I thought, *The door's open, we'll get burgled and we'll get cold; people might come in and take our possessions.* Then I remembered we had none.

Chapter Forty-four

He was drinking Perrier and I had whiskey and outside the moon was shining on some other city; hidden to London this night by thick clouds. He held my hand over the table. A woman came in carrying an empty basket. She looked sort of empty herself; hollow, dead behind the eyes.

'You have ruined my life,' she said and scooped up the fruit from our plates and put it all into her basket. She wore a dress not unlike a shroud, so tattered she might have lain dead in it for a whole year.

'Champagne, please,' she shouted to the waiter, and looking down at me she said, 'The champagne's for me. I'm celebrating.'

When she moved away I noticed she was barefoot and her feet were bleeding. She left a trail of muddy, bloody footprints all the way to the door.

He finished his Perrier and I finished my whiskey and we walked out into the night and in a street off Leicester Square we held on to each other like the wind might choose to blow us apart and we would've had sex in the doorway to the surgery of a twenty-four-hour emergency doctor, only before we could a woman in a white coat came through the door. She spoke to us, though I couldn't quite hear what she said and neither could he.

At his flat there was a note stuck to the door which said

This property has been broken into.
Everything was taken. Burglars.

And inside, all the drawers and cupboards were empty,
all the plants dead, all the fruit. The only thing living there
that night was me.

We sat down and drank each other in; such a beautiful
man I had never even dreamed of. Such love I could never
begin to describe.

'Such a love as this could never die,' he said to me, and I
believed him, and amidst the empty cupboards and shelves
we slept, woken only once in the night by a woman, a
woman we hadn't heard approach because her feet were
bare. She cried out *No!* several times, and when we didn't
stir she padded away and we slept on and he held on to me
as though I were a dead woman, come alive again for him for
just this night, and I clung to him as though he were a
drowned man. I clung to him as though by loving him more
than all the world I could give him back his life.

I was fussed over by various nurses and a doctor who looked
as though he was about to drop dead from exhaustion. He
looked very young. Younger than me. He probably was. I
wondered if he'd passed all his exams; should he really be
there? Was he a student? I didn't envy him his job.

'Where is he?' I said. 'Aedan. Where is he?'

'You should try to sleep. You've had a—'

'*Sleep?*' He had to be joking. 'Tell me where he is.'

'He's in the ICU.' I worked out what that meant. 'Perhaps a
little later, I'll get someone to take you round there, and
maybe you could give one of the nurses some details.'

'About what?'

'Well, your full name. Your friend's full name, that sort of
thing. Nothing to worry about.'

'What about her?'

'She's been taken to another hospital.'

'Then she isn't dead.'

'No.'

'Pity.' I closed my eyes because it seemed easier than keeping them open. I remembered her face in the doorway. She'd looked desolate, standing there. Utterly desolate. She had turned around almost immediately. I remembered hearing the front door slam shut and later what I thought was a shot, some sort of gunshot, but maybe I'd dreamt it. Where could she have got a gun from?'

'How do I get to Intensive Care?'

'On a stretcher usually.'

'That's really not funny.'

'I'm sorry.' He looked it.

'I have to see him.'

'He's asleep. We don't expect him to wake up till the morning.'

'What time is it now?'

'About four.'

'Afternoon?'

'Morning.'

'He's OK, isn't he? I mean, he won't die . . . will he?' What would I do? I went dizzy, suddenly struck by a sharp toothache sort of pain in my right arm.

'I think you should try to sleep. You've had a shock.' I noticed my arm was bandaged up. I couldn't remember why.

'I don't remember what happened. We were in the flat and . . . I remember she came in, and the music and . . . I have to see him, I've got to be with him.' Had I been drunk? 'What happened?'

'We don't really know. We thought you might be able to tell us. There's a bullet wound from some sort of gun in your arm and one in your right thigh. We got most of the actual bullet out. There was also some glass embedded in your thigh. We haven't worked out quite how that happened.'

'The champagne.'

'What?'

'Nothing . . .'

'You're lucky to be alive.'

'And Aedan?'

I saw him think about it for a moment.

'I'll take you there. I'll have the nurse bring a chair for you.'

'I can walk.' He helped me to my feet. Dizzy again I nearly fainted from the pain in my leg and in my head and almost asked him if he could get the chair after all but I thought it would probably take ages and I didn't want to waste time.

A police woman was waiting outside the room.

'When you're feeling a bit better, Mrs O'Brien,' she said, 'we need to ask a few questions.' I didn't respond. 'If that's all right,' she added. For a second I didn't register. She'd called me O'Brien. *Ellen O'Brien?*

'That's not my name,' I said. Aedan O'Brien. O'Brien. Aedan's name.

The doctor intervened. 'She's not really ready for you yet. Tomorrow?'

Further down the corridor a photographer leapt out in front of us both and clicked away at his camera until the tired young doctor told him to piss off. A woman in a huge multi-coloured anorak shouted after me. I looked back. She was being held back by a man in some sort of uniform. 'Ellie, is it true it was his ex-wife who shot you?' I stared down the corridor as she was dragged away. 'You and Aedan,' she shouted. 'Was it his ex-wife? We want to hear your side of the story. Is Matthew Howard here? Has he been to see you?' I turned around quickly to the doctor and then back to her and screamed, 'She's not his fucking ex-wife. That's bullshit.'

'Leave it alone,' the doctor said. 'Don't tell them anything. They'll print what they like anyway, whatever you say.'

We limped on. I looked over my shoulder to see if she had come back. No-one in sight.

'He's in here. I can't promise he'll wake up for you, but

you never know. He's got three holes in his back. We're worried about his spleen.'

'His spleen?' I didn't even know what a spleen did. Was it like a liver or something?

'He's seriously ill. Don't expect the moon.'

Ah, the moon. It always seems to come down to the moon . . . *since all things lost on earth are treasured there* . . . The eclipse. The moonshine we'd eaten with such greed. The moon. Nights spent watching it from my kitchen window. Watching the wolves howl up at the sky. At the moon. I'd always expected the moon and more.

He didn't look alive to me at all. Maybe they were trying to break it to me gently and this was their way. He lay there full of tubes looking quite dead, his skin a sort of blueish purple. Nothing moved. Even his eyelids were still. The monitor at the side of his bed flickered. Was that his heartbeat? It looked exactly as they always did in the films.

'It's the first time I've seen one,' I said to the nurse who was hovering behind me.

She looked blank. 'What?'

'One of these,' I said, pointing to the machine. I smiled at her but it turned out to be a mistake because she obviously saw this as a green light for her to chat.

'I really loved that programme you were in about the American. I almost didn't recognize you. Your hair was different, wasn't it? Was it a different colour?'

'Yes.' I didn't know what she was talking about.

'We had that Scottish actor in here about two years ago. The detective. I expect because we're right near the West End. We get a lot of actors passing through. Have you ever worked with him?'

'Who?'

'The Scottish bloke. The detective.'

'I don't know who you mean. Look, you couldn't get me a coffee or something, could you?'

'No problem. I'll get you a snack as well if there's anything

241

you fancy. I'm off duty in about ten minutes, I could take you in the staff canteen if you like.'

'No. Thanks. I'd like to stay here. Thank you.' Get out get out before I kill you.

She disappeared through the plastic doors and left me alone with Aedan and the machine.

'Aedan?' He was so still. I took his hand. It was cold as ice. I wrapped a bit of my robe round it and squeezed it. 'Aedan?' I squeezed tighter, willing the life into him. I thought I saw one of his eyelids flicker. I waited for it to happen again. He didn't move at all. I doubted he had any idea I was even there.

The young doctor came in with the coffee.

'I hijacked Sandy and sent her on her way.'

'What?'

'The nurse. Thought you might not feel up to chatting.'

I didn't bother answering. I looked back at Aedan. He seemed to have moved slightly.

'He seems to have moved,' I said.

The young doctor pulled up a chair for me and then got one for himself. I sank down like I had no choice in the matter.

'Mrs O'Brien.'

'Ellen . . . Ellie.'

'Ellie. Sorry. Can I ask you a few questions?'

'What about?'

'Your husband's medical history.'

'Oh. Yes. I suppose so.'

'OK. Right. Now . . . What's his full name?'

'Aedan. A-E-D-A-N. It's pronounced Aidan. You'd better tell the nurses. They might not be able to pronounce it if they just read it from his chart.'

'I'll let them know.'

There was a long silence, filled with bleeps and carpetless corridor noises and the sound of emergencies in the building.

'Aedan what?'

'Sorry. O'Brien. Aedan Patrick O'Brien. He's Irish.'

'Do you know his blood type?'

'No. Sorry.'

'Not a problem. We have it on the other chart. Now . . .' He looked over the papers on his clipboard. 'Is he allergic to anything?' My tongue was stuck in my jaw. 'Ellie? Do you know if he's allergic to anything?'

'No. He might be. I don't know.'

'Apart from his appendectomy do you know if he's been hospitalized for any reason before?'

'No.'

'His date of birth?'

'December the . . . nineteen fifty-five . . . six . . . I . . .' I couldn't work it out. 'He's thirty-six. Seven, sorry, he had a birthday.' When? When did he have a birthday? The eclipse. His birthday followed the eclipse. Had he had another one? 'What's the date today?'

He looked at his watch. 'The second. Just. September the second.'

'Oh.'

'Does he have any other family we could notify? Do you?'

'Dead.'

'Well . . . if you think of anyone . . .'

'It was our anniversary.'

'Today?'

'Yesterday.'

'Has Aedan ever had any respiratory problems?'

'What?'

'Breathing trouble. Trouble with his chest.'

'I know what respiratory problems are.'

'Do you know if Aedan's ever had any?'

'No.'

It seemed that all I actually knew was his name. I didn't even know his shoe size; not that he was going to be doing any walking for a while.

'Ellie?' He'd put his hand on my shoulder.

'I didn't know him at all. He's my husband. We were married. I don't even know his shoe size. I can't even remember if he takes sugar in his coffee.'

'You should sleep. You'll be better equipped to look after him in the morning if you get some sleep now. Try to have an hour.'

'Can I sleep here?'

'It's not really . . . there's a bed in a room about two doors down the corridor . . .'

'I'll stay awake then. I'd rather be here. I want to be with him.'

Chapter Forty-five

I was warned not to try to leave the hospital. The doctors said this was for my own benefit as a posse of press had camped outside and didn't look like they were going anywhere until I did. I asked if I could see Frances. Nobody seemed to be able to come to a decision on this. In the staff toilet I overheard one of the nurses saying to a friend that the woman who tried to kill the actress had been admitted to the same hospital. I caught up with her in the corridor and asked her if what I'd heard was true and she said it was more than her job was worth to tell me that. I hunted down the tired young doctor who'd dealt with me when I first arrived. I said, 'Why will no-one tell me the truth? Do they think I'm going to kill her?' He said nothing. 'Do I look like a woman who would murder someone?'

'Frankly, yes, at the moment you look like you would. Especially the woman you want to see so much. Why do you want to meet her now? It can't help Aedan. It won't help you.'

'It might.'

'Wouldn't you rather I arranged for someone to get a message to her? You shouldn't be walking around anyway, you've been hurt yourself. How are we expected to mend that leg if you won't rest it? And you shouldn't be talking to anyone, you should be asleep now. You've been here nearly three days and you haven't slept in your bed even for a night.'

'I want to be with Aedan when he comes round.'

'That mightn't be for days and days. You'll have collapsed by then.'

'You think he's going to die, don't you?'

'I really don't know.'

'But you must have an opinion, a professional opinion. Look at me. Tell me the truth.'

'I think your husband is dying. I'm sorry, Ellie.'

'I promise you, I won't hurt her. I have to see her. Tell me where she is. *Please*.' We'd developed some sort of relationship and I think he felt he owed it to me.

'Look, unofficially, someone you might want to see is two floors down from us. Ask a nurse . . . tell them I sent you and ask for Annie Smith.'

'Who?'

'She's registered here under that name because of the press. She's been admitted because she cut herself rather badly on a garden rake while she was at Springfield. Do you want me to come with you?'

'No thanks.'

'I think there's some police watching her. You mightn't get past them.'

'I will.'

'Look, I'm trusting you, Ellen. You'll be careful?'

'Of course.'

'Will you let me get Sandy to take you down there in a chair?'

'There's no need. My leg's fine. Really it is. I won't let you down.'

'Good.'

'Let me know the instant there's any change with Aedan and I'll come straight back up.'

'Have this then.' He gave me a bleeper from his coat pocket.

'That's very sweet of you. How clever. What will you do without it?'

'That's only a spare. I'll bleep you if we need you here. Don't do anything stupid.'

'No. It's all been done.'

She looked tiny. She was so small her feet only just touched the floor. I wondered why they hadn't given her shoes to wear, or even a pair of socks; her feet would get filthy and hurt, bare like that. I found her sitting on a blue plastic chair in an empty room at the back of the hospital. It was a large room with enormous windows all the way round it. It looked like it might have been a function room of some sort. The policeman sent to keep an eye on her was deep in conversation with an old man in a wheelchair halfway down the corridor and so there were no questions to be avoided and no-one to stop me going in.

She looked as though she was wearing a hospital nightie; it had a papery look to it and it tied at the back round her neck. My footsteps on the wooden floor were a surprise to me. I stopped about ten feet away from her, expecting her to turn around.

'Is it you?' she said.

'Yes.' Still she didn't move.

'Why did you come?'

I didn't know. Curiosity? Revenge? Neither. Both. I didn't know.

'Is he dead yet?'

'No.'

I walked over to the chair and stood directly in front of her. She smelled of mould.

'Frances . . .' She didn't look at me. She didn't even blink. 'Frances.' Louder now. She would have to look at me. I would make her. 'Frances.' Almost a shout.

'You're angry.'

'Look at me. *Frances.*'

She raised her eyes and met mine. I wished she hadn't. I've never seen such pain. Big, watery, grieving grey eyes, begging me to be somebody else.

'Why?' I said.

Huge tears plopped out of the eyes and rolled down her face till they dropped off her chin onto the nightie. They came so quickly and in such quantity they didn't seem real. We stared at each other. I wanted to look away but couldn't. I wanted to swear at her and slap her and shake her and smash her head against the floorboards but I couldn't move.

'He's going to die, isn't he?' she said.

'I don't know.'

'I wanted . . .' She looked away, her mouth hanging open as though she'd forgotten what it was to build a sentence. I felt something like relief to be out of her gaze. 'I wanted . . .'

'What?'

'To be old with him.'

'So did I.'

'He was mine.'

'He didn't belong to anyone.'

'He married you. I wanted . . .'

'Why did you do it?'

'I loved him.'

'He might die.'

'I hope he does.'

'Why?'

'I'd rather he was dead than alive without me.'

'You'll be put away.'

'I'm already in prison.'

'Yes.'

'You'd help me though, wouldn't you? Aedan always said, "She's a good woman. A really good woman." You'd help me, wouldn't you?'

'I don't know.'

248

'Get me some pills. Get me something to do myself with. They won't let me near anything. They think I'm a nutter. But they'd let you.'

'No. I won't do it.' I would save her life. I would make sure she lived for a long time; at least as long as me. Longer.

'But . . .'

'Never.'

'Don't you want me dead?'

'I hope you live for ever. I hope you live for ever with your pain and your loss and I hope your grief chokes you every time you wake. Like mine does.'

'Would you let me see him? Today? Or tomorrow?'

'No I wouldn't, and if you come anywhere near us I'll get you arrested.'

'I loved him so much.'

'Me too.'

'We have a history together.'

'I know that.'

'Then you'll know he loved me once.'

'Yes.'

'We did our first theatre job together . . . I was married though. I wasn't free.'

'You could've left your husband.'

'We made promises, Aedan and I.'

'And you were already married.'

'Oh, what do you know? You're only twenty-four.'

'Twenty-five.'

'Whatever.'

'Why did you do this to us?'

'How long had you known Aedan before you loved him, before you were sure?' I looked out of the window. 'A minute or two? Not much longer. I thought you of all people would understand.'

'If you loved him so much, why this? Why did you do this?'

'We made promises.'

'So you said. And now he may die. Because of some promise.'

'He broke them all.'

I turned around to go and walked to the door with some difficulty. Before I managed to get out of the room she whispered my name. I didn't turn around. I couldn't look at her.

'Ellen . . .' I stopped, unable to ignore her. 'He kept all your letters, y'know? Every one. I hated it. He carried them around with him. I read some of them.' I couldn't speak but nor could I move. I had almost forgotten that she *knew* him, she had spent time with him. 'He talked about you. Too much. Said you were like a recurring dream. He said you were thin.'

'Not always.' It came out involuntarily. 'I . . . I pined . . . when he went from me I didn't eat.'

'Me neither.'

I turned to go again. Again she stopped me.

'He told me he loved you more than all the world.' She paused and the room was so silent it might have existed only in my head. 'He said you had the key to life. Did he tell you that?'

'Yes.'

'So if you ever doubt . . . I mean . . . He did love you. It wasn't a fantasy. That's why I let him go . . . only of course I didn't really. I came and found you both.'

I left with a bad taste in my mouth. The gift she'd handed me, the gift of her admission, did not atone for her ultimate theft. I wondered how difficult it had been for her to say. Perhaps it hadn't been difficult at all, now she had achieved her aim. But she was ill. She loved him possibly as much as I did. Maybe I would let her see him tomorrow. She was a mad woman after all and that bit I could understand.

I went straight back to Aedan, who looked somehow different. There was colour in his cheeks. The doctor said it was because he'd contracted pneumonia and something else I couldn't pronounce but I didn't believe him. The chatty nurse came in and put her hand on my shoulder. I expected her to start twittering on about the West End or something but she didn't, she just looked at me and smiled very slightly and kindly and carried on with her jobs. I started to talk to him. I talked about *Romeo and Juliet* and the weather outside and all the fuss with the press and the photographers at the front of the building. I told him my leg was much better and that I was walking about without the fucking Zimmer frame they'd given me. I laughed and squeezed his hand and said come back come back come back to me Aedan.

'Ah, dear Juliet,' he said. God, my God, my God. I started to shout for the doctor but no sound came out. The young one came in and I waved to him and managed to say, 'He spoke! He knows me! He isn't dead—'

'Ellen . . .'

'Look at him, I told you he looked different today.'

'Don't get too excited . . . it's early days yet.' Oh, what did they know? The doctor hovered for a second or two and then took his leave and Aedan said another word which I couldn't quite hear. I moved closer so our faces almost touched and he said, 'It's Juliet. Back from the dead.'

'Thank God, Aedan, thank God for this. Jesus Christ, thank God, I love you, Aedan, I love you I love you.'

'I can't hear you.' I smiled and almost laughed and got even closer and gripped onto his hand and said it again.

'I can't hear you.'

'I love you,' I said, tears falling, relief.

'Again.'

'I love you.'

'For how long?' he said, quiet, breathless.

'Always. More. Longer.'

'My *wife*.'

'I love you.'

'For ever?'

'Yes.'

'I can't hear you.'

'For ever.'

'Are you holding my hand?'

'Yes.'

'Don't go off again.'

'I won't. I'm with you.'

'I can't hear you.'

'I'm with you.'

I said it eight or nine times. I kissed his mouth and smoothed his hair away from his face and crushed his hand in mine.

'I'm with you.'

I said it again and again and kissed his face and his hair and his hands.

I told him again, 'I'm with you,' I said. I said it two or three times more before I realized he was dead.

Chapter Forty-six

I was late for the first rehearsal. People drank coffee and ate toast in a dirty room with a lot of mirrors in it in an old church hall near Waterloo. Only about five minutes from my flat so people were curious as to why I was late. I had things to say to you but the job was there to be done and I've never missed a day's work.

We discussed the tragedy of Shakespeare's plays and also the humour. I couldn't find anything funny until about eleven o'clock when someone said something and I laughed and in the middle of the laugh I nearly choked on my own guilt and thought I might not make the whole day but the job was there to be done and I've never missed a day's work.

I tried to pretend you had never been in my life. I tried to pretend but found I could not. I walked home every night with Shakespeare in my head instead of you, but when I reached the flat you were always there at the door. You stared at me from all the mirrors. I went to bed to sleep away the thoughts of you but you were always there. I tried to pretend life could continue with you not in it but found it could not.

I cannot forget.

Aedan. We made promises; such promises I try to break. I try not to remember and not to forget. You are in every doorway on every London street. I feel like a woman drowning, lying on the water dreaming of rescue.

A mad woman, a woman madder than myself, approached me in the street the other day and said, 'You must not dream of the dead, lady, dream of the living.' So I went home and dreamt you were alive. You came to me (a dream) laden with fruits and told me such sweet fruits could not die. Such fruits I could feed from for ever. And I believed you. I am a mad woman, a woman mad. You came to me (alive) and fed me moonshine, and I ate. Into my home you walked and painted all the woodwork with your promises, upset every glass and bottle, broke the windows, tore my heart in two and in the night while I dreamed you loved me still you took yourself and your sweet fruits away (burglar). Still dreaming I screamed come back come back come back come back. Awake now my home is barren; drenched in fear and anger and pain and I miss you I miss you I miss your smell, the way you smelled when you were alive, when life had not the guts to run out on you.

And so it's easier not to sleep. Twenty-four hours of each day I am awake. I watch the minutes as they are born and as they die and if the hands of the clock could go back for me I would go back to the canteen of a studio in Holland Park and I would choose to meet you again and again. I would live all of you all over again. Even in this darkness, lying alone, pressed to the earth, an iron bar on my chest I would choose to do it all again. Twenty years, fifty years from now, forever I will remember the taste of you. I will smell you in London streets and in my home and in my bed and in my sleep you will bring me fruits that will never die.

You were ripped away from me some dank September night, a night that was born of a sunny day. You were gone from me not for the first time, only the first time I watched you leave. Tried to photograph you but all the pictures died before they were born. I would've given anything to have you back, would've done anything to bring you home. I will still. December dying here without you I still hear you, still feel your touch. Your breath here I can almost see. Could've had your child. O to have the chance again. Your child in me. Dead before she was born. Would've done anything to have her back, to have the time back. Lost hours carrying a child you left behind. She died. Lost hours with you beside me inside me and out.

It rains here. It rains and rains and rains and even in summer it freezes on the streets and if it thaws I think if it thaws I dream you will wake and I will sleep again. People tell me I should go away somewhere; they tell me I should leave death by itself for a while, leave you alone, forget you, let you be dead.

But I cannot leave you.

I cannot sleep or wake or eat, I cannot breathe. I cannot leave you alone, forget you, let you die, let you be dead, since what am I but dead without you? A dead woman.

A woman drowned;

Lying on the water, dreaming of rescue.

Acknowledgements

For help in a variety of disguises and for all the love they've bandied around, I would like to thank the following people, who have all, for one reason or another, been awake at four in the morning when everyone else slept.
My lovely Grandmother, Helena Josephina McKiernan (Nell), who once sent me twenty-seven bars of chocolate in a Jiffy bag; Rebecca Nagan, Alison Johnston, Lucy Brazier and Sasha Paul, for encouragement and hilarity and all that coffee; Fay, for showing me kindness I never knew existed; my agent, David Daly; Neil Daglish who once saved my life; Graham Reid for unforgettable memories of leaves and mad dogs; Alan Strachan for blind faith; Bill Almlie; Susie Blake; Karma Brown; Margaret Potter; Dame Alan, for giving my evil twin Betty all that work; Billy Grayson for introducing me to obsession; Peter Winstanley (I still think of you); Andrew Hewson, Ursula Mackenzie and Alison Tulett for getting the show on the road; Howard Saddler, without whom this book was written; Clare Cathcart, who was there and Pip, who wasn't but was lovely nonetheless,

and Thanks to The Irishman, for cherished moments.